THE
LEGACIES

THE
LEGACIES

JESSICA GOODMAN

RAZORBILL

RAZORBILL

An imprint of Penguin Random House LLC, New York

First published in the United States of America by Razorbill,
an imprint of Penguin Random House LLC, 2023

Copyright © 2023 by Serenity Lane Corp.

Visit us online at PenguinRandomHouse.com.

Library of Congress Cataloging-in-Publication Data is available.

ISBN 9780593619506 (hardcover)
1 3 5 7 9 10 8 6 4 2

ISBN 9780593696071 (international edition)
1 3 5 7 9 10 8 6 4 2

Printed in the United States of America

BVG

Design by Rebecca Aidlin
Text set in Adobe Caslon Pro

To Maxwell,
who makes it all possible.

THE
LEGACIES

AFTER THE BALL

THE LEGACY BALL *had never ended in a murder—obviously. Usually, the seniors from New York's elite institutions capped off the night by watching the sunrise at some elaborate after-party. An all-nighter at a mansion in Bronxville. A beach bonfire at a sprawling estate in Southampton. A strobe-lit rave in a Ridgewood loft. This year, the nominees were supposed to be whisked away in a fleet of Suburbans heading to someone's country manor in the Hudson Valley.*

But that's out of the question now, with the body and all.

Bernie Kaplan stands on the corner of Sixty-First Street in glittering four-inch stilettos and a green tulle gown, Skyler Hawkins's tuxedo jacket hanging off her shoulders, even though it's warm for September. If you look closely enough, you can see she's trying not to shiver. A light breeze whips at the diamond drops dangling from her ears. The sirens from the cop cars wail, and Bernie glances down at her pale pink manicured fingers, now flecked with blood and dirt. Her bright red hair is messy, out of place. Her mother usually whispers for her to tuck back the flyaways before onlookers can snap photos, but Esther Kaplan is nowhere to be found, so Bernie lets them go free.

Bernie's eyes move to the curb as the rest of the attendees of the Legacy Ball spill onto the street to see the commotion. She wishes Tori were by her side. A week ago, that girl was no one. A scholarship senior from Queens who had stayed in the background for three whole years. Now, it's obvious that all of the Legacies underestimated her.

Bernie opens her mouth as if to say something but snaps it shut when the whispers around her erupt into frantic, excited chatter. The wondering, the gasps, as police roll a stretcher away from the side entrance of the Legacy Club, away from the Ball. The body's on it, covered by a white sheet. An outline of lifeless fingers, legs, arms. The medics push the corpse into an ambulance and shut the door. It speeds north.

The commotion gets louder. People are screaming and sobbing, drowning out the crackling voices coming in over walkie-talkies. Bernie longs for Isobel, what they had lost. For Skyler, too. For what he represented.

But she can't think about them right now. Because in this moment, there are questions. So many questions. And no one seems to have the answers.

All anyone knows for certain is that as the clock strikes midnight, a member of one of New York City's oldest, most exclusive institutions is dead, and that Bernie Kaplan is the one with blood on her hands.

FOUR DAYS
BEFORE THE BALL

Bernie

"ISN'T IT WEIRD?" Isobel asks, her voice lilting. "To see all these strangers here, at *our* school? At Excelsior Prep?"

We're standing together at the entrance of our high school's cafeteria, though *cafeteria* isn't really the right word to describe this room, with its sky-high marble entryway and custom round oak tables that seat twelve. *Dining room* is more apt, though *Architectural Digest* once called it "the prettiest place to eat in all of the five boroughs." Across the atrium, floor-to-ceiling picture windows overlook the lacrosse fields down below, freshly mowed to a uniform length.

On the western side, you can see the turrets of the lower school peeking through the orchard across campus, the weeping willows and tall apple trees swaying through the glass. Headmaster Helfrich likes to say that Excelsior's campus is a fifth the size of Central Park and just as beautiful, a massive sprawl north of Manhattan, over the Bronx border.

If I close my eyes, I could walk right out that door and all over Excelsior's grounds without tripping or falling or bumping into anything. We're only a few weeks away from the start of senior year, and coming here, even today before classes begin, feels like coming home.

Except I can't help but feel a wave of anxiety building in my stomach. Isobel and I inch forward in line, and I look behind me at the other nominated seniors from different schools in the Intercollegiate League. They're dressed in their most appropriate luncheon attire, standing up straight, smiles perky. Skyler's at the back of the line with Lee, Isobel's boyfriend, since they were late and I refused to wait for them. I spot the other Excelsior nominee we know about, Kendall Kirk, in a heated conversation with the debate champion from the Quaker school, Manhattan Friends, over by the drinks table. There should be six of us from Excelsior, but no one's figured out who the last nominee is. Not yet. I crack my knuckles, tuck a stray lock of hair behind my ear. I remind myself that I'm wearing what I'm supposed to wear, acting how I'm supposed to act. Everything will go exceedingly well this week. It must. But my sense of unease won't go away.

"They're not strangers," I whisper, leaning close to Isobel so none of the students behind or in front of us hear. "At least they won't be by the end of the week."

Isobel nods, considering this assessment. If I were feeling a little less on edge, I might take the time to remind her to not be so snippy, which has been her default defense mechanism since I met her in fifth grade. After all, first impressions start *now*, as my mom told me, and can last until the final donation is made during the Legacy Ball in only four days. If you want to win—and we all *do*—you have to start on a good note, even with your peers. You never know whose parents or aunts or family friends are already in the Club or how deep their pockets are.

Plus, most of the other nominees are people we've seen around our whole lives—other seniors at schools in the Intercollegiate

League we've played in field hockey or competed against in Model UN. There are only thirty-six of us here—six chosen from each of the six sister schools—and half of these kids summer out east with me, and the other half I recognize from Skyler's party scene.

The ones we *don't* know, we sure as hell will soon. And if we're smart, we'll keep them close for the rest of our lives. That's what Mom says, at least. Those chosen for the Legacy Club will be our college roommates, spouses, business partners, and investors. They'll be our allies in not only New York society, but in our long, storied futures that are only just beginning.

"Never forget, that's how I met Lulu Hawkins," Mom likes to say, while giving Skyler's mom a little elbow nudge in the ribs. And the single one of us who wins the presentation competition will ascend to the top of the Club immediately, gaining not only a board seat that helps determine future nominees but also a cash prize. Though no one really cares about the cash—no one here needs to. Mom says it's tradition for the winner to donate it back to the Club to fund scholarships. But winning is an honor. A distinction that you are the elite among the elite. And I want it.

Isobel looks like she's about to say something else, but the line moves quickly, and I reach for her elbow before she can blurt out something sarcastic. "Come on," I say. "We're next."

I lead Isobel up to the registration table in front of the Wall of Fame, an eighteen-foot-tall panel that has the names of Excelsior's most adored alumni chiseled into stone. Among them are a Supreme Court justice, two Academy Award–winning actors, three long-serving members of the House of Representatives, a Pulitzer Prize–winning playwright, a celebrity chef, and more start-up founders and heads of banks than I could possibly count. When

I was little, I asked Mom why *her* name wasn't up there. She told me it was because being the best mom didn't count as an accolade, even though it was the most important job in the world.

One day, I'll find my name on that wall. Ideally as a renowned politician. A senator, maybe. Or even New York City mayor. Though, to be honest, Isobel has a better shot of making it for her art, since she's already had a group show at the Brooklyn Museum when they honored young city-bred artists. She sold four charcoal pieces that week. And she didn't know a single one of her buyers. Even Mom was impressed.

I look up and see Jeanine Shalcross sitting behind the registration table, a smile spreading across her face when she recognizes me as Esther Kaplan's daughter. Most people do, thanks to the fact that we could basically be twins with our curvy builds and long, strawberry hair.

"Bernadette Kaplan," she says. "So nice to see you! Shani wanted me to say hi. She just moved into her dorm at Cornell, you know. First class was this week. Excelsior certainly prepared her for the rigorous coursework, I can tell you that." Her mouth grows wider, overeager, and I fight the prickling sensation crawling up my spine.

"Hi, Mrs. Shalcross," I say, extending my fingers. Her eyes flit down to my perfect pink manicure, the emerald ring on my middle finger, and she shakes my hand heartily. Mom always said Jeanine had been a total follower since they were classmates at Excelsior all those years ago. But they went to college together, were in the same sorority, and moved back to the Upper East Side at the same time, so she'd been a fixture in my mom's social life forever.

"Lovely to see you. My mom said Shani's Legacy presentation was wonderful last year."

If I recall correctly, she also said Jeanine Shalcross is a pushover who would lie down in the middle of Fifth Avenue in couture if Mom asked her to.

Mrs. Shalcross beams with pride. "Ah yes, Shani didn't win, of course. But did us proud. Your mother, though, her presentation was legendary when we were seniors. Won by a landslide." She flips through the name cards in front of us and hands me mine. "She winged it. Came up with the whole thing on the spot. At least that's what she told me. But that's Esther for you. Flakey as a croissant but always sticks the landing." She pauses, then purses her lips, like she didn't mean to say that out loud.

I smile politely and glance at my name card, handwritten in cursive. I've heard that story dozens of times: how Mom got up on stage and made some charming, hilarious speech totally off the cuff. Skyler's mom said it ended with a standing ovation.

"You girls must be so excited," Mrs. Shalcross says, changing the subject. "Finally, your turn to participate in one of the city's most illustrious traditions." She sighs and looks past us, and for a second, I wonder if she's remembering her own Legacy Ball, and how it was likely the best night of her life, even if she didn't win.

Mom always said it was hers—that it would be mine, too. She even promised me that, for the occasion, I could wear my grandmother's beloved diamond necklace, the one that's been in her family since they fled from the pogroms in Russia—that even more than my bat mitzvah, the event would mark my entrée into adulthood. And for seventeen years, I've believed her.

Isobel clears her throat. "Isobel Rothcroft," she says, looking at the stack of cards. Mrs. Shalcross gives her a once-over, taking in Isobel's dark blunt bob and her silk V-neck jumpsuit. Even though it's vintage Halston, pulled from her mom's outstanding collection, I should have warned her that it would be a little too bold—too Brooklyn—for the Legacy crowd. Not that it would have stopped her from wearing it. I smooth out my own dress, a nautical-inspired sleeveless A-line number my mom had steamed last week, and stand up a little straighter in my espadrilles.

"I hope your mother feels better," Mrs. Shalcross says, leaning in. "She texted me yesterday that she had a nasty cold and couldn't make it. I have to tell you I was shocked. She must be extremely ill if she'd miss the welcome luncheon, especially since it's your year as a nominee."

My cheeks burn and I bite down on my tongue to keep from lashing out.

A girl from Tucker Country Day clears her throat behind me, and I give Mrs. Shalcross a little shrug before excusing myself to make way for the other kids.

"That was rude," Isobel mutters. "Can't your mom be sick for once?" She rolls her eyes and I loop my elbow through hers, grateful that Isobel has the guts to say what I'm thinking out loud.

Isobel and I walk farther into the cafeteria, which has been transformed into a full luncheon with boxy flower centerpieces sitting on each table. Every place is set with round gold chargers, china plates, three different types of forks, and printed menus with handwritten names at the top, indicating where each guest should sit.

Isobel grabs a glass of iced tea off a tray passing us by. "I wish they had something stronger," she says as she takes a sip through a metal straw, then stabs at a mint leaf that had been propped up inside.

I look around the room at everyone trying to be so prim and proper and realize I couldn't disagree more. If there were booze here, I'd make a fool of myself somehow. Flub a name or stumble in my heels. That's why I don't like drinking so much or really at all. The whole losing-control thing. Not my vibe. I'd rather know exactly what's coming my way, so I'll be ready. Prepared.

Isobel, though? Whole other story.

Is looks at me and pouts. "This is all just so . . . formal."

A waiter walks by with a silver platter full of poached shrimp on skewers and little pots of bright red sauce. Mom likes to say that shrimp cocktail is just a sign that the hosts decided not to pay extra for oysters, which she mentioned dozens of times this summer as she went back and forth over the luncheon menu with the other board members. She was so pissed when she was outvoted, calling the whole week gauche as a result.

"We're in Legacy Club territory. Of course it's going to be stuffy." All around us kids are doing their best preprofessional impressions, fiddling with their ties, making small talk with strangers, and smiling with all their white teeth on display. I try to imagine my mom's commentary if she were here, how she'd tell me to stand up straight but then make fun of Jeanine's dress in the same breath.

"*Is* your mom okay, by the way?" Isobel asks, looking around the room. "Last week, she said the only thing that would keep her from all the events would be nuclear warfare."

"Super contagious," I say. "Doesn't want to give it to any of us before the big night. Totally sucks." The lie rolls off the tip of my tongue, hot and fast. Isobel has always been able to tell when I'm fibbing—when I said I had a migraine but really just wanted to skip an all-night rager or when I told her I had five tequila shots at last year's junior prom and was *so* wasted but really was dead sober. Now she's so distracted, I'm hoping she won't notice.

She turns to me, a concerned look on her face. "Everything okay?"

Guess not.

"Of course." I flip my hair over my shoulder and flit my eyes around the room, landing on Skyler, laughing in a corner with Lee. I need to get out of Isobel's presence ASAP or else she'll start to suspect something's up, and I don't want to have to lie to her any more than I already have. We've come so far since that big blow-up fight in Shelter Island at the beginning of the summer. We've both done everything we could to come back to each other, and I'm not going to let my mom's whereabouts affect that.

I nod to her card. "What's your table?"

She glances down. "Four."

I look at mine, a bit relieved. "One. We should probably sit down."

Isobel looks at me, skeptical, but nods. "Text me for a bathroom break?"

"Mm-hmm," I say, but I'm already walking away from her to find my table at the front of the room, where a few kids from other schools have taken their places. As everyone else finds their seats, we make small talk and sip our goblets of ice water, pick at the bread basket in front of our plates. I catch two of the kids from Manhattan Friends staring, their eyes lingering a bit too long on me, my dress, my hair.

I should be used to it by now. The curious gaze. Comes with the territory of being Bernie Kaplan, daughter of legal megastar slash always-on-TV pundit Rafe Kaplan and Esther Kaplan, one of the city's most prominent and covered socialites. When they catch me looking, they turn away. I paste a smile on my face, but under the table I wring my hands around my thick white napkin. All because I can't shake the gnawing, pulsing secret I'm keeping: the fact that Mom disappeared last night without a word.

I thought it was strange that she was missing from her bedroom at midnight, when I went in to curl up beside her like I sometimes do on nights where my insomnia kicks in. But her room was empty, and I didn't want to knock on Dad's door even though his light was still on. Maybe she was at the Legacy Club, going over last-minute details with people like Mrs. Shalcross.

But when she was still missing this morning, I knew for certain that something was wrong. Really wrong.

She's the kind of parent who volunteers as class mom every single year, who runs the PTA and is on a nickname basis with half the teachers. She texts me forty-five times a day with funny musings about the tourists in Central Park or the hot new barista at our favorite coffee shop. We share clothes and jewelry and handbags, big bowls of buttered popcorn on the couch, and memes about Bravo shows. She goes on unexpected trips all the time, but she always texts me while she's en route. Not hearing from her for twenty-four hours is not just uncommon, it's unimaginable. Especially only five days before *my* Legacy Ball, which she's been planning since last September and talking about since I was in preschool.

The only secret she's ever kept from me is who she nominated this year, telling me in a singsongy voice that I'll find out along with everyone else the night before the actual Ball.

When I confided in Dad this morning that I thought maybe something had happened to her, he scoffed and waved his hand at me. Then he went back to his laptop, perched on his standing desk inside his wood-paneled home office. "Don't worry. She's fine."

He's surely right. Almost certainly.

Tearing apart a piece of focaccia, I get a sinking feeling in my stomach that everything is about to change. Mom always said the Legacy Ball is where the chosen ones become adults. It's when life starts, where opportunity begins. And since I was lucky enough to have her, I'd never have to worry about going through it alone.

Suddenly, my clutch vibrates in my lap, and I reach for my phone, a desperate pulsing in my chest. When I see my mom's name on the screen, I let out a breath.

Sorry to skip the luncheon, but fear not, love. I'll be back soon. Enjoy the oysters for me! Bet you're glad we skipped the shrimp, ha! xo Mom

My stomach settles, realizing Dad was right. Mom's probably just pampering herself before the Ball or taking one of her solo weekends out east. She'll be back. She's fine.

But when I read her message again, I frown. She knew the menu—went over it painstakingly with Jeanine and complained about losing the oyster war. She never would have written this.

So, if she's not texting me . . . who is?

Isobel

The voice is low and menacing, even though I know who it belongs to. I spin around in my chair and see Skyler Hawkins sliding into the seat next to me, unfolding his napkin in his lap. His white button-down is crisp against his navy jacket, and his dark hair swoops down over one gray eye. Without looking, I know that he's got the attention of dozens of our peers, seated around the room. He always does.

"No." I fold my arms across my chest, indignant, even though yes, of course, I'd kill for a Xanax. But I don't want to let Skyler know that. Not today.

He probably suspects I'm lying, but he doesn't push it. He knows where he is—who's watching. He smirks and reaches for his water glass, nodding at the other kids at our table, saying hi and introducing himself as the class president at Excelsior Prep.

I can't believe I'm forced to sit with him at the Legacy Ball kickoff.

Bernie warned me that they usually separate people from the same school during this event, so I didn't expect to be with her, Lee, Kendall Kirk, or whoever else our sixth nominee is—no one seems to know. But it didn't even register that I could possibly be stuck next to Skyler for an afternoon.

Since that party in Shelter Island a few months ago, I've tried to keep my distance—to make sure we're never alone together. It hasn't been that hard, since Lee's his best friend and Bernie's his girlfriend, making it extremely normal for me to dip out with either one of them. But the occasional moment at the end of a park picnic or the brief periods when Lee decamps for the bathroom during a kickback . . . they always leave me on edge.

I look around the room and see Bernie sitting at the middle table, sandwiched between a kid from Lipman, who is rumored to have been cast in a leading role in the next HBO prestige drama, and another from Gordon, who discovered a new set of galaxies for NASA over the summer.

I try to take in all the other faces, identifying people I've met at Skyler's parties or when I've spent the weekend in the Hamptons at Bernie's. Immediately, I realize this crowd is just as boring and predictable as I thought it would be, another reason why I didn't even *want* a nomination in the first place. But I could never admit that to Bernie, who had been talking about the Legacy Club since I met her and had been promising that she would drop hints to her mom that she should nominate me. I've had years to tell her, *no, please don't*. But I never got the courage to explain that even though we were best friends, there were some things we didn't need to share—*this* being one of them.

And so, here I am, taking a coveted spot in this ridiculous club.

Usually, at these types of things, Bernie's all about making small talk, flipping that long red hair of hers over her shoulder and ingratiating herself with everyone. It's something I love about her. Her ability to talk to anyone about anything. It's useful when you're someone like me, who'd rather be alone with a set of charcoals and a sketchpad. But now, Bernie's staring down at her plate, disengaged from whatever conversation's happening at her table.

Maybe she's nervous, being the ball's student chair and all. Or maybe . . .

No. There's no way.

But she *was* rather weird with me just now, wasn't she? Avoiding my questions and dismissing me to sit down early. I got the sense she was lying about *something*.

I yank at Skyler's elbow, pulling him away from a conversation with a student from Tucker Country Day that ends with the kid saying something about his squash team.

"What?" Skyler asks, ducking his head toward mine.

My throat is scratchy, and I wish I had thought to bring a nip of vodka to slip into my iced tea, though Bernie warned me I'd get caught in a second.

"Do you think Bernie knows?" I ask, my voice small.

Skyler's head snaps up and his wide gray eyes find mine. When he looks at me like this, it's easy to remember why Bernie fell in love with him—why she's been with him since freshman year. Despite the fact that their families are so intertwined, there's more to it. His beauty. The way he looks at you with that intense gaze, those high cheekbones. His cupid's-bow lips. In another life, maybe I would have been the one who garnered all of Skyler's affection. Maybe I'd be Bernie. But in this one, we're tied together only by her—and our desire to keep our shared secret.

"What makes you think that?" he asks, masking a fear I know is there.

I look over at Bernie, who's now fully engaged in conversation with the actor kid, nodding along to whatever he's saying, smiling, laughing at all the right moments.

"I don't know, she seemed weird before."

"Weird how?"

"Distracted." I pause. "And did you see Esther's not here?"

Skyler looks around the room. "She's probably sick or something. You know how she is." A waiter reaches over his shoulder and sets down a plate of frisée lettuce dotted with little pieces of bacon and blue cheese.

"Maybe I'm just paranoid."

"Self-medicate or something. But don't start twisting shit."

"Hey," I say, slightly hurt. "Asshole."

Skyler narrows his brows. "You didn't tell her anything, right?"

"Obviously."

He purses his lips, and for a second it looks like he doesn't believe me, like he's trying to suss if I'm telling the truth. But I am—because I don't really have a choice. Telling Bernie was never an option. After a beat, he nods. "Neither did I, which means that Bernie doesn't know shit, okay? Let's just get through this week alive. You know how much the Ball means to her."

I push a piece of lettuce around on my plate and chew on the inside of my lip. Skyler's right. Bernie has no idea what happened at that party at Lee's house on Shelter Island. At least not what happened after she left. And what's been going on since.

Her words from that night still sting, how she told me I was acting like a *fucked-up fool*. But that was nothing compared to what I said to her. We apologized to one another the next day and sheepishly, with hesitation and our guards up, decided to move forward.

Because that's the thing about Bernie. She stayed loyal to me, even when she shouldn't have.

I wasn't supposed to be at Lee's house that night. That was my first mistake. Telling her I was home in Brooklyn when I was really at Lee's. It wasn't like we planned to throw a party. Or that we intentionally didn't invite her. It just sort of . . . happened.

"Hey, gorgeous."

I jump at Lee's voice as he plants a soft kiss on my bare shoulder. When I spin around in my seat, I see him crouching behind me in a rumpled linen button-down, his charcoal-gray blazer fitting perfectly over his muscular arms. He's got dark skin and beautiful brown eyes that never break contact, thanks to the confidence instilled in him by his dad, the renowned artist Arti Dubey, and his mom, Arti's gallerist Lizzie Horowitz. Arti, who was born in Goa but came to the States to study fine art at Yale and never left, is best known for his work in the mid-nineties in which he smeared bodily fluids onto eighteen-foot-wide white canvases. He once did a performance piece at Brooklyn Academy of Music that was an allegory about climate change. Except, he performed it nearly nude. Lee hated that project, but I thought it was kind of brilliant.

Arti's pretty revolutionary in the contemporary space and was one of my artistic heroes even before Lee and I got together last year. Since then, I've probably spent more time with Lizzie and Arti than I have with my own parents. Two art world icons are way more interesting than a magazine editor and a cardiologist.

It's not that I started dating Lee only because of who his parents are—or because they showed interest in my work after my exhibit at the Brooklyn Museum. But I'd be lying if I said that I didn't at least *think* about the fact that being with Lee means I get to hang out with one of my idols.

"Where are you sitting?" I ask.

Lee nods over to one of the tables on the side, under a wall of windows that overlooks Excelsior's Olympic-size indoor swimming pool. The only person over there I recognize is Kendall, who looks up and smiles in our direction, giving a little wave.

Kendall and I met in a mommy-and-me music class in Fort Greene Park and even had a nanny share together. But while I stayed in Brooklyn for elementary school, he started at an all-boys prep school uptown in kindergarten. After his dad's health tech company went public, the whole family moved to Tribeca, and then I barely saw him or his little sister, Opal, at all. Not until we both started at Excelsior. Now he spends most of his time working on science experiments or popping by the very occasional party. He's friendly with Lee and Skyler, even though based on what happened in Shelter Island, he should probably want to claw Skyler's eyes out. Though he has no idea. He wasn't there.

All of a sudden, the violin music that had been pumping through the speakers starts to fade away, and someone taps the microphone set up at the front of the room.

Mrs. Shalcross, from the registration table, smiles brightly and addresses the crowd. "Lunch will be served momentarily, so please take your seats. The Legacy Ball kickoff luncheon is about to begin!"

Lee squeezes my shoulder and heads off to his table, and as soon as he's out of earshot, Skyler leans over so his breath is warm against my skin.

"Now you want that bar?"

I elbow him in the side a little too hard, and he winces but doesn't pull away. Finally, like my body has a mind of its own, I nod and watch Skyler pull out a slim pill from his pocket. He presses it into my palm, and I feel its familiar grooves against my skin. It calms me, the little pharmaceutical. The possibilities within. I'm tempted to eat the whole thing now, here. But I already had one today, downed it with my morning coffee a few hours before we got here. And I *did* eat a small hunk of Adderall to get a little more pep just before I entered the building.

But looking around . . . eh, I need this.

I slip it into my mouth and swallow a gulp of water. "That's the last one I take from you," I whisper, already feeling relief.

He laughs softly, mostly because we know that's just another lie shared between us.

Tori

I THOUGHT I was prepared for the kickoff luncheon. I thought that having an odd fascination with the Club—one that led me down YouTube rabbit holes where old dudes claimed the Club was part of the Illuminati and back to my scholarship pamphlet where I first heard mention of the Club—would mean that I was ready to be part of this world myself.

But stepping into Excelsior Prep today, it was immediately obvious that I was foolish to think that stalking alumni on LinkedIn and hunting through our school's digital archives for any mention of the Club could make me feel ready for *this*, an event so over-the-top, so elegant, so extreme that it's hard to believe it's only the first in a series of many that will soon dominate my week.

Who am I kidding? My *life*.

My heart beats faster than usual, and I can't tell if it's from anticipation or dread. Probably a bit of both. I'm seated at a table with eleven other nominees, kids I've never seen before, though apparently, they go to schools just like mine throughout the city.

I wonder if I make eye contact with them long enough, they'll be able to smell the inauthenticity coming off of me in waves. I wonder if they'll know that I don't deserve to be here, not in my simple black sheath dress and Doc Marten loafers, or worse, if they'll assume that I'm a recipient of one of the scholarships we'll spend this whole week raising money for. That thought turns my stomach.

"Tori?" says the preppy-looking kid next to me.

"How'd you know?" I wipe my sweaty palms against my thighs.

He points to my name card. "Tori Tasso, Excelsior Prep."

"Oh. Right."

He extends his hand. "I'm Chase Killingsworth. Gordon Academy."

I take it, even though my skin must be slick. Somehow his grasp is perfectly room temperature, which furthers my girlfriend Joss's theory about all rich people: They somehow stay climate controlled no matter the circumstance.

I'll have to remember to tell her it checks out when I get home to Queens later.

"So," he says. "Any idea who nominated you? I'm pretty sure my dad's golf buddy Anders Lowell put my name in." He says it like I'm supposed to know who Anders Lowell is, and unfortunately, I do, since if you have half a brain cell, you know that Anders is one of the anchors on the *Today* show. But I don't want to give this Chase kid that satisfaction.

"No idea." Chase frowns and I sneak a peek at Skyler sitting over by Isobel Rothcroft, with a look of composed disdain on her face. I wonder how it feels to be him, to be *any* of the other kids here. The ones who take their place in this room for granted, who have assumed from birth that they will become Legacies.

Skyler's eyes flit toward mine and I look away, embarrassed. My chest tightens, but I try to keep my breathing calm. I wish I could say I earned my spot at this table. That I deserve to be here. But he and I both know that's not true—and maybe that's why I can't help feeling like someone's going to pop out from under the table and banish me from the luncheon any second.

Chase shrugs. "Guess we'll find out for sure at Nominations Night, huh? I hear they do a whole big presentation where every senior has to guess which member of the alumni committee nominated them and if they *don't* get it right, they're banned from the Ball."

My stomach drops. "That can't be right."

"You're so full of shit, Chase." The girl to his left leans over and smiles at me. "He's been looking forward to this week since he was ten, so please excuse him." Chase shrinks in his seat, but before the girl can keep talking, that bug-eyed woman from the registration table who looked at me like I had three heads when I said my name walks up to the microphone and gives it a little tap.

I say a silent prayer that I don't have to make conversation with Chase anymore and focus my attention on the woman up front. Behind her, a dozen or so adults are standing in a neat little row, smiling and clasping their hands in front of them.

"On behalf of the Legacy Club Nominating Committee, we want to welcome you all to the annual kickoff luncheon!" Mrs. Shalcross says. Behind her, the adults applaud, gazing out at the tables full of students.

"As you know, every year, the Nominating Committee taps thirty-six Legacy members to select one senior from the Intercollegiate League high school from which they graduated to join the Legacy Club, an honor that begins now but lasts long after you leave high school. Though you won't have access to the actual Club on Sixty-First Street until the Ball itself, after Saturday, you'll get your full membership and a key—yes, a real working key!—which will let you in all hours of the day for the rest of your lives. Inside the club, you will find hotel rooms, a restaurant, a squash court, an indoor pool, a historic library, a ballroom, and so, so much more."

She pauses, a hitch in her breath, and presses one hand against her heart. "We can't tell you how much it means to us to invite thirty-six new, young members into our fold. Look around. These are the people you will go through this week with, the people who will be alongside you through the good and the bad, the fun and the stressful. If you're lucky, they will become some of your best friends, your colleagues. Because Legacy Club members always look out for their own."

I do as she says, zeroing in on all the other students, people who've overlooked me for years. Isobel Rothcroft, who I'm not sure knows my name. Lee Dubey, who called me Taylor when I showed up to his Shelter Island party. Kendall Kirk, who's too busy pining after Isobel to notice anyone else. Bernie Kaplan, who's basically the queen of this whole thing. And Skyler Hawkins, whom I can't look at without feeling like he's the only one who sees me for what I really am: an outsider who's so desperate, she'll do anything to claw her way in.

None of these people are my friends. The idea of them being part of my life forever is . . . impossible.

But I try to remember why I wanted this, why I used all the power I had to score a nomination, no matter the cost. The Club can open doors for me that not even Excelsior can. Sure, I have a perfect GPA, a stellar track record on the debate team, and a full slate of AP courses. But even I know that all of those accolades mean nothing if the right people have no idea you exist. An outstanding resume can get you an interview at a prestigious job or a second look from a college admissions counselor, but growing up in New York City, going to a school like Excelsior, I've learned decisions are made based not on how much you know, but who.

And the only *who* that matters are members of the Legacy Club.

I swallow the lump in my throat and remind myself of one thing: I need this.

I straighten my shoulders and shake my dark hair down my back, listening to Joss's voice in my head. *You're Tori Tasso from Astoria, Queens, whose family has owned the best diner in the neighborhood for the past forty years. You know how to fight for yourself. You deserve a place in this world—now and always. Don't let them tell you otherwise.*

Mrs. Shalcross cedes the mic to a tall Black woman in a navy skirt suit and blouse printed with some sort of coat of arms. "I'm Yasmin Gellar, an Excelsior alum," she says. "Proud to be up here with our nominating committee, even though I'm filling the imposing shoes of our chairwoman Esther Kaplan today."

I sneak a peek at Bernie, whose cheeks are now as red as her hair, though a smile is still plastered on her face. Across the room I see Isobel look my way and do a double take, her mouth forming a small O shape. I avert my eyes, clench my fists. Of course she didn't expect me to be here.

"It's my distinct pleasure to walk you all through this week's schedule and the rules that come with being part of this year's nominated class." Mrs. Gellar pulls a pair of glasses out of her pocket and begins to read off of a few note cards.

Some of the kids around the room start to zone out, like it's obvious they've heard the spiel before from their parents or siblings, aunts or uncles, people in their inner orbit who have been through the mysterious, shrouded Legacy Ball week, which I'm told always takes place during the last few weeks of summer vacation. But I spy a few nominees who perk up, eager to learn more about what they're getting into, what parts of ourselves we'll have to put up for auction, how much we'll have to put on display.

"At the Ball, each of you will be asked to give a short presentation about the value of one of the scholarships the Club funds," Mrs. Gellar says. "Then, all the members in attendance will offer donations to help boost the endowments of those scholarships. But here's the catch." She smiles devilishly and leans in. "Each member has the chance to make a donation in one of *your* names based on how excellent your presentation is."

My stomach jolts. I received one of those scholarships, the Arts and Letters one, the summer before entering Excelsior. It's the only way I got to go here, and I've done my best to keep it hidden. I still remember reading over the pamphlet, a small paragraph on the back of the glossy paper jumping out at me:

> *All Intercollegiate League scholarships are funded by the Legacy Club, one of New York City's premier institutions for independent education. Members of the Club are delighted and honored to welcome in a new class of recipients, who will follow in the footsteps of past students to leave their mark on the Intercollegiate League.*

That was the first time I heard about the Club, the first of *many* times I googled them and read every single word I could find, trying to figure out what it was, who was part of it, and how they became members.

I asked Mom about the Club once, if she thought it was strange that a group of random people decided who got this money, but she told me not to worry about who was in it or why and to just do my best and be glad I got a scholarship. But after I got to Excelsior, it became clear to me how much the Club lords over the school—the city.

All around Excelsior's campus, there are little plaques posted on trees, benches, lunch tables, doorways—GIFTED BY THE LEGACY CLUB. At all-school assemblies, there are always Legacy Club members, holding those signature gold keys, sitting on the dais. They are everywhere, running banks and law firms, museums and talent agencies, and they all came from schools like mine. Once, I overheard an admissions counselor complaining about how they *had* to let in every single Legacy member's child, even if they didn't pass the admissions test, how she heard they even gave out no-interest loans to certain members.

Over the past three years, it has become obvious to me what the Club means, that it affords you not only a permanent place in New York elite society but also a surefire way to financial freedom. And it's also impossible to get nominated if you don't know anyone.

Or so I thought.

It all started with that scholarship, all because of Mom. I wonder what she'd think about me being here now. I fight the stinging in my eyes. I can't let myself cry. Not here. No matter how much I miss Mom.

"Alumni are told to judge the presentations based on your argument, knowledge of the Legacy Club, commitment to scholarship, and, of course"—she pauses, smiling wide—"charisma."

A titter of laughter passes through the room.

"While you will all end this week with a membership in the Club, only one of you will win the cash prize."

I sit up straighter in my seat, leaning in. This is what I have been waiting for.

"The student who earns the most donations in their name will also receive twenty-five thousand dollars, outfitted by the generosity of our nominating committee."

I suck in a breath of air, shock pooling in my throat, and expect those around me to do so, too. But none of the kids at my table stir. A few of them pick at the plates of poached salmon that appeared in front of us while Mrs. Gellar was speaking, tearing the pink flesh with their sterling silver forks.

I guess, for these students, twenty-five thousand dollars might be spending money in college or a few first-class flights to Europe. It may pad their trust funds, their dining budgets. But for me, that money could help buy the twins new laptops, fund Helen's tuition at her soccer clinic, help Dad get through a few mortgage payments, a month of payroll. A sour, bitter feeling swarms my stomach. The people around me have no idea what that might be like.

No one in the house denies that things have been tight since Mom died last spring, and Dad always says he doesn't want me to help—that I shouldn't take up extra shifts at the diner—but this money could give us some much-needed breathing room. This money might change things.

As Mrs. Gellar continues talking about the week's events, how tomorrow we'll all pick up our outfits, and on Thursday we'll convene for the Acts of Service Day, how Friday's dinner will reveal our nominators, all I can think about is that I need to earn that prize—and how far I'm willing to go to get it.

AFTER THE BALL

THE POLICE DO *their best to keep everyone on the corner of Sixty-First Street, which, before tonight, none of the officers had any idea was a significant location. One rookie detective, a young woman with a short dark ponytail, eyes the plaque bolted to the limestone exterior.*

LEGACY CLUB, it reads. MEMBERS ONLY.

The detective pauses and looks around at the teenagers in their ball gowns, their diamonds, their tuxedos, rumpled from a night of dancing— or whatever it was they were doing inside this mysterious building. None of it looks right. None of it looks real. But she should be used to this by now, having worked dozens of cases on the Upper East Side, where the biggest problems have to do with white-collar criminals or rich people yelling about the unhoused neighbors who sleep outside their townhouses.

An older policeman with a graying beard pulls out a megaphone. "We're going to ask everyone to go back inside the building," he says. "No one is allowed to leave the premises. Not until we ask some questions."

A murmur breaks out, and some of the adults, pulling their teenagers along with them, begin to balk at orders coming from a nobody, even if he has a badge. These are people who are unafraid to break the rules, to bend them to their will.

That's what these people do, after all. Break things.

But this isn't one of the crime scenes Homicide usually deals with— the ones where no one cares about the John Does. Tonight's death is different. This lost life was one of the city's best. Most important. Or at least that's what these people will have you believe.

Despite their protests, everyone is nudged back inside the six-story townhouse, gleaming white in the thick, humid air. Along the entry-way, there are no identifying characteristics—no bulletin board pro-claiming upcoming events, no welcome sign, no indication of what it does. What happens inside.

The crowd moves slowly, against their will, until finally, all of the guests are corralled inside the lobby, where a half-eaten ice cream sundae bar melts against the wall, dripping bright green, pink, and brown on the granite floor. A bowl of maraschino cherries sits un-touched, urns of coffee cooling beside them.

"Looks like a great party," one cop mumbles to the detective. "Except for the dead body."

She doesn't laugh. Instead, she looks around at the crowd, their sniffles echoing throughout the room. "Time to divide and conquer?" she asks. The rest of the officers nod.

They've got questions, and perhaps these people have answers.

Bernie

THE LUNCHEON ENDS with slices of warm apple pie made from fruit picked at Excelsior's orchard, but I'm too anxious to eat a single bite. Mrs. Gellar didn't have to call out my mom's absence, but she *did*, and now all I can hope is that no one else noticed.

I glance at my phone for the millionth time today, willing my mom to text me again. I toggle over to Find My Friends and expect to see her icon pop up somewhere in the city, but just as I saw this morning, there's nothing. She's nowhere, and I can't fight the feeling that still, something's wrong.

Around me, wooden chair legs screech against the floor as students stand up, shake hands with one another, and prepare to pick up slim black leather folders, which are sitting at the registration table. Even from here, I can see they have our names on them, lined up in alphabetical order. Inside, our scholarships will be revealed, as will the rest of the rules for the week. When I was little, Mom would show me *her* folder that she kept from when she was a Legacy nominee and tell me stories about what was inside. I always thought when I got mine, we'd pore over it together.

Guess not.

Isobel appears by my side, her eyes hooded slightly, which makes me wonder what kind of fun she and Skyler got into at their table. I can't help but feel a small ball of desperation forming in my stomach. It's always been this way with Isobel—me wanting to protect her, to save her mostly from herself. I've succeeded at times, like when I convinced her to wear one of my tasteful silk tea-length dresses to homecoming instead of her metallic plunge-neck mini, which made her look a little trashy, or when I successfully paired her up with Lee—a huge win for all of us, really—so she would stop making out with those going-nowhere art students always hanging around her neighborhood.

And, of course, there was the time when I forced her to puke up everything she had consumed after it was very obvious she was on the verge of alcohol poisoning at last year's junior prom. Or when I was able to get her into a cab after finding her passed out in some senior's bedroom during a Halloween party freshman year.

But recently, she's been unwilling to take it easy, and I'm not so interested in telling her to cool it. I tried that during the Shelter Island party and that almost broke us. It's exhausting taking care of Isobel.

"Did you see who the sixth nominee is from Excelsior?" She drops her head toward mine, shielding her face with her short hair.

"Nuh-uh," I say. I was too busy trying to keep my composure during the presentation to look around and care.

"Tori Tasso," she whispers.

"Tori Tasso?" I repeat. "She's not . . ." I stop myself before I finish my sentence. There's no point, since both Isobel and I know what I was going to say.

She's not one of us.

"Isn't she from Queens?" I ask instead.

Isobel swats my arm. "I'm from Brooklyn."

"I just . . . I didn't peg her for a Legacy."

Isobel shrugs. "Guess someone did."

I spin around the room and spot Tori in the back by the bay window with her long dark hair and chunky lace-up shoes. She's walking around, not really talking to anyone, looking sort of lost, the same way she did during freshmen orientation. She stuck out then, too, like she didn't know that you should always walk with your shoulders back, your chin tilted up. You could tell she wasn't used to the grandeur of a place like Excelsior by the way she gawked at all the open spaces, the pristinely kept rooms. Even though she's been our classmate for all of high school, she still has that wide-eyed, unsure look about her. Except this time, it's directed at our peers, the other Legacies.

Tori and I have barely said more than two words to each other since freshman year, but maybe I should go talk to her and say hi. If someone thought she deserves to be here, then maybe she does.

Isobel tugs on my arm. "Lee wants to go find somewhere to get a drink," she says, lowering her voice. "Wanna join?"

I open my mouth to say yes, of course, because that's what we do most of the time—hit up the places that have been passed down from generation to generation as *the* bars that don't card or don't care. There's the Mexican spot on the Upper West Side that Skyler loves because they make their margaritas extra strong, and the tapas place near Lee's townhouse in Chelsea that always gives us free mezcal because Arti Dubey is a regular. Isobel doesn't play favorites, though she's always begging us to pop by the natural wine bar near Fort Greene Park so she can walk home for once. Even if I don't like to drink, I still need to be part of it. Because if I'm not, I'm nothing.

"Where are you going?" I ask.

Skyler slinks up behind me and wraps an arm around my waist, which causes Isobel to flinch. "Taking the party elsewhere?" he asks, planting a soft kiss on my cheek.

Isobel looks at me, waiting for my response.

I nod to Isobel and Lee, who's appeared by her side, lacing his fingers into Isobel's. "They're heading out."

Skyler bounces on the balls of his feet. "This thing was stiff as fuck." He loosens his tie. "Let's *do* something."

Lee wiggles his eyebrows at Skyler, and I can already tell they're scheming about what they can get up to for the rest of the evening, but something inside me rebels against the idea of following them.

We don't have any other Ball obligations today, but tomorrow's our final dress fitting, and if my mom isn't there, then everyone will *really* start to wonder where the hell she is and what's going on. I have to find her today. Or at least try.

I shake my head. "You guys go on without me. I feel a migraine coming on." The lie rolls off my tongue and I reach a hand to my forehead, feigning ill.

Isobel cocks her head. "You sure?"

I nod. "Of course. I'll catch up with you guys tomorrow."

Skyler pouts but leans toward me to give me a soft kiss on the mouth, one that sends a fizzling, crackling sensation all through my stomach. I didn't always think we'd be together. Not in the second grade, when Mom told me she and Lulu had already started planning our wedding, but Skyler had just pantsed me on the playground. ("He has a crush on you!" she insisted, though I knew better.) But Skyler was always the person I had run around in diapers with, the boy who let me help decorate his Christmas tree because we didn't have one. We were intertwined in ways we both realized but didn't fully understand.

Not until the summer before ninth grade, when Skyler had a growth spurt and I grew breasts larger than any girl in our class. One August night, a few weeks before school was due to start, we met on the beach between our houses in the Hamptons to watch a meteor shower and share a French chocolate bar my mom had gotten from the boulangerie in town.

We were lying on the blanket together when Skyler rolled over, propping his head up with one hand. I was worried about how I looked to him then, if I was all flattened out, lying like that, or if my hair was too wild from the sea salt misting in the air. But Skyler just looked down at me and smiled, as if he had been waiting for that moment all summer long.

"Bernie." He said it in a whisper, like it was a secret.

I sucked in a breath of air, afraid to say his name back.

"Should we make our parents happy for once?" He bit his lip, devilish and sweet, sending a spasm straight to my stomach, heat throughout my core.

I wanted to play dumb, but it seemed ridiculous. Of course I knew what he meant, and there was only one thing to say.

"Yes."

He closed the space between us, pressing his soft lips to mine, his warm hand to my bare stomach, under my sweatshirt.

We stayed like that for a while, listening to the wind, the waves, the sound of our breathing. And when he pulled back, we both laughed and flopped back down on the blanket. He grabbed my fingers and rubbed his thumb against the back of my hand. "It's just the beginning, isn't it?"

Falling in love with Skyler felt like fulfilling a prophecy, like walking toward my predetermined future. With Skyler, all of these things felt easy: Watching old rom-coms in his bedroom as his hand snaked up my back to undo my bra. Whispering about our future children and if their hair would be fiercely red like mine. Laying my head on his shoulder as we took the crosstown bus to Barney Greengrass on Sunday mornings.

So much has happened since we decided to seal our fate three years ago. But one thing has always stayed constant: our unwavering understanding that we were meant to be together.

Skyler raises his hand and rests his finger pads against my neck. I turn my face up to his. "I'll see you guys tomorrow, don't worry."

"Love you," Skyler whispers into my ear, and for a moment, that settles me, the reminder that even though Mom is missing on the most important week of my life, at least I have Skyler. I'll always have Skyler.

† † †

The penthouse is still and silent when I push open the heavy front door. Thirty-five flights up, this whole floor has been ours since before I was born, since Mom and Dad purchased it with a few million dollars of the fortune they inherited from my maternal grandparents. Over the years, it's become a party venue, hosting Legacy Ball gatherings, and a boardroom for when Dad was working until the wee hours of the night with Lulu Hawkins on some of the biggest cases of his career. It's been home to political fundraisers, private performances from Broadway singers, shivas for some of the city's most iconic personalities, and the best sleepover setting in all of New York, complete with lox and bagel spreads that Mom has catered for Isobel and whoever else has stayed over in one of the many guest rooms.

But to me, it's home.

I step out of my heels in the entryway and set my purse down on the velvet-covered bench. My bare feet echo across the hardwood floors as I make my way past the grand piano toward the kitchen. I plunk a C chord and listen to it echo through the empty rooms.

I yank open the fridge to find it full. It's almost a tease, the fact that all of Mom's weekly deliveries still arrived this morning even though she's not here. The CSA box showed up at eight, full of end-of-summer tomatoes and melons and fresh loaves of sourdough bread. The flower arrangements appeared an hour later in their elegantly wrapped white paper. And just before I left for the luncheon, Damien the doorman rang up with a pink box full of chocolate croissants. That one stung the most. Weekly pastries are *our* thing, pinching off buttery bites of flaky dough from the tucked-away French bakery on Seventy-Fifth. Eating one without her felt like treason.

Mom is big and happy, with elegant features and stark red hair, just like me. She passed her body down like a legacy, and together we revel in our many curves, our strong, wide builds. Sharing croissants before school is a celebration of our bodies, that's what she says.

"I will never catch you counting calories, Bernadette Kaplan," she told me once when talking about her own mother, who was obsessed with being thin and died when Mom was a teenager. "Grandma Rachel was a wonderful woman, but she never learned that food makes you strong, that it is meant to be fun—not a weapon."

Our fridge always reflects that. I pull out a plastic tub of white-fish salad, grab a box of everything bagel chips from the pantry, and set them on the marble island. I wonder for a second if I should get some utensils, but then I remember Mom's the only other person in the house who likes smoked fish, and I dunk a chip right into the dip.

The open container doesn't make the smell go away, though. Mom's scent. Her lilac perfume. It's everywhere. Dabbed on napkins, on the drapes, on the tablecloth. She's always here, even when she's gone.

Gone.

Where *is* she?

"There you are."

I nearly jump as my dad pads into the kitchen wearing no shoes and a suit, his tie sloppily hung around his neck. His forehead is dewy like he's been sweating, and there are bags under his eyes.

"I thought you were at work," I say.

He gives the whitefish a funny look but reaches for a cracker. "Remote depositions today."

I nod like I care what that means. There's a tension between us as the wet sounds of chewing fill the air. Dad rests his hands on the counter and flexes his fingers. He peers at me over his glasses.

"Everything okay?" I ask.

"Work stress." He doesn't offer much else.

There's an awkward pause, and I fill the void. "I got my scholarship assignment. Arts and Letters."

Dad grunts. "That's what your mom had when she was your age. Never shut up about it."

An unsettled feeling rises in my stomach. Dad didn't grow up like Mom, with her private schooling and the inherited Hamptons house. He comes from a working-class suburb of Detroit, where most everyone he knew was employed by an auto company. Dad always says he was ostracized for caring more about his math textbooks than changing motor oil. As Mom tells it, Rafe Kaplan was a star student and earned a full ride to Cornell, which is where he met Mom, who knew she would go there since she was a child, thanks to the donation that helped fund the library renovation.

Dad pretends he's above all this Legacy Club stuff and everything that comes with membership, but after three martinis last year, Mom told me that's how he and Lulu Hawkins were able to start Hawkins Kaplan in the first place. After Mom introduced Dad to Lulu one winter break home from college, Lulu and Dad were determined to start their own law firm that "takes down bad guys," as Dad likes to put it. After law school and stints at big corporate law firms, they finally were able to do that, thanks to some hefty networking done at the Legacy Club.

Hawkins Kaplan struck gold twenty years ago when they won a suit against a major gas and electric company that was contaminating the water in a small town in Idaho, which gave thousands of people cancer. The plaintiffs in that case walked out with huge settlements, while Lulu and Rafe became heroes, landing the cover of *Time* magazine, a visit to the White House, regular TV appearances, and even more high-profile cases that keep them in the spotlight. Now it's hard to turn on the news without seeing my dad talking back at me.

But all their success can be traced back to the Club. It's where they were able to get their first celebrity clients all those years ago, thanks to Yasmin Gellar being one of the top talent agents in New York. It's not a coincidence that Anders Lowell has Dad on the

Today show every other week. It's the Club connection and he knows that.

Dad starts to move back toward his office, where I know he'll stay for the rest of the night—the week, if he had it his way—but I can't let him go. Not yet.

"I got a text from Mom," I say.

Dad stops, his bare feet flexing on the floor. He turns around, his mouth a firm, straight line. "See?" he says. "She's fine."

"It didn't sound like her. She got the menu wrong."

Dad winces, running a hand through his hair, gray but still thick. He licks his lips, looks up to the ceiling.

"What?" I ask.

I can tell he's mulling over a few different lies, playing out each one in his head.

"I'm not one of your clients, Dad, I can handle the truth."

He opens his mouth, then shuts it, and looks me right in the eye. "You think you're old enough?"

I nod emphatically, though as soon as he asks, I'm not sure I am.

Dad's face relaxes, and it's as if something inside him releases. "I sent that text."

"What?"

Dad shrugs. "From her iPad. No oysters, huh?"

Fear rises in my throat. "I don't understand. Where is she?"

He shrugs. "I have no idea."

"Don't you think we should call the police or something?"

Dad laughs and shakes his head.

"How is this funny to you? Your wife is *missing*."

"Sweetie, your mother has done this before."

I blink once, then again. "What are you talking about?"

Dad sighs. "That time she went to the Hamptons to finish the bathroom renovations when you were in sixth grade?" He throws up his hands. "Had no idea."

I shake my head, remembering the texts she sent me while she was gone during that trip.

Dad points his thumb back at his chest. "Me," he says. "I texted you. Same thing when she left for that sailing trip to Spain. There was no renovation, no sailing trip. She turns her phone off and goes . . . wherever. She does this, and I've always covered for her."

I press my palm to my temple. "I don't understand. She just . . . disappears? And you text me, pretending to be her?"

"We made a deal years ago. Your mother needs her space. It's just something about her that I gave in to a long time ago." He says it bitterly, and I know what he means. That marrying Esther Baum, marrying into her world meant that he had to defer to her needs over the years, acquiesce, make himself smaller. It was the price he paid for gaining access to her wealth, her network, even after he became *the* Rafe Kaplan. "It's one of her . . . quirks. A selfish one."

"But where does she go?" My heart is racing, and it feels like the ground is moving beneath me.

He waves a hand around. "Oh, wherever. I often find out later. Some spa in Arizona. A villa in Mexico. The Soho Farmhouse in England once. I think she gets off on keeping it a secret, knowing no one in the world can find her. Not even you."

I step back, almost like I've been hit. "But Mom tells me everything."

Dad sighs. "Turns out, she doesn't." He reaches over and pats my hand awkwardly. "That's why I'm *not* worried."

"So, what? We just wait around until we figure out where she is? If she's coming back?"

Dad looks annoyed now, crossing his arms over his chest and checking his watch, like he has to get back to work. But then he looks at me with a pang of pity on his face. "I'm sorry to let you in on the secret that your mother is less than perfect, Bern. But maybe it's time you found out. See who she really is. You said yourself that you were old enough."

My jaw drops open and my head swims with questions, but before I can ask them, Dad looks at his watch, a frustrated scowl coming over his face. A few beads of sweat form at his brow. "I have to get back," he says, and begins to disappear down the hallway. Then suddenly something dawns on me—one question I must ask.

"She comes back, though," I call. "Right? She's always come back."

Dad turns around and nods. "She does," he says. "We just don't know when."

He closes the door to his office, and the kitchen is suddenly cold, colder than it was before, and now all I want to do is find Mom and prove him wrong. She would never leave me stranded this week of all weeks.

With shaking hands, I pull out my phone and let my muscle memory move through it, pulling up our texts, where nothing has changed, and Find My Friends.

Sure enough, no one's there, just an empty map of New York City. But then something blinks—a photo of a woman who looks just like me, with bright red hair and dark sunglasses shielding her eyes. My mom's icon photo.

It appears fast, a moving target as it heads up Madison Avenue, stopping at Seventy-Sixth Street. But just as quickly as it appeared, the icon vanishes. No location found.

I pull up Google Maps, trying to remember what the hell is on that corner. Could she possibly be *here* only a few blocks away? Not in some faraway paradise, forgetting all about the Legacy Ball? About me? I zoom in, and when I see what's there, a beat of hope thumps in my chest. The Trinity Hotel, Mom's favorite place to get a drink or a massage.

Before I can think too hard, I'm back at the front door, stuffing my feet into my platforms and grabbing my bag. If I time it right, I'll be there in fifteen minutes, and with any luck, my mom will be, too.

Isobel

"OHMIGOD, NOT BARTHOLOMAY'S." I groan as we hop out of the taxi in front of the Trinity Hotel. I know my way around the Upper East Side almost as well as I do my own neighborhood, Clinton Hill, but I wasn't really paying attention to the address Skyler gave the driver, thanks to Lee's wandering hands in the back seat.

Skyler and Lee think this place is the most fabulous bar in all of New York, but in reality, it's an overhyped, old-school spot known for serving twenty-five-dollar cocktails and ignoring our ages thanks to the fact that Skyler's family owns one of the long-term rooms that they let relatives stay in when they come to town. Putting our orders on the Hawkins tab didn't always feel so bad, but since Shelter Island, I've bristled at the idea.

Skyler waves me off and Lee grabs my hand. "Come on," he says. "It'll be fun." He rests two fingers on my chin and smiles, which is all it takes for me to give in. Plus, I know he's right. It *will* be fun, and right now I'm itching for something to change my mood—a drink, a buzz, anything to turn this afternoon into something *fun*. He grabs my hand and I let him pull me inside the hotel lobby, past the guests with their Louis Vuitton luggage and their dozens of dress bags. No one stops us as we head to the bar, dark and luxe, with mahogany woodwork and thick, hand-painted wallpaper. No one bats an eye when Skyler plunks down in a booth and wiggles his fingers up to the waiter, who comes right over.

He orders us martinis, and as soon as the frosty coupe glasses arrive, my adrenaline kicks in, and the promise of this boring, stuffy day turning into a full-on *night* takes hold. I take a big gulp, feel the cold briny liquid slide down my throat, and let the familiar feeling wash over me. The one that tells me to *keep going, don't stop, more, more, more.* It's like there's a pilot light inside me and one sip, one pill, one *anything* has the power to set me on fire.

It's the same urge, the same rushing, churning hunger that keeps me on the hunt for the greatest party, the latest night, the most fun anyone has ever had in their entire lives. I've always been this way, even when I was little—constantly searching for a greater power, a better time. And often it has come in the form of altering my reality and exploring what else is possible.

Sometimes I wish I could moderate myself like Bernie does, have a bit more control. But then I wouldn't have the stories—the *life*. Sure, sometimes those stories end with little memories and a few moments in front of the toilet bowl. But it sure beats acting like every decision is one that might set off a sequence of events that could alter the course of your life for the worse. Being Bernie must be exhausting. All I want is a little adventure, and I sure as hell didn't find it at the Legacy luncheon.

I drain the rest of my martini and lean into Lee, feeling his warmth. He wraps an arm around me and laughs at some story Skyler's telling. But all of a sudden, Skyler stops talking and looks right at me. "Want another, Is?"

Lee turns to me, curious.

I kick Skyler under the table, but he doesn't take the hint.

"I'm fine." I reach for my drink but realize it's empty.

"We had a little party at the luncheon." Skyler nudges Lee's side but Lee frowns. He may not mind that my dad's diagnosed anxiety means that I know exactly where he keeps his stray

medication—old refills he's forgotten about hidden in dressers—
and that we can enjoy them together, just us. But whenever Skyler gets involved and starts feeding them to me, Lee's quick to
harden. Good thing he doesn't know that most of my stash comes
from Skyler—or what secret I'm keeping to make sure it stays that
way.

"I'm good," I say, pressing my fingertips into my glass.

Skyler narrows his eyes. "Liar," he says. But before he pushes
it, he stands up abruptly, knocking over my glass. "I'm gonna go
to the bathroom." He steps out of the booth and walks toward
the hallway, but not before checking out every single woman in
the bar, even though they're all nearly twice our age. I slide farther
down the booth, suddenly not wanting to be here at all.

There's an awkward silence now, one that tends to creep into
our dynamic more and more these days when it's only Lee and
me, free from Skyler or Bernie, or his parents to fill the void.
We *do* have things in common—friends, art, partying, our physi-
cal chemistry—but sometimes when it's just the two of us, alone
without buffers, I wonder if we would be together if it weren't for
our friends. I try to think of something to say, but then Lee turns
to me. "You gotta be careful at Legacy stuff this week."

My stomach seizes, and I already feel the excuse coming up
my throat. *I get anxious.* Which is true, even though I don't have a
diagnosed disorder like Dad. *I needed to take the edge off.* Also true.
I was bored.

But I say none of those things and instead tap my empty glass.
"Should we get another?" I ask.

"You sure?"

As if I don't know my limits. But the last thing I want to do
right now is pick a fight with Lee.

"I'm fine," I say. "But if you want to dip, we can head back to your place? Watch a movie or something?"

I slide my hand onto his thigh, knowing just where to squeeze to get a reaction, but Lee stays still and shakes his head.

"I promised Dad I'd go over my Yale essay with him tonight."

"Oh?" I say, perking up. "I could come with you. I've been meaning to talk to Arti about—"

Lee clears his throat, cutting me off, and for a second there's another uncomfortable moment of quiet between us. "Sorry," he says. "I gotta do this one-on-one with him."

"Oh yeah," I say, worried my desperation to talk shop with Arti is a little too obvious. "Of course."

He checks his watch. "Shit, I should probably get going soon, anyway." His eyes flit to mine. "You finish your application yet? My dad said he'd look it over. Put in a good word with the fine arts school."

A lump forms in my throat as I nod, the lie swelling in my brain. Just a few months ago, when Lee and I were still new and shiny, he wanted us to promise that we would both apply early action to Yale. That way I could follow in his dad's footsteps in their art program, and he could pursue environmental science just like he planned—and we'd only be a few quick hours from New York.

But even though it's where Arti studied *and* he said he would help me with my portfolio, I'm not so sure I want to go to Yale. Or college at all right now. The more I think about it, the more I want a reset—a break in the form of a year away from basically everything I grew up with. My brother, Marty, suggested this gap year program in Australia, where you help kids who've been through trauma heal with drawing. I even started filling out an application.

But I can't say that to my parents, who are obsessed with the idea of me getting a degree immediately. And I certainly can't say that to Lee, who's convinced the best years of our lives await us together in New Haven.

"I'm almost done."

Lee smiles, the unease that was there a minute ago gone. "Good." He looks around, then gets up. "Don't tell Skyler I left. He'll kill me for ducking out early." He leans down and kisses me before I can protest. "See you tomorrow."

"Wait—" I say, but he's already gone and suddenly I'm sitting here, very aware of the fact that I'm about to be alone with Skyler, feeling the need to get the hell out of here as soon as possible. But before I can follow Lee out the door, Skyler slides back into the booth.

"Where'd fucker go?"

"Home. I should probably get going, too." I make a move to pick up my purse, but Skyler grabs my wrist a little too tightly.

"One more drink. You can't leave me alone." He pauses, raising an eyebrow. "Unless you'd prefer I call my other friend?"

I try to wriggle my wrist away, but Skyler doesn't let go. His grip is tight and his eyes flash a warning, a sign that he loves that he *owns* me in this sick, twisted way. I wish I could tell Bernie the truth, but even if I did, I'm not quite sure she'd believe me. There's a risk she'd choose Skyler over me, especially after what I said to her that night. And I'm not about to take it.

Right now, his smirk is menacing, but the martini has hit me harder than I'd like to admit, so when the waiter comes around, I let Skyler order me another one as he drops my arm. The second drink makes it easier to ignore him and the way his eyes keep glancing down to my chest, the way he licks his lips as older female guests walk by in heels.

But when he stops talking and elbows me in the side, causing me to spill half my drink down my jumpsuit, I zone back in. "What the fuck is wrong with you?" I hear myself slurring as I drop a wad of napkins into my lap, hoping to soak up the spill.

Skyler points to the front desk. "Didn't she have a migraine?"

I follow his gaze to find Bernie, with her bright red hair, talking closely to the concierge, her brow furrowed and her fingers clenched around her purse.

I nod. But why was she lying?

Tori

I LOVE THE way the diner smells during the dinner rush, like meat grease and French fries, mixed with the sweet, clean scent of lemon Pledge coming from a spray bottle.

All the servers are moving in a swift, graceful choreography I've known since I was thirteen, when Dad finally started letting me put on the white apron and hand out laminated menus bound together with plastic spirals. Tasso's is the most welcoming place in all of New York City. At least to me.

There are mermaids painted on the walls, mint-green tiles on the floor, navy booths made of leather that never cracks. At first, it was hard to come here after Mom died. I saw her in every corner, screwing in fresh lightbulbs, laughing with the regulars, manning the pastry display. Sometimes I thought she loved this place more than my dad did, even though it had been passed down through *his* family. She always said it saved her, appeared in her life at a time when she needed it the most.

But after she died, coming back here was the only thing that made sense, made me remember her laugh and her smell and her smile. Being here now makes me feel like she's with me. At least for a moment.

I plunk down at the bar with a platter of fries and gyro meat and drop my bag to the floor.

"They didn't feed you at that fancy lunch-y thing?" Marina, the hostess who's been around since I was a kid, leans over the bar and wipes down a few coffee and ketchup stains. She waves goodbye to a couple over my shoulder.

I drag a fry through a puddle of tzatziki and pop it into my mouth.

"Eh, none of it was as good as this."

Marina clucks her tongue and shakes her head, causing her frizzy dark curls to bounce around her face. "You're ridiculous, you know that?"

"I know."

She laughs and glances over to the simple wood door that leads to my dad's office. No doubt he's in there, triple-counting yesterday's haul, going over food orders and shift lineups.

"He okay?" I ask.

Marina gives me a little grimace.

"Tell me."

She props her elbows up on the bar like she's going to say something but then leans back, as if she's changed her mind.

"Oh, come on. I can handle it." But there's no way Marina's going to tell me whatever's going on. She's known me since I was in diapers and still sees me that way. Especially since Mom died. She took it upon herself to stock our chest freezer with forty-five frozen spinach pies and just as many trays of moussaka.

"Why don't you talk to him yourself, huh?" She nods to the door and leaves the bar to help an elderly foursome find their seats. I finish the last French fry and bus my dish so the servers don't have to worry about it, and then linger by the door to Dad's office for a second before knocking.

"Tori," Dad calls from inside. "Come on in."

I turn the knob and poke my head in. "How'd you know it was me?"

"You think I don't know my own daughter's footsteps?" He shakes his head, which is hanging down low over his desk, covered in yellow legal pads and an old computer. I can see some sort of spreadsheet displayed on the screen. "Nah," he says. "Marina texted. Said to prepare for a line of questioning."

I shut the door behind me and sink into the brown leather chair opposite his desk. I smile, grateful for these still moments when it's just the two of us. It's dorky to say but my dad's always been my best friend. He used to schedule Tori Time, where we would spend the whole day together while Mom took diner duty for the day. They were the best—Mister Softee cones, trips to Coney Island, visits to the Socrates Sculpture Park, lazy days spent playing board games by the waterfront. I always told my dad everything.

Until this year.

When the nomination for the Legacy Club came, he first thought it was a notice related to my scholarship. But when I told him about how the Club selected high school seniors to be life-long members, he was straight-up confused. "Sounds like a place where children of billionaires can get tax write-offs." He laughed at his own nonjoke and went back to making scrambled eggs at the kitchen, turning away from me.

Part of me was miffed that he didn't seem to understand the weight that the invitation held, but the other part felt vindicated by the fact that he *didn't* know anything about the inner workings of the Club. In some twisted way, this confirmed to me that it really *was* the type of thing whose importance could be fully comprehended only by those in the know. My dad was not one of those people.

But perhaps I could be.

We didn't talk much about the Club after that, but I couldn't let go of the gnawing guilt I felt about the way I got my invitation—that I didn't really deserve access to that building, that lifestyle.

"Harold?" someone calls from outside. "Light's out in the bathroom!"

Dad shakes his head. "Gotta do everything around here," he mumbles before stepping out into the hallway.

I give him a half-hearted smile, but when he leaves, I take a closer look at the papers strewn about on his desk. There are a few new menu mock-ups and some seating charts laying out the streetside tables. But underneath all that are papers, stamped with bright red letters that make my stomach flip. They all say OVERDUE.

I pick one up and try to decipher the rows and rows of numbers, each climbing higher and higher into five digits. I fumble around for another one, a letter from the Queens Savings Bank addressed to Harold Tasso. When I start reading, my stomach lurches.

> *This letter is to remind you that your mortgage payment is due and payable on the 1st of every month and late if paid after the 15th day of every month. To date we have not received your full monthly payment, just as we did not receive payment for the last three months. Your total owed bill is $21,890.*
>
> *As you know, your failure to pay this month's principal will result in a default. Please contact . . .*

Before I can keep reading, the door opens, and Dad steps inside and flops back down in the chair.

"I swear, these guys—" But then he sees me holding the letter. "Hey, Tori. Put that down."

I shake my head. "Are we gonna lose—"

But Dad cuts me off with a steady hand on my shoulder. "Everything's fine, Tori."

"I know things have been tight since Mom died. I'm not a child."

Dad looks at me hard. "I know you're not a child."

"Then treat me like an adult. Tell me how bad it is."

Dad pulls off his glasses and rubs his eyes, and for a second, I think he might cry. When he looks up, I see exhaustion on his face.

"Tori," he says again. "We're gonna get through this. The money is coming, you know. The lawyers promised. Any day now."

My eyes sting and my throat becomes scratchy. He's been saying that forever, like these lawyers are about to drop us a golden parachute. But as the days have turned into weeks and now months, I can't help but feel like the tiny amount of hope in my heart is more juvenile than realistic. And yet . . . and yet, I'm desperate to believe him, to make money a nonissue for us.

It wasn't always like this. Not when Mom was healthy, before she fell down the stairs while taking ingredients into the diner's basement and fractured her hip. It wasn't a life-threatening injury, just an unfortunate accident. A huge pain in the butt that would keep her off her feet for months. The ER doctor said it would require only one surgery and some inpatient rehab. Dad even made her a special cushioned stool so she could sit behind the hostess stand at the diner while she healed.

But the doctor admitted her to a hospital that was overcrowded and understaffed, and during her weeklong stay, no one realized she had contracted pneumonia. She'd had asthma all her life, and even though Dad threw a fit, the hospital didn't do much of anything to help. The staff barely looked in on her at all. The infection spread quickly, and within two weeks she was on a ventilator, dying right in front of us.

It was preventable. A devastating case of malpractice and negligence. That's what the lawyers said when they contacted us a few weeks after her funeral, after the platters of meat and hand-wrapped dolma stopped arriving on our stoop. Two twentysomethings in dark suits and shiny hair came to our house and told Dad we had a case against the hospital, that we could sue. That we'd get millions of dollars in relief. They flashed some business card, and I watched from the staircase as my dad, stooped over in shock, shook their hands and said yes.

It didn't take long for those lawyers to settle with the hospital system so the case wouldn't have some prolonged public trial, but the money hasn't come yet. We're still waiting, trying to pay off her medical bills while the reality of her death has barely sunk in.

"It's been months," I say, my voice small. "Can't they give you a timeline?"

Dad swallows and runs a hand back and forth over his bald head. "I keep calling and . . ." He throws up his hands. "Nothing."

"Maybe you should take *them* to court," I mumble, half joking.

I expect Dad to laugh but he just nods slowly, his arms crossed over his chest. "I don't want you to worry, Tor," he says. "We're gonna be okay."

I nod, knowing he's lying, that if we don't come up with this money fast, we could lose everything my family's worked for.

And if I'm being honest, it's not just that. Losing the diner would be like losing my mom all over again.

"Especially now that you have that fancy Club membership, huh?" He pats my arm, like he's proud. Like he *gets* it, even though he doesn't. "You're gonna run some business one day that's gonna make us all millionaires. But until then, we'll always have Tasso's."

"Sure, Dad."

His face falls slightly, but then he nods toward the door. "Why don't you help Nico with gelato service. Good tips tonight."

I stand up and leave his office, closing the door gently behind me, but not before hearing him sigh a little too loudly, his chair squeaking as he leans his weight back.

But he doesn't know that I can help. I can *do* something. I can win that money.

Twenty-five thousand dollars.

An obscene amount of money to most people in the world, to everyone I know. Everyone except the other Legacy Club kids. The students who didn't even raise an eyebrow when Mrs. Gellar mentioned a cash prize.

It would be more than enough to help float us for a few months.

I reach into my backpack and pull out the heavy leather folder I got at the end of the luncheon and open it up to reveal my scholarship assignment. *Arts and Letters*, the very one I was awarded three years ago.

> *Your job is to persuade donors to fund the Arts and Letters scholarship in your name by showing them why this scholarship can help those in need*

*experience the incomparable education you received
at one of the Intercollegiate League schools.*

I look up, a wave of realization passing over me. There's no one who can do this better than I can—no one who can convince these rich assholes better than me. A determination sets in to my core. I'm going to win.

AFTER THE BALL

THE FOYER IS *cavernous, full of tulle, tuxedos, and smudged lipstick. All around, there are stifled sobs, whispers, the drifting winds of gossip, as the cops bring each guest, one by one, into side rooms for questioning.*

No one really knows what's happened, but everyone is desperate to find out, to dig through the events of the evening—the week—for clues or excuses.

One group of students huddle together, their wide-eyed expressions hidden behind curtains of hair, manicured fingers.

"She did deserve to win," one young girl exclaims to another.

"I just didn't think he would go that far," another says.

"Drop that bomb here? She knew better."

One boy approaches the group. "Have you seen Tori? Tori Tasso?"

The first girl shakes her head. "No." Her face goes white. "Wait, was it her?"

A hint of hope punctuates her words, noticeable only to those who feel it, too, who know that if the deceased was someone whose presence had signaled a shift, who was new and unusual, and thus an outsider, that perhaps news of a death may not be a tragedy but a relief. No one here dares disturb the atmosphere, the tradition, the peaceful transfer of generational power. But Tori . . . well, Tori did.

The girl cranes her head to see above the crowd toward the back of the room, where no one tries to venture. There, oversized windows extend from the marble floor to the ceiling, illuminating a garden down below.

But in that garden, out through those spectacularly shiny windows, one could peer straight onto the patio, where pools of blood have stained stone and shards of glass, where flower beds have been trampled and smushed, where a body landed after being thrown from the roof.

Bernie

"ARE YOU SURE you haven't seen her?" One hand grips the front desk tightly while the other stays wrapped around my phone, the screen bright, waiting for my mom's icon to appear again.

But the hostess shakes her head. "Sorry, no."

"You're certain? Long red hair, just like mine? She's here all the time, usually for spa appointments."

The woman purses her lips. "I'm so sorry but no one has checked in here under that name."

"You can't ask again?" My heart beats so fast, I feel frantic, like it's going to thump right out of my chest. This is my only clue, the only indication that Mom is still somewhere in the city, that she may come back in time for any of the events taking place this week.

The woman shakes her head yet again. "So sorry, Miss Kaplan. Perhaps you are mistaken."

A lump forms in my throat, but I bite the inside of my cheek to stop the tears from coming. If Mom were here, she'd tell me to roll my shoulders back and tilt my chin up. To project confidence even if there is none. I smooth out my expression.

"Of course," I say. "Thank you."

I spin around and let my face fall as I take a few steps toward the door, pulling my jacket around my middle. But when I look up and into Bartholomay's, where I've spent way too many nights with Skyler, I come face-to-face with him and Isobel staring right at me.

Shit.

They both look stunned, and I get that gnawing feeling in my stomach that I've had ever since the day after that Shelter Island party. My chest tightens as I think about that night.

I hadn't planned on going out, but when Skyler sent me a text, begging me to join him at Lee's, I figured what the hell. It was only a quick Uber over the ferry, and I was bored at the house since Mom was attending a fundraiser dinner at the Parish Museum.

But when I checked the Excelsior group chat, I saw someone had posted photos of Isobel wearing a bikini doing a keg stand, and I realized Lee was throwing a full-blown rager. Suddenly, I was short of breath in the car as we inched forward across the Long Island Sound. She had told me she was at home in Brooklyn when she was really *here*, making a fool of herself and, by extension, me.

Something inside me hardened, and when I arrived at the party, walked in, and saw Isobel sprawled across not only Lee's lap, but Skyler's, too, jealousy pooled in my stomach. The three of them looked like the perfect little trio, laughing at something uproarious, tossing back shots, and spilling all over one another as Isobel looped her arms around both of their necks.

Fury started to build until I found myself walking over to them and pulling Isobel off Skyler.

"Bernie!" she squealed. "You came!"

"Seems like you really care," I said, the words sharp on my tongue.

Isobel stood on wobbly feet. "Stick up your ass or something?" she asked, laughing.

My face grew hot and I was so mad, my vision started to blur. How could she not understand how mortifying it was to show up and find her all over Skyler? To not have been invited by her?

Isobel started walking toward me, but I backed away just as she tried to hug me. "Get off," I said, and she tumbled to the ground, her knees landing in a sickening thud on the hard slate.

"Fuck, Bernie." Isobel struggled to stand and by now there was a group gathering around us, Lee and Skyler whispering to one another. "I was just trying to give you a hug."

A desire to keep this from being a whole *thing* made me help Isobel up. When I got close to her, I whispered in her ear. "You lied. You told me you were home."

It was easier to say I was mad about *that* than the real reason, that Isobel had acted out my worst fear: that Skyler would realize soon that I wasn't fun or exciting enough to be with, that all of our family history and intertwined lives wouldn't be enough to keep him with me, someone who was desperate to keep up appearances even when no one else in my life seemed to care.

Isobel laughed. "Seriously, Bern? It's not like this party was a secret." Her voice carried through the night and people turned to stare, inching closer toward us.

"Come on," I said, blinking back tears. "Don't be like this."

"Like what?" she said, laughing. "Fun? You should try it!"

"You're acting like a fucked-up fool," I said loud enough for everyone to hear. Isobel's drunk eyes blinked in shock and stayed on me, my face, even though she was swaying back and forth, her bikini strap slipping down her shoulder. "You should be embarrassed of yourself."

"Me?" Isobel laughed, regaining her stance. "You're the one who should be embarrassed. Showing up here and yelling at me for what? Not deigning to make sure you knew every detail of this party? Grow up." She paused to finish whatever was left in her cup. "You think you're God's gift to Earth, that you're *so* much better than everyone else."

I took a step back, heat rising in my chest. Isobel had never spoken to me like that.

"Fuck you," I whispered.

Isobel walked toward me, her fists clenched by her sides. She was messed-up but alert, which made everything she said next so much worse because I knew she meant it. "Do you really think anyone here would be friends with you if you weren't *the* Bernie Kaplan?"

Lee walked up then and put a hand on her arm. "Come on, Is. You don't mean that."

Isobel stopped then and brought a hand to her mouth, her eyes growing wide. "Shit," she said, and I knew she was about to apologize. But I wasn't going to stick around to hear it. Not after she said my worst fears aloud for everyone to hear them.

I looked for Skyler in the crowd that had gathered and found him, heading toward me, a stunned expression on his face. But he was a moment too late, and by then I had run off toward the street, tears streaming down my face, where my Uber hadn't left yet and I was able to hitch a ride back home. As I looked out the window, I could see Skyler running to the car, and soon after we turned down the street, I received a dozen texts from him, apologizing and offering to come after me. Isobel didn't reach out. Not until the next day when she asked to come over and apologize.

She blamed the whole thing on alcohol and Xanax, and admitted that she sometimes thought I hated her, that she wanted to hurt me in that moment. She said she didn't believe those things, that she regretted them completely.

It took a few weeks for us to come back together, for our bond to heal slightly. But the scab's still there, threatening to scar, and we both know that we can't go back to the way things were before that night, can't even talk about what she said to me. Sometimes when I see her alone with Skyler, or partying with Lee, I worry that she was right. That no one would be friends with me if I wasn't *me*.

But now, Skyler's the first to spring up from the table, and he bounds toward me, his face morphing from surprise to delight. It's just enough to settle my nerves, to convince me that he's genuinely glad to see me, that he knows I can live a little, just like Isobel. But as the space between us closes, I realize that I'm going to have to lie about why I'm here—what I came here to find.

"Babe," he says, wrapping his arms around my waist. "You're feeling better?"

"*So* much better."

"How'd you know we were here?"

"A little birdie," I say, coy.

Skyler's grin deepens, believing whatever the hell he thinks that means, and he tightens his grasp on my waist, nuzzling his chin into my neck. I feel eyes turn to look at us, to take in the scene. Some of them may recognize us, may know who our parents are. But it's the others who intrigue me—the ones who glance sideways and know that whoever we are, we're important, relevant.

It's because of the way our parents showed us to carry ourselves, to dress, to speak. It's been hammered into us since we were children—how to tilt your chin up just a little and walk straight and make eye contact. To omit *like* and *um* from our vocabulary and to have bodily awareness in every room we enter. All of this helps portray sophistication, poise, the idea that we are worthy of being among New York's elite one day. That we already are.

In moments like this, my heart swells with the weight of *being* Bernie Kaplan. It's almost as if my life was predestined—that when we were in our mothers' wombs, Skyler's parents and mine decided we would be together, that our lives would converge and explode in a dynamic partnership intended to solidify our families' loyalties toward one another for generations to come.

"Come on," Skyler says, directing me back to the booth where Isobel waves eagerly.

I slide into a seat so I'm sandwiched between them like I have been so many times before. This *should* feel natural—like there's nowhere I'd rather be than between my best friend and my boyfriend—but something feels off. I shake the feeling, knowing it's only because I'm keeping something from them.

That has to be it.

Isobel rests a hand on my arm. "I'm *so* glad you're here," she says, cuddling into my side. "Lee just left and this day was *dead*." Her words run together like mush, and for a second, I'm grateful that she doesn't suspect a thing about my mom or why I was here in the first place. "But now you're here! Everything's coming up us." She holds her glass up in the air and hugs me hard. I lean into her, letting her envelop me.

A tumbler with something bright yellow, garnished with an orange, is placed in front of me, and I take a sip gingerly, slowly, feeling the booze hit my brain in an instant. My lungs are on fire and everything in my body is telling me to push the drink away. But Skyler squeezes my knee beneath the table, and I decide to have one. Only one.

"Give us a toast, Bernie," Skyler says, his thumb grazing my bare skin.

"Yes, yes," Isobel says, jumping up and down in her seat.

I pause, wondering what to say to these two, the people who are closest to me in the world.

"Well," I start, holding my glass in the air. "To . . . us and whatever comes this week. To our future in the Club."

"Amen," Skyler says, downing the rest of his glass.

Isobel follows suit, and I'm left glancing at the entrance, hoping that any minute my mom will walk through the revolving door with a squeal and a hug, letting me know that the past twenty-four hours has all just been an elaborate prank.

But she doesn't come. And neither Isobel nor Skyler notice anything strange. So, I continue sipping my drink, and even though it tastes like poison and I can already feel my control waning, I stick around while Isobel calls out to the waiter, "Another!"

THREE DAYS
BEFORE THE BALL

Isobel

I WAKE UP with a sandy throat and a pounding headache that seems like it's about to split my brain in two. My eyes blink open and all I see is pink. Familiar blush and peony tones coating everything in front of me. For a second, I wonder where I am, but then I roll over and realize I'm in Bernie's bed, her pretty, pale comforter shielding my gaze from the morning sun streaming through her window.

"Argh," I groan, and flop my arm around, expecting to find her next to me, but the bed's empty and I just hit plush feathertop.

I reach around for my phone and find it hiding beneath the pillow, the battery down to 5 percent. The clock reads ten a.m.

Shit.

Bernie's probably been up for hours, a special little skill of hers being that she wakes up at seven a.m. every single day without an alarm, and will probably judge me for sleeping this late and being hungover as hell. But as last night comes back to me, I remember *she* was there with us, going drink for drink. Or . . . was she? I definitely remember her making a toast. So unlike Bernie. So free. It was almost unnerving.

Bernie raps her knuckles on the doorframe. "Oh, good. You're up."

"Barely," I moan. But when I peek at Bernie, I'm grateful to see that even though she's padding into the room with a mug of coffee, she's still in her polka-dot pajamas, her bright red hair tied in a sloppy topknot, depuffing strips stuck to the skin below her eyes.

Bernie laughs and tosses me an electrolyte-filled bottle of water, which I guzzle while sitting up in bed.

"Please tell me your mom set out a full spread," I say, suddenly craving an everything bagel with scallion cream cheese.

Bernie bristles and turns away from me, shedding her pajama top and pulling a bra over her chest, hooking it behind her back.

"Is she feeling better?" I ask.

"She's staying at the Trinity," Bernie says. "Didn't want to get anyone else sick before the Ball. That's why I was there yesterday, dropping a bunch of stuff off that she forgot."

"Huh." Most of the time I sleep at Bernie's, her mom is bopping around in the kitchen, ready to greet us with a carafe of freshly squeezed orange juice and a platter of bagels served with lox and whitefish. She rarely engages with me but loves to spend hours peppering Bernie with questions about the night before— who hooked up with who and which new restaurants were considered cool. She would have loved hearing about the party in Shelter Island had the drama *not* been about her own daughter. I was so grateful Bernie said she didn't tell her.

Watching Esther with Bernie always made me a little jealous since my own mother was so rarely interested in the social aspects of life. Instead, she spends most of her time working as the editor in chief of *Glam*, the biggest women's magazine in the country.

She doesn't quite get that no one in my generation is into magazines, but that doesn't stop her from trying to mine my brain for ideas about how to turn their long-form features into viral

TikToks. Mom's parents are from Mexico, and that made her the first woman of color to run *Glam* in its hundred-year history, which even I can understand is a big fucking deal. Since she took over, she's appeared *everywhere*, talking about fashion, politics, and women's issues on TV, panels, and red carpets.

"So, your mom's not coming to the fitting?" I can't help that my voice sounds surprised. Traditionally, all the femme nominees get their outfits at the only Ball-approved atelier, Madame Trillian's Custom Gowns, which just so happens to be down the block from the Club. Nominators fund our looks, which are sewn to fit our exact measurements by Madame Trillian and her team. We have one final try-on today, where the nominating committee gets final approval. The whole ordeal is supremely formal and outdated, but it's basically the only thing Esther has talked about for the past few weeks.

Bernie scoffs. "And get the whole nominating committee *and* half the nominees ill? No way."

I chug the rest of the water bottle and wipe my mouth with the back of my hand. I look down and see I'm wearing one of Bernie's old Excelsior Field Hockey T-shirts, weathered and soft from so many runs through the washing machine. My jumpsuit is in a crumpled ball on the floor, and I realize I didn't plan to sleep here so I don't have anything to change into.

Reading my mind, Bernie tosses me an oversized linen tunic she knows I like. "This will look fine with the mules you wore yesterday," she says.

"Thanks." The fabric is soft in my hands, and I know I should be grateful that Bernie always thinks of everything, that she always has a plan. But even when she's being kind, I can't help but feel that she enjoys when I fuck up just a little bit so it makes her look better. She'd run my life if I let her.

"What time do we have to be at the fittings?" I say, plugging my phone into the charger next to her bed.

"Hour and a half," she says. "But no offense, you should probably shower."

I toss a pillow at her. "You don't think the *famed* seamstress Madame Trillian will enjoy my new perfume, eau de champagne?" I breathe out my dragon breath all over her, and Bernie laughs before letting out a gag.

"Madame Trillian might, but Mrs. Shalcross and the nominating committee won't."

Bernie looks at herself in the mirror, peeling off the under-eye strips, smoothing her eyebrows down with her pinkies. She looks concerned for a moment, uneven. "Your mom coming?"

I glance at my phone, wondering if I should give her a call to ask. Esther told us a few weeks ago it was customary for mothers to attend the final fitting, and my mom seemed to brush it off completely. But when I check the screen, I see her assistant has texted me: Your mother will arrive at Madame Trillian's at 11:45 a.m. She will have to leave no later than 12:15 p.m. for a lunch downtown.

"Thad says she's on it."

"Bless Thad."

I rub my eyes with the back of my palms and vow to dunk my face in ice water as soon as I get to the bathroom. And take two Advil. Maybe a little nubbin of Vicodin if I can find one from when Skyler handed me a few the last time we all went out for sushi.

"Did your mom give you any advice?" I ask. "Words of wisdom to get through?"

Bernie's mouth curls down into a frown and she shakes her head. "Just what she always says."

And together, we chime in unison, "Be yourself because no one else can."

Maybe it's my hungover state, but a bubble of warmth fills in my chest as I lean back against Bernie's soft pillows. Despite the past few months, how we fought and found our way back to one another, Bernie's the best friend I've ever had, probably *will* ever have. Even if she drives me crazy with her perfectionism, her need to control, she's always looking out for me in her own precise way.

I open my mouth, my heart rising in my throat. *Now. Now's the time to tell her.* It would be so easy—to admit what happened at that party and what's gone on since then. She would understand why I kept it a secret. Wouldn't she? But as soon as I feel the words in my mouth, the way they might sound out in the open, I know I can't. Of course I can't. Not only would Skyler stop supplying me, but if Bernie found out I had been lying to her this whole time, I don't know if she would forgive me. Especially after I said all of her worst suspicions—the ones she admits late at night when it's just us in the darkness of her bedroom, our features visible only by moonlight. I said those things to hurt her, not because I meant it. Not really. Not all the time.

But we almost didn't come back from that betrayal. And if I came clean now, I'm not sure we ever would.

Tori

I'M SORRY, YOU'RE telling me that trying on frilly dresses is more fun than this?

A photo appears on my phone of a pretty Japanese girl with a big pink smile and long dark hair, holding up a forkful of waffle bites. She's cheesing at the camera, an arm thrown over my dad's shoulder in our favorite booth at Tasso's. Her sparkly green nail polish matches the menu on the table. When I zoom in, I can see the top of my little brother George's head peeking out the side of the photo, no doubt a platter of extra-crispy bacon and sunny-side-up eggs sitting in front of him. Seeing Joss there with my family gives me a sense of calm and security, a little reminder of who I am outside of Excelsior, at home. I bite my lip and smile at the photo, wishing I was right there next to her.

You know there's nowhere I'd rather be, I text Joss back, along with a pouty emoji. But beauty calls, babe. I snap a selfie as I climb the steps of the subway, emerging on the streets of the Upper East Side, only a block away from where the Legacy Club is head-quartered.

I stuff my phone back into my pocket and try not to think too hard about what I'm missing with Joss and my family. There've been countless mornings like this one, where we all pile into the booth at the diner with our binders and textbooks, studying and joking as we pass around platters of French toast and home fries the size of our heads.

Joss doesn't go to Excelsior, but we met in fourth grade when we were placed in the same classroom at the elementary school that's within walking distance of both of our houses. We've been inseparable ever since.

She's the only one from my old school who didn't treat me differently when I started at Excelsior freshman year. The others were quick to whisper behind my back that I thought I was too good for them, even though I was desperate to keep some semblance of normalcy as my entire life seemed to change overnight. Joss said all the other kids in our class were jealous—and that she was, too, in her own sort of way—but that rooting for me and wanting to change her own shit weren't mutually exclusive activities. It was only a few weeks into ninth grade when our relationship went from friends to something more, two months before I admitted I loved her.

That's still the case now more than ever, even if she thinks waffles are more important than Legacy Ball fittings.

I follow the directions to the tailor that I memorized the first time I visited when Madame Trillian took my measurements a few weeks ago, and when I get to the storefront, with its floor-to-ceiling windows and its mannequins in the window, my chest tightens.

It's one thing to be at a luncheon with all the other nominees, but to come to the final fitting, well, that's a little more "pageant" than I think I can handle.

Thank goodness Madame Trillian helped me pick out some fabric that felt like it was really *me*—simple, smooth, and dark. I reach out to pull the door handle, but a security guard with a black earpiece beats me and ushers me in with a white gloved hand.

"Right this way, Miss Tasso."

I blush and scurry inside the storefront, which has been a custom dressmaker in this area for decades. During my first appointment, the tailor told me that Michelle Obama had a gown made here once. Apparently, it's been *the* designer to the Legacy Ball crowd since the seventies, and in the back room, sketches of past dresses are framed along the wall.

All around the entryway are mannequins wearing regal floor-length gowns with sheer illusion sleeves, sequins, and handmade silk corsets. They sparkle as the light catches them at different angles, and I hold my breath as I make my way to the back door, which leads to one giant fitting room.

Unlike the kind of guidance I assume people like Bernie get about the Ball, I had no idea dressing up was such a *thing*. But when my nomination came, it also came with a letter telling me to report for my first fitting here and only here, where my outfit for the event was to be handmade to my specifications and paid for by my nominator. All I had to do was show up and stand still and not get pricked by the straight pins. Easier said than done.

The first fittings weren't so bad, since it was just me and Madame Trillian, but she warned me that the final try-on would be a bloodbath. Officially, it's so the nominating committee can approve all dresses and the tailors can make final alterations before Saturday, but unofficially, Madame Trillian said, it's so we nominees can size each other up and get out all our superficial shit-talking before the event actually happens.

I push open the door and walk through to find a massive room, covered in mirrors that reflect nearly thirty of my peers in various stages of undress, beautiful, delicate fabrics flying all around as plastic packaging that once held Spanx and tags to strapless bras float limp to the floor. Those framed sketches nearly obscured by the glare of the morning light.

The group is mostly cis girls, though Mrs. Shalcross was quick to tell me that I was not the only queer kid in attendance and that two nonbinary students were also nominated, and how *exciting* for the Club that they would get to embrace such diverse sets of experiences.

I wanted to laugh in her face, though some part of me sort of appreciated the effort. But now, looking around, I've never felt more out of place, and I know it has nothing to do with my sexuality.

Because there's one thing here I wasn't expecting, and that's a horde of moms.

All around me, mothers stand with their mini-mes, running hands through the ends of hair, folding up discarded T-shirts, pulling pumps out of shoeboxes lined with tissue paper.

A shooting pain pierces my chest and I clutch my tote bag tight to my side, feeling my one pair of fancy shoes press against my hip.

"Tori!" Madame Trillian approaches and kisses me on each cheek. "Oh, good, you're here. I've been *dying* to see you in your gown. Come with me."

She takes my hand and leads me over to a quieter corner of the room where there's an empty space near one of the mirrors. But then she disappears down a staircase, and I'm left alone in this frenetic swarm of limbs and pins and trailing fabric.

I look to my left and my stomach sinks, seeing Bernie Kaplan sitting perched on a velvet ottoman wearing a white silk blouse and camel-colored slacks. Her hair is long and fluffy, held back by a silk headband, and she's scrolling on her phone, intently reading something on her screen. But when I realize she's alone, without her mother, too, a wave of relief passes through me. Suddenly she looks up, startled to see me, and a warm smile forms on her face.

"Tori," she says, which I'm pretty sure is the first time I've heard her say my name. "Congrats on the nomination."

"Thanks."

"We were all curious who the sixth was."

My cheeks redden, wondering if that was a slight.

"It's so cool you're here. Really exciting."

I have no idea how to respond to that in a way that doesn't make me sound like I'm as surprised as she is. So instead, I just ask, "What color did you go for?"

She looks around the room at all the periwinkles and magentas. "Emerald green. You?"

"Navy," I say. "Madame Trillian thought it might complement my skin tone, and I was like, 'Sure, as long as it's not pink.'"

Bernie's mouth turns into a frown. "I love pink."

Shit.

I try a different tactic. "What's your scholarship?" I ask.

"Arts and Letters."

My heart drops, realizing I'm going to have to go up against Bernie Goddamn Kaplan on the same topic. "Oh, me too."

She cocks her head. "Have you started working on your presentation?"

I could lie and tell her no, that I didn't spend all of last night writing out a first draft and then revising until I finally had something promising enough to show Joss, who's the editor in chief of her high school newspaper and said she would read a copy for me. But instead, I try the truth.

"Yes. It's going to be great."

She arches one eyebrow playfully. "I love a little competition."

Before I can respond, Madame Trillian approaches with a garment bag draped between both arms. "I think you're going to adore it, dear. Quick. Get changed."

I do as she says, trying to hide my body as much as I can, because even though I'm not a prude, the idea of all these people seeing me nearly naked is mortifying.

Madame Trillian unzips the bag and pulls out two thin blue straps holding up a slim, silky dress that has a shape I can't quite make out. She opens it up from the back and holds it out for me to step into. Coming behind me, she pulls it tight and hooks the sides together. As she zips it up, I can't bring myself to look in the mirror, not yet. It's only when she smooths the fabric down over my hips and takes a step back, making a satisfied little sound, that I blink open my eyes and find something shocking looking back at me in the mirror.

The dress is majestic in its deep dark blue, with a simple square neckline and elegant little straps that rise up over my shoulders and meet together in between my backbones. It hugs my hips but not too tightly and falls in perfect pleats down my front, swishing as I move my body side to side. It's simple and stunning, something I would have picked out for myself had I been able to afford it.

Wearing it now, I feel like I've been given a coat of armor—or an excellent disguise.

Maybe *this* is what will help me feel like I really, truly belong here.

"It's perfect, isn't it?" Madame Trillian says, clasping her hands in front of her chest. "Your mother would *love* it."

I whip my head around. I didn't tell her anything about my mom, but based on the way she's looking at me now, it's clear someone on the committee did. I bet that nosy Mrs. Shalcross made sure that everyone was aware of my mother's untimely passing.

I shake my hair down over my shoulders and blink a few times, trying to stop my eyes from growing wet.

"Thank you," I say softly.

"Madame!" someone calls. "We've got a corset emergency!"

She shakes her head and leans in toward me. "I'll be back. Just stay put until the committee comes around and approves you."

I nod, but as soon as she leaves, I feel my self-consciousness take over, the stares from people all over the room. Most of all, I feel Bernie's eyes land on me and stay there, analyzing every single inch of my look. A bitterness takes hold inside my heart. There's no way she'd feel like I do—like everyone is watching her every move, waiting for her to fail, to prove to them that she really doesn't belong, no matter what a nomination says. People like Bernie never have to wonder if they deserve what they're given. They just take it. Even if it's not theirs. But if this dress is armor, now that I'm in it, I can at least pretend like I'm ready for battle.

"Thoughts?" I ask.

Bernie nods. "Classic but contemporary. Striking and elegant. A solid choice."

"How'd you describe yours?" Bernie's dress bag still hasn't shown up.

Bernie shrugs as if the whole thing isn't of that much interest at all. "Girly," she says. "And frilly."

"Your idea?"

Bernie smiles. "My mom's. But I don't mind."

It looks like she wants to say something else, but then another seamstress motions for her to come to the other side of the room where a poofy dress bag is hanging off a velvet hanger.

I stiffen as Mrs. Shalcross and a team of adults walk by and stop in front of me, standing on this little velvet pedestal. I hold out my arms like I'm about to be examined, but when she gives me a strange look, I snap them by my sides again.

She pauses with a legal pad in her hand and looks me up and down, her brow furrowed. Another one of the committee members, a tall white woman with long silver hair parted in the middle and a boxy suit that looks like it belongs in a museum, nods furtively and turns to one of the seamstresses running around with a pincushion strapped to her wrist. She takes off in a different direction.

"Tori," Mrs. Shalcross says. "What a delight. Absolutely exquisite."

I feel my cheeks redden and murmur a quick thank-you.

"Approved," she says, "obviously." But then the other woman whispers something in her ear. "Oh, yes, right. Of course."

The seamstress rushes back with a small velvet bag and hands it to Mrs. Shalcross. She reaches inside and pulls out something I can't quite see. Something small that fits in the palm of her hand. She takes a step closer to me and extends both hands, and that's when I see she's holding out a thin silver chain with a diamond the size of my thumbnail hanging between it.

I can't help but let out a little rush of air as she reaches around and clasps it behind my neck.

"Your nominator wanted you to have this," she says, her voice betraying no emotion. "To complete the look."

I shake my head, looking at the enormous jewel dangling between my collarbones. "It's . . . it's too much."

Mrs. Shalcross laughs. "It is. But sometimes nominators give little gifts beforehand. Of course, *your* nominator went a little overboard but . . ." She shrugs, which elicits some laughter from the chorus behind her. "It's perfect."

AFTER THE BALL

"PLEASE BACK AWAY *from the crime scene." Someone in uniform waves her hands away from the garden, away from the blood, the imprint of a body, the marks where fingers clawed at dirt. She unfurls a roll of yellow tape, separating the violence from the party. It's stark against the regal interior, the lights that had so recently illuminated a stunning evening.*

"Crime scene?" one girl asks a little too loudly. "Do they think it's a murder?"

All around the room, spines straighten. Jaws clench. The truth settles in: Everyone is a suspect. No one is safe.

The adults are supposed to be in charge. They were supposed to uphold the traditions of the Club, the elegance. The congeniality. But instead, they let this *happen. Jeanine Shalcross stands in shock against the wall. Her eyes roam the lobby, meeting Yasmin Gellar's, and they exchange furtive glances.*

A death can be explained. But a murder?

This will not be good for them, the Club. A murder threatens their future.

And being threatened changes everything.

But still, despite the sense of urgency to act and save themselves, no one in the room can deny that every Legacy is wondering what happened, the possibilities percolating. Dying like that, so gruesomely, so horribly . . . well, it made them all think about why. Everyone knows the deceased had enemies—especially after what transpired this week.

It would have taken a tough, persistent sense of grit to move past that. But no one doubted that they would. After all, they were in the Club. Untouchable.

And yet . . .

One would be in denial to assume that no one else could be involved, that no one else who had access to this building wanted revenge, justice. No one was supposed to go past the second floor of the Club. But at least one person broke the rules. Now they have to figure out whether anyone else did, too.

Bernie

IN THE MIRROR, I'm accosted by a forest of green. The dress Mom helped me design is strapless with a sweetheart neckline and a low back, sewn together with a gold thread that picks up the light at all different angles, especially when I twirl. Last week, it seemed like this gown was absolutely perfect, but now it's itchy and claustrophobic, like the layers of tulle and lace will suffocate me under their weight.

I look at the other girls around the room reflected in the mirror. Some seem even more uncomfortable than I do as their mothers cock their heads and whisper to the seamstresses, motioning for their child's breasts to be lifted, waists to be tucked, straps to lie flatter. Others look regal, like they have been waiting their whole lives for a Legacy Ball gown, which they *have*, as they swish and swirl their skirts around their ankles, press their hands to their stomachs and admire their curves. But among the sea of dresses and few tailored suits, I can't stop looking at Tori Tasso, the girl who shouldn't even be here. She stands still, looking at herself in the mirror, her pretty reflection staring back at her with no expression at all.

Her dress is undeniably beautiful, with its understated elegance. We've gone to school together for the past three years, but I've never really thought about her at all. Not until now. But her nomination . . . it makes no sense. Who on the committee would even know she exists?

Isobel and I spent most of the summer wondering which of our classmates would get the invites. I was a shoo-in since my mom is a Legacy. Skyler, too, thanks to Lulu.

We assumed Lee would get chosen since one of Lizzie Horowitz's most devoted buyers is a ninety-five-year-old socialite named Gertie who was one of the first women to be accepted into the Club, and she had vowed to choose Lee when the time came.

Isobel kept insisting that she wouldn't get picked and that she would be totally fine if that happened, but I knew she was just trying to prepare for the worst and that she'd be heartbroken if she didn't get nominated. She must have been worried that no one would choose her, and secretly, so was I. It's against the rules to pick your own blood, so over the years I dropped hints that Mom should tap Isobel. But Mom's affection for Isobel hasn't always been obvious. On more than one occasion, she confided in me that she thought Is was too edgy, a little *weird*. Mom even admitted that she thought Isobel was only friends with me because I made life easy for her—I planned our social calendars, introduced her to the right people, got Lee to ask her out. With me, I gave her an entire world, one she didn't even have to think about gaining access to.

That was the worst recurring fight between Mom and me, because of course I defended Isobel. I *always* defended Isobel. Even when she blacked out on July Fourth freshman year and puked in the pool at our Hamptons house.

But I never told Mom what Isobel said to me at that party. It was too shameful, too horrible. After that night, though, Mom's suspicions started to become my own. They popped up when Isobel declined to come over for a sleepover or when she blew me off to hang out with Lee.

Or like that one day over the summer, when we biked to Montauk to see the lighthouse at sunset and Isobel confided in me that she was worried we'd drift when I joined the Legacy Club and she didn't.

"Will you still be my friend?" she asked.

I had to laugh. We'd just made it through the biggest fight of our lives. "You're joking, right?"

She shrugged and looked out toward the water.

"You'll get a nomination," I said, trying to sound sure. "If not from my mom, then probably Lulu. Plus, isn't one of the editors at your mom's company in the Club?" It didn't occur to me then that Isobel could get picked because of her own talent, her own merit. Mom had always said that it was about who you *know*, who your parents *know*. The idea reeked of nepotism but none of us questioned it. None of us cared.

"Maybe," she said. "But, really, what's so great about the Club anyway? Like, you *will* still want to hang out with me, right?"

I threw an arm around her, ignoring the gnawing feeling in my stomach, the one that told me her suspicions were right. Things *would* change if I got in and she didn't. Even though the Ball signals the end of Legacy Week, there's still what comes after. The membership, the monthly events, the secrecy of what goes on inside those walls. If I couldn't share them with Isobel, who knows what else I might keep private?

But I lied. "We don't have to worry about that because you're going to get in. And even if you don't, we'll still be best friends."

My allegiance was never tested though, because Isobel's nomination came on the same day mine did in the form of thick cardstock invitations, addressed to our homes. I called her as soon as

I saw mine, breathless and relieved, as she told me that she had received one, too.

I nearly screamed, and she told me I had been right all along.

"Of course I was," I said, clutching my own nomination.

Later that night we met for a celebratory kickback at Lee's place, where we spent hours trying to figure out who else would make up our sixsome from Excelsior.

It didn't take long to find out that Kendall Kirk, the sweet brain-iac who I often asked to explain AP Physics formulas to me, had gotten the nom, since he texted Isobel asking if she had intel on what he could expect.

But Tori. Tori was the surprise.

Looking at her now, it's hard to read her expression—how she feels about being here among all of *us*, the kids who've grown up together since the beginning. But she's been around us for three years. She's acclimated by now. At least I assume so.

It shocks me, though, that even with all that time passing each other in the halls I don't know much about her at all other than the fact that she has the highest GPA in our class, lives in Queens, and her mom passed away in the spring.

In the mirror, I see Mrs. Shalcross step back, admiring Tori before moving on to the next student. Tori cocks her head to one side, her full neck coming into view. There between her col-larbones is something big and sparkling, a hunk of diamond so shiny, it glints in the mirror. I lean into my own reflection to get a closer look.

She wraps her fingers around the stone tightly until I can't see its shimmering angles anymore. Her eyes shoot around the room, as if embarrassed, and for a second my heart lurches for her. She must not know anyone, not really. It's not like Isobel and I have been so welcoming.

I wonder what it's like to walk through this world as a tourist, never inhabiting your own space. At least that's how I imagine her life at Excelsior is. I've never had that feeling. Never once had to question my place right in the middle of everything.

But then my thoughts take a turn. Maybe she hasn't either— and I'm the one who's ostracizing her without even realizing.

"Bernie, don't you look marvelous." I spin around to see Isobel's mom standing there, her leather work tote hanging in the crook of one elbow. She's clutching her cell in her other hand.

"Thanks, Gloria," I say, stepping off the velvet pedestal and out of my pumps. "Glad you could make it."

She smiles and holds up her phone. "Gotta go make a few calls, but I *had* to see Izzy in her dress." She nods to Isobel, who's in the process of wriggling out of a sleek one-shoulder silver number and into the clothes I tossed to her this morning.

I'm about to utter a response, but then she turns on her heel, blows Isobel a kiss, and rushes out the door as fast as she can, her earbuds in and already connected to whatever editor in Italy she needed to call.

Isobel plops down next to me, her limbs splayed out on the armchair. I fight the urge to tell her to sit up straight and mind her manners—that there are nominating committee members here, after all. But I'm not her mother. And I'm certainly not *my* mother.

"Can we go yet?" she asks. "Lee said we can come by to hang out. Skyler's there." She pops a piece of gum into her mouth and starts chewing loudly. "They invited Kendall, too. A whole nominee situation."

I look around the room and see Tori now in her street clothes, gently tucking her dress back into its garment bag, zipping it closed with care.

"Let's do it," I say.

Isobel pops up, a devilish grin on her face. "Thank god. I was—"

But I'm off, not waiting for her to finish her sentence. In a few steps I'm back at Tori's station.

"Come to Lee Dubey's with us," I say. "The rest of the Excelsior nominees will be there. We can all . . . get to know one another."

Tori crosses her arms over her chest, one eyebrow arched. "Haven't you guys known each other since, like, kindergarten?"

I redden, embarrassed, but try to shake it off. "We'll get to know you."

Tori pauses long enough for me to realize I've offended her. Like she knows that only now, after she's been nominated for the Club, am I trying to befriend her. My stomach flips, shame building in my gut. But then a small smile crawls across her mouth.

"Okay," she says. "I'll come."

Isobel

TORI IS SANDWICHED between Bernie and me in the back of a black car, heading downtown on the West Side Highway toward Lee's townhouse. The radio is blaring some pop song that's so repetitive it starts to give me a headache, and our driver is mumbling into his phone in Spanish.

My cheeks burn as I realize what he said. *These rich brats better tip well.*

I reach into my pocket and find half a Xanax, which I slip into my mouth. I don't think anyone notices.

Bernie leans forward from the other side of the seat and props her chin up on her fist.

"So," she asks Tori. "What do you think of the events so far?"

Tori picks at her fingernails. "I don't know." She pauses. "About what I expected."

Bernie cocks her head. "How so?"

Tori looks out the window like she's trying to mull over what to say, how to act. She seems so unsure of herself and the words coming out of her mouth. Part of me wants to shake her and tell her to relax—that this week isn't *that* big of a deal. But then I'd be lying. Because even if I don't really care about being a Legacy—even if I didn't want it in the first place—I still know what it can afford you and the kinds of doors that it can open. If I make it through this week, I'll have easy access to a dozen gallery owners in the city and some of the most prolific art collectors on the East Coast. None of *them* will care if I go to Yale or college at all. I'll be set.

But the idea of becoming a success because of the Legacy Club turns my stomach. Especially since I know I only got a nomination because I'm Bernie's best friend. Esther probably picked me out of pity.

"It seems like everyone already knows each other," Tori says, her voice clipped. "Like you all have been preparing for this for a long time."

Bernie mulls this over and then nods, agreeing. "I guess that's true. I mean, most of us *have* gone to Intercollegiate schools forever. You know, my mom is on the board of the Club. So is Skyler's. Members rotate who gets to nominate seniors, so it was just lucky that they both got this year I guess." But when she clocks the flushed look on Tori's face, she starts to backtrack. "That doesn't mean there's no room for new faces." She smiles wide, trying hard.

Tori nods but she doesn't look like she believes her.

We're all quiet for a second and I try to think of something to say, but everything in my body rebels, feeling suffocated in this back seat. I glance out the window and see we still have a ways to go before we get to Lee's exit.

Bernie changes the subject. "So, what does your dad do?"

I close my eyes and lean back against the headrest. I hate that question. The only people who ask are the ones who want to know if your parent works with their parent—if your family is on the same level as their family when it comes to vacations and houses and where they like to eat dinner. Most of our peers have a simple answer like "finance" or "private equity," but everyone knows that just translates to "money." When I say that my mom is a magazine editor and my dad is a doctor, I'm often met with bulging eyes and big noises signaling surprise, like they're unsure how two upper-middle-class professionals could launch children into *their* world, one of the uber-wealthy. It's only when I reveal that my mom actually *runs Glam*, and if anyone asks, yes, my dad *did* inherit a bunch of money from his real estate developer aunt that my presence makes sense to them.

But now, as Tori's forced to answer the question, I wish I could block everything in this car out.

"He owns a diner in Astoria," Tori says. "It's been in my family for decades."

Bernie's eyes look like they're about to pop out of her head. "That's so cool." She's using her fake voice and I bet Tori knows. "My mom *loves* diners. Her favorite is Edna's in the Fifties, where they make *the* best Greek salad with pita."

"You should come to Tasso's sometime," Tori says. "It's *actually* Greek."

Bernie nods and then we all go quiet in an awkward pause.

The silence is unbearable until finally we get off the highway at Twenty-Fourth Street and make a few quick turns, pulling up in front of Lee's home. The bar is hitting me, and like magic, I feel so much more relaxed, ready for what's next. I lean forward in the seat so I can hop out of the car as soon as we stop.

The streets in Lee's neighborhood are wider than they are in mine. It's a sparse part of the city, populated by art galleries and townhouses, buildings that look like UFOs, setting trends for the rest of the world.

The Dubeys have been here since the nineties, before the High Line and the Whole Foods and the big box retailers turned the eastern parts of Chelsea into Murray Hill Lite. They've stayed put all the way over here on Eleventh where the subways are far and the views of the Hudson River are unbeatable. It's private, they say.

More so than the massive doorman buildings on the Upper East Side or the neighborly vibes in Clinton Hill.

The driver hits the brakes and I climb out of the back seat, taking a few steps toward the Dubeys' townhouse, which is really the whole building to my right. On the outside, it looks like a classic Italianate brownstone, but on the inside, it's a sleek minimalist's dream, with a skylight that directs sun through the whole building thanks to an interior cutout that creates a massive tube in the middle of the space. It was designed specifically for the Dubeys by a famous Japanese architect, and their home has been photographed in every major design magazine. In July, they opened it up for tours and private viewings that attracted most every A-list celebrity and art collector.

Now, Lee's standing on the stoop of his home wearing waffle sweatpants that hug him in all the right places and a loose white T-shirt. His bare forearms are sculpted and his hair is a little tousled. Smiling at me like that, he calms my nerves. Reminds me that things are easy with him. Simple.

Well, for the most part.

There are still the lulls in conversation. The secret I'm keeping from him about Skyler. But maybe Lee doesn't realize, maybe he's still thrilled he chose me, even if I don't totally understand why.

But if I'm being honest with myself, I do know why.

It's because of Bernie. Everything's because of Bernie.

"You made it!" Lee calls from the top stair. Based on the flash of curiosity that appears on his face—quickly and then not at all— he's as surprised as I was that Bernie invited Tori Tasso along to hang out. But Lee, never flustered, doesn't bat an eye. Instead, he bounds down the steps barefoot and rushes to us, embracing Tori in a hug before greeting me. I step back, surprised.

"Tori Freaking Tasso, the sixth nominee we never knew we needed," he exclaims, releasing her in a dazed state of confusion.

"Uh, thanks," she says, stiff.

Lee throws an arm around me, and ushers us all into the foyer of the townhouse, which is covered in stark black marble slabs. Past the entryway is a bright white living room, devoid of any color at all. Over dinner once, Lee's dad, Arti, told me that he wanted to simulate the birthing experience by forcing his guests to walk through a completely dark space and then be shot out into the world, born anew in bright light.

After he said that, Lizzie leaned over to me and whispered in her wine-drunk voice, "He wanted fluorescent lights to emulate the hospital. That's where I drew the line."

Lee leads us through their home—past the framed handwritten letter from Marina Abramović in the hallway, the Cy Twombly painting above the breakfast nook, and out the back doors to the deck, where Skyler and Kendall are sitting on outdoor sofas. Skyler offers him a joint, but Kendall looks away, awkward.

My stomach clenches looking at Kendall, and I reach for Lee's hand, grasping it in mine.

"It is absurdly unfair that we had to get up early and go have a freaking fashion show while you guys had to do *nothing* today," Bernie says, pushing past me to sit down next to Skyler, who I can't help but notice is looking at Tori with a confused, curious expression. Tori doesn't even glance his way.

"Oh, come on. Trying on tuxedos with fucking *tails* is its own kind of hell," Skyler says, taking a hit of the joint and passing it to Bernie, who declines.

Kendall leans forward and gives me a nod. Nothing like the

familiarity we experienced when we were kids. Back when we were little, we all played together—Kendall; his sister, Opal; my brother, Marty; and me. We'd gather at Fort Greene Park while our parents shopped at the farmers' market on Saturdays. Marty, the oldest, would boss us around and march us up and down the big concrete steps near the monument like a drill sergeant. Opal, a good five years younger than him, was always the first to fall in line, giggling and smiling, unafraid to get dirty as she took roll-around breaks in the grass. Opal was sweet then. A little weird, even.

But at Excelsior Prep, she became someone else. A tenacious, obsessive student with perfectly dewy makeup, barely visible pores, and a natural charisma that charms teachers, coaches, and all of her classmates. She was freshman class president, captain of the JV field hockey team, on track to be the next Bernie Kaplan. She's polished. Professional. Perfect.

I'm supposed to hate her for a million reasons, but I don't. I can't. She's still little Opal Kirk to me.

"Oh please," Bernie says. "You have no idea the kind of absurd expectations that come with being a *girl* associated with the Legacy Club. Even the idea that we have to have our outfits approved by some committee is absurd."

Lee hands me the joint and I take it eagerly, desperate to make Bernie stop talking. It's so hypocritical—like obviously the Club doesn't care that they're upholding outdated stereotypes and here we all are, partaking in its outdated BS. I suck on the joint harder, focusing on the lightheaded feeling floating to my brain.

Bernie nods toward Tori. "Right?" she asks. "We were all put on display today like little dolls."

Everyone turns toward Tori, and I watch her straighten her

spine, the skin on her chest redden. I glance back at Bernie, a bubble of resentment forming in my stomach. She didn't have to put Tori on the spot like this, but deep down, I know that Bernie doesn't even realize what she's doing. In her mind, she probably thinks this little pivot to Tori is *kind*, an effort to bring her into the conversation. But I wish she realized that it's not.

"Well," Tori starts slowly. "I didn't really expect anything less."

Lee leans in, his elbows resting on his knees.

"It never occurred to me that today would be anything more than that," she says, her words coming faster, like she's gaining confidence as she talks. "I feel like if you accept your nomination, you're submitting to the idea of performing outdated gender roles, at least for this week. Don't even get me started on the whole class aspect. So we have to own up to our part in that. We can't pretend like we're not different, or better, when we're submitting to it. Maybe we're the ones who are supposed to change it from the inside. Doesn't really do any good to complain about it here just among us, right?"

Everyone is quiet, stunned, and Bernie's neck reddens, the telltale sign that she's uncomfortable. Embarrassed. But then she nods. "Tori's right. Maybe *we're* the ones who will change it."

The others mutter some sort of agreement, but it's obvious no one here—certainly not Tori—is on a crusade to rework the whole Legacy Club this week. We're all just trying to survive.

"Bathroom," I mumble, and head back into the house. I walk past the ridiculous birth canal situation and into the powder room, where I push my head between my knees and breathe a few times deeply. It's not that I'm anxious. Not right now. I just need space from all these people, some of whom are supposed to know me better than I know myself.

But if that's true, then why do I always find myself wanting to flee?

Finally, I pick my head up, wash my hands, and throw open the door. But when I see Kendall waiting there, I take a step back.

He pushes his black round glasses up on his nose so I can see his eyes a bit better. Kendall's always been studious, uninterested in going to parties or snorting lines off a mirror or staying out too late. Back when we were kids, I was always trying to get him to take sips of my mom's left-out bottles of wine with me, while he stayed watch, never partaking.

"What's up, Ken?"

"I was going to see if you wanted to come with me to the bodega," he says. "Skyler says we're out of ice."

"Oh. Okay."

"Cool."

Kendall spins on his heel and starts walking fast toward the front door. I take off after him, my brain buzzing, my feet bouncing off the concrete.

After a few moments, I catch up to him and we fall in step, walking leisurely to the next avenue, where the closest corner store carries just about everything, including Lee's favorite snack, chocolate-dipped digestive cookies from England. I make a mental note to pick some up. And a bag of Doritos. Maybe a few Haribo bags, too. Shit, maybe I *am* high.

Kendall glances at me sideways, and as we walk, there's a quiet between us, the kind that comes only when there are no expectations, when you don't really care what the person next to you thinks about you. It happens so infrequently at Excelsior Prep. But it's always been this way with Kendall. Even when we were toddlers,

Mom said we'd play together wordlessly, passing plastic measuring cups back and forth and stacking them one by one, a strange activity we became obsessed with after Kendall's dad tossed them at us one Sunday afternoon while all the adults were trying to play a game of Hearts on our patio.

When we hit the traffic light, I keep walking, but all of a sudden, I feel a yank on my elbow pulling me back to the curb just as a biker whizzes by, screaming at me over their shoulder.

"It's red," Kendall says, his voice harsh.

I look up. "Shit. Sorry."

"You could get killed."

I shrug him off me. "It's fine."

Kendall stops and looks at me. "It's *not* fine."

"What's up with you?" I cross my arms and look at him hard. His brow is narrowed, and his button-up is rumpled, half tucked in to his khakis.

Kendall runs a hand through his short dark hair and sighs, frustrated. "I need to talk to you," he says.

"Okay," I say, fear churning in my stomach.

The light changes green and he starts walking, so I follow, trying to catch up to his fast steps. My mind spins with what he could possibly want to talk about, but deep in my core, I know what it is.

When we get to the other side of the street, Kendall makes a left, away from the bodega. "Opal told me what happened," he says, confirming my worst fears. "At that party in Shelter Island."

I close my eyes. "I don't know what you're talking about."

Kendall clucks his tongue in disbelief. "Come on," he says softly. "Be honest with me."

But I don't know if I can. Because if I do, then I'll have to admit what happened, what I've been keeping from Bernie.

On that fucked-up summer night, I had been walking around Lee's property in my wet bathing suit, dripping pool water on the slate patio, looking for Lee. My head was cloudy and confused after my fight with Bernie, and I just wanted to find him, to have him tell me everything was okay, that I hadn't made a fool of myself. I padded into the house where dozens of kids were pounding shots and snorting whatever off the glass coffee table. I swiped a beer from the cooler and cracked it open as I walked up the stairs, my bare feet soft against the plush carpeting.

I popped open Lee's bedroom first, the one that was covered in framed photos of various ponds, bays, and beaches. But it was empty. I debated crawling right under his white bedspread and falling asleep, waiting for him to cocoon himself around me. But I kept going, chugging half the beer as I walked farther down the hallway, the music from downstairs pulsing in my brain.

Passing the primary suite, where his parents usually slept, I heard noises inside. Laughter and soft music—different from what was blasting in the living room, where the rest of the party was full of couples dry-humping on the couches.

I twisted the knob and stepped inside, expecting to see Lee and Skyler starfished on the floor, giggling up at the ceiling, but instead, what I saw caused me to drop my beer in a loud crash.

There on the bed was Skyler's bare ass pumping wildly into someone who was very obviously *not* Bernie.

It took a second for him to hear the can hit the floor, but when he did, he turned around and looked right at me with fire in his gray eyes, his dark hair flopping around on his forehead.

I knew I should run, but I was stuck in place, in shock, my wet bathing suit suddenly cold against my skin.

"What's . . ."

A girl's voice broke through the air, and as I kept staring at them, she seemed to prop herself up off the bed on her elbows and poke her head around so her pretty face was visible in the dark, flushed and vulnerable.

Opal Kirk was lying there, under a naked Skyler Hawkins, her dark hair messy from the pillows, her eyes wide with shock. I'll never forget that look, the way she pleaded with me without saying a word. *Don't tell.*

Standing on the corner of the deserted street in Chelsea, Kendall's looking at me expectantly. But I can't let on what I know, not when I'm relying on Skyler.

"What are you talking about?" I ask as innocently as I can.

Kendall cocks his head. "Opal told me," he says softly. "Last night."

I look at him blankly.

"She said you know. That you saw."

I open my mouth, then snap it shut.

"Did you know she says she loves him? That he sneaks into our apartment every other night? The idea that he's in my home makes me want to puke." Kendall shivers. "He keeps telling her he's going to dump Bernie. 'Just wait a little longer.' First it was 'before school starts.' Now it's 'after the Ball.'" He shakes his head and bites the inside of his lip. "I told her he's never going to do it. He and Bernie are . . . destined or whatever it is they say."

I shake my head, wishing I had taken another hit of that joint, that we were back at Lee's with everyone else. That I had never been burdened with what I saw.

But mostly that I had told Bernie when I had the chance.

Instead, I've been keeping his secret, listening to him talk about Opal for months.

I don't know what to do except walk as fast as I can into the bodega, where I grab a bag of ice and leave a five-dollar bill on the counter, ignoring Kendall's calls behind me.

"Hey," he says, walking fast after me. "Isobel, stop."

I push his voice away and keep walking back to the house—back to Bernie and Lee and Skyler and the rest of the week that we still have to get through.

"Why are you being like this?"

Tears prick my eyes, but I keep going, hearing his footsteps pick up behind me.

"You *know* Opal. She's heartbroken. Came to me crying, begging me not to tell anyone."

"So, why are you telling me?"

"Because *you* know already. You can do something," he says, practically begging. "You can tell Bernie. She'll break up with Skyler, and Opal will finally see what a dirtbag he is, that Bernie had no idea about any of this."

I stop short and Kendall bumps right into me. "You don't think I've thought about this? All you can do is tell Opal to get over him. He's never going to want her like he wants Bernie. He'll use her some more, but she'll never get what she wants. Tell her to give up now."

"Fuck, Is. When did you become like this?"

"Like what?"

"Cynical and mad at the world."

"I'm not."

I reach down to pick up the ice but so does Kendall, and for a second our fingers make contact, hot from the city sun, pressing down on us. I pull away and stand up straight.

"The Isobel I used to know would do the right thing. If not for Opal at least for Bernie, her quote-unquote best friend of all time. Aren't you guys like blood sisters?"

I shake my head, tears pricking my eyes. "You have no idea what my friendships are like."

Kendall snorts. "That's for sure."

"What's that supposed to mean?"

"It's not like you stayed *my* friend when you came to Excelsior."

"Oh please, as if you wanted to hang out with Bernie and Skyler when we were twelve."

"No," he says, his voice small. "But I wanted to hang out with *you*."

My face feels hot, and I realize we're almost back at the house, to safety. "Why are we even talking about this?"

"I just thought . . ." Kendall shakes his head. "Never mind."

"What?"

"I just thought that maybe you'd still give a shit about Opal. Or at least Bernie. But I guess not."

"Why don't you say something?" I ask. "You tell Bernie that her angelic boyfriend of a million years has been fucking a sophomore. Huh? *You* can be the bearer of bad news."

Kendall looks at me, disappointed. "Everyone would blame Opal for breaking up *the most perfect couple in all of New York City*," he says with disdain. "You think Bernie wouldn't make Opal's life a living hell after this?" He scoffs. "She'd turn everyone at Excelsior against her. I don't want that for Opal."

"You don't think that would happen if I told?"

He shrugs. "Bernie trusts you. You like Opal. Or at least you used to. Maybe it'd make her realize this is Skyler's fault, not hers."

We're standing in front of Lee's townhouse now, the soft wail of a siren a few blocks away.

"Shit," he says.

I stay silent, itching to go inside, to get away from him, from the truth.

He shoves the bag of ice toward me. "Tell them I had to go."

I take it from him and open my mouth to say something, but by the time my voice rises in my throat, he's already turned on his heel, walking away, and the only thing I can register is overwhelming relief.

Tori

I'M RELUCTANTLY LISTENING to Skyler go on and on about what frat he thinks he'll probably join when he heads off to Penn's undergrad business school next fall, even though he hasn't even sent in his application *or* been accepted, when the patio door slams shut and Isobel bounds down the steps with a bag of ice dripping condensation on the ground. She plops it down next to Skyler and slumps back on the couch, pulling her sunglasses over her eyes.

"Kendall had to leave," she says.

"You guys were gone a long time. Everything okay?" Skyler asks in a tone that puts me on edge.

He's looking at her with a harsh steely gaze, and I wonder if anyone else notices. Based on the fact that Lee's now stretching out his limbs in some sort of yoga pose way on the grass and Bernie is scrolling through her phone intently, neither of them give a shit.

Isobel nods and makes herself another drink, sloshing orange juice onto the ground as she mixes it with vodka in a red cup and drops a handful of ice right on top.

"Yup."

Skyler nods but keeps his eyes on Isobel, who's chugging her drink, spilling droplets down the front of her shirt.

I never knew she was sloppy until that night in Shelter Island when I stopped her from falling headfirst into the shallow end of the pool after she did a keg stand in the grass.

I don't even think she noticed me. Certainly not enough to say thank you.

I hadn't wanted to be at that party at all but stayed to prove a point. To show that I could. I wouldn't even have gone if the events of the day had unfolded differently, if our vacation hadn't started to take a turn.

It was a random coincidence we were out in Shelter Island that weekend anyway. After Mom died and the funeral came and went and all the frozen meals from our neighbors were eaten, Dad, the twins, and I were left alone with our grief and the emptiness of our house. It was unbearable, the absence of her laugh, her smell, her nagging me to turn all the lights off.

One of our loyal customers, a big-shot real estate developer in Long Island City, must have gotten deep, talking with my dad one night, because the next day, he gave us the keys to his beach house on Shelter Island and said to head out there for a few weeks. Thought we could use a break from the city. From everything.

Dad didn't want to go, but the twins begged, and I was secretly looking forward to getting out of the city and staring at the water, reading some of the sci-fi paperbacks Joss picked out for me at the bookstore. So, one weekend in early June, Dad relented and the four of us packed up our old station wagon that Dad keeps parked in the street and drove out east, down the Long Island Expressway, and onto the ferry to Shelter Island, a thirty-square-mile stretch of land between the wineries on the North Fork and the oceanside mansions in the Hamptons.

It was a little more rugged and quiet than its bougie neighboring areas, with overgrown nature preserves and secret swimming ponds, and we spent two weeks floating in the bay and eating burgers Dad grilled over an open flame. We played cards and watched movies and made s'mores on the deck.

Near the end of our stay, we were all crying less, talking about Mom more—focusing on who she was, not how she died. We almost felt . . . normal.

It was our second-to-last day there, and I offered to take the twins out for mini-golf to give Dad some alone time. Together, we rode bikes to the course and stood patiently in line as Helen went on and on about making sure she got a lavender ball, and George made me promise we could get ice cream after dinner. I placated them, just happy to see smiles on their faces, hear their laughter in the air. I didn't even get annoyed when two guys wearing Lipman Academy sweatshirts bumped into me in line, spilling a Diet Coke on my shirt. "Whoops," one said, an apology, I guess.

Everything was fine—lovely, even—as we putted hole after hole until we got to one of the final stations, where we were supposed to hit the ball through a whale's mouth to reach the end.

Helen made it through first, in one putt, but soon it was clear George would take a while. After several swings, he started to get agitated, his shoulders wriggling, his voice quavering.

"We can go," Helen said, bored. "You don't have to finish it."

But George stood stoic, frown lines deepening as he tried and tried to get that ball into its hole. His face reddened as he let out a frustrated little sigh, an indication that whatever grief and sorrow had been simmering beneath the surface was threatening to spill over right here on this mini-golf course. I approached him and wrapped an arm around his shoulder, holding him lightly.

"Get a move on!" someone shouted behind us. I spun around to find those boys with the Lipman sweatshirts, backward baseball caps on their head, snickering in our direction. They rolled their eyes and motioned for us to pick up the pace. "Hurry it up, townies," one said.

I released George and gripped the club tight in my hand. "We're from the city." I don't know why that was my response, loaded and futile, but it was what came to mind first—the disgust at being called out, wrongly, for not having the same area code as they did.

One laughed. "All right," he said, clearly not believing me. I watched as he reached up and spun his cap around so the brim was facing me, and when I saw what was emblazoned on its front, I stopped. A simple word, LEGACY, embroidered in a neat white cursive, every stitch perfectly sewn in.

My throat was scratchy, and I had no response. "Finally," George called. "Come on, Tori." Face red and eyes stinging, I turned and hustled Helen and George out of there, not daring to look back at the Lipman boys, whose laughter bleated through the air.

As we biked back to the house, I was glad to be riding behind the twins so they couldn't see my eyes blinking back tears. What shocked me most about the encounter wasn't that it had upset me but *why*. It wasn't that they were rude to George or that they were impatient. It was that they didn't see me as one of them. I wasn't mad. I was embarrassed. Because, for some dark and twisted reason, I wanted them to like me. I wanted them to see me as a peer, because in most of the technical ways, I was.

I also went to an Intercollegiate school and was from the city, my whole life formed inside those five boroughs. They had no idea that I was at the top of my class, with grades good enough to go to any college I wanted, that I had reference letters my classmates would kill for, an unrelenting work ethic. But they just assumed I was no one.

Why hadn't they been able to tell I was *one* of them?

The answer was obvious: Because no matter what, I wasn't. I wouldn't be. Not unless something changed. Drastically.

As we neared the house, I pictured the boys. Their hats. The word *Legacy*.

My heart raced as I realized what it meant. The Legacy Club. *That's* what would change things. A surefire way to not only lay claim to acceptance but keep it with a tight-fisted grip for an entire lifetime.

But as quickly as the realization came, heartbreak followed. I wasn't the type of person who earned a nomination, who got noticed. That went to the likes of Bernie Kaplan or Skyler Hawkins, people who were *actual* legacies to the club, who wore their parents' Legacy class sweatshirts to dress-down day at school.

Dropping my bike near the house, though, I made a decision: Senior year was my last chance to finally feel like an Excelsior student. And fuck if I was going to go off to college not fully belonging to this world and all of its privileges. I had been given the scholarship three years before, but for the first time, I was ready to be part of everything Excelsior had to offer, even if no one else thought I should.

So, when the Excelsior Prep class chat lit up with an invitation for anyone to come to a party in Shelter Island, I shoved my feet into sandals and trekked the half a mile down a stretch of Ram Island Road that abutted the pond, courage pushing me forward down the street.

I had rarely been to an Excelsior party, but I walked into that night feeling different, bold. It was a chance to start over. To launch into senior year feeling fresh and shed the pain that junior year had brought me. The isolation I had forced on myself the years prior. This was my chance to show those boys—everyone—that I deserved to be here.

By the time I got there, the party seemed to have just slipped into a heightened, hedonistic phase, and I spotted dozens of classmates in various stages of undress, jumping into the pool or doing body shots off the Ping-Pong table, which seemed like it was about to collapse.

The house was dark and full of sweaty bodies, and it made me claustrophobic. But I forced myself to stay. This is what fun was supposed to be, right?

I wandered around and found my way upstairs, lingering for a moment against the banister. That was when Isobel rushed out of that room, her face full of shock, and pushed past me, nearly falling all the way down the stairs.

"You okay?" I called after her, but I heard no response.

Only a moment later, Skyler exited the room, his shorts up but not buttoned, calling to someone still in the room. "Stay put!" he said harshly.

I watched it all unfold, the wheels in my head turning, putting the pieces together, until I realized I had come to a crossroads.

With only a few choices, I might be able to solidify my standing in this world and never leave it.

I had never done something so brazen, so wrong, but I had watched my classmates closely over the years, realizing the shortcuts they took, how their connections worked in their favor.

For once, I wanted them to work in mine.

"Tori?" Bernie asks now, her voice tinged with a hint of mild annoyance.

"Sorry, what?" She's looking at me with a strained smile.

"I asked who you think nominated you. Do you know anyone in the Club?"

I glance sideways at Skyler, who averts his eyes and tosses an ice cube at Lee, who's now doing a headstand against a tree, his linen shirt dropping over his face to reveal a muscled abdomen.

I shake my head. "Nope," I lie. "No idea."

Bernie

EVERYONE IS BEING so weird today. At least it's not just me. Maybe people are freaked about the Ball and making those presentations on Saturday. But even so, Skyler's distracted, and Isobel is getting drunker than she should for a random afternoon. Only Lee is his normal, carefree self. And who knows how Tori usually acts, but she seems strangely unenthused for someone who I would assume is trying to get into all of our good graces.

At least tomorrow's Acts of Service Day will be a little more chill. Less room for error.

A clattering rings out, and I turn around to see Isobel reaching through a maze of glasses, sending them crashing to the ground, as she grabs for a bottle of vodka on the table.

"Don't you think you're good?" I whisper to her, placing a hand on her shoulder. But she shrugs me off. Except in that moment, she loses her balance and tips over in her seat, onto the table, hitting her head on the corner with a loud *thwack* before falling to the ground.

"Isobel!" I jump to my feet to help her up.

"I'm fine," she says, yanking her arm away from me. But she's holding her hand to her head, and I can see she's bleeding through her fingers.

"Let me help you." I reach for a napkin amid the shattered glass and spilled liquid. But she stumbles to her feet and pushes me away.

"Fuck off, Bernie." Any sympathy I had for her curdles, and

I'm left with that same feeling I had toward her in Shelter Island, when I saw her spiraling, morphing into something ugly.

But then she turns toward the bushes, where she keels over and barfs straight into the hydrangeas. By now the rest of the group has realized what's going on. Skyler's looking at her with disgust, while Tori's eyebrows shoot up in surprise. Lee rushes to her and wraps an arm around her.

"Aw, babe," he says softly, sad. "Let's get you cleaned up." Lee leads her inside, away from us, the onlookers.

"Can I help?" I call halfheartedly, but Lee looks over his shoulder and shakes his head. "Better not," he mouths to me.

"I'm gonna take that as a cue to go," Tori says, gathering her things before rushing out the door. Honestly, I don't blame her.

An unsettled feeling washes over me, like I'm torn between wanting to help Isobel and wanting her to grow up. Being a messy drunk was fine when we were freshmen and no one expected us to know how to handle our booze. But she should be able to control herself by now, especially if she's going to be a Legacy . . . if people are going to be judging her as *my* best friend. I thought she learned her lesson at the Shelter Island party.

But as I watch Isobel stumble inside, her weight mostly on Lee's shoulder, something in my chest begins to burn, and I start to wonder if this is more than the standard get-fucked-up-and-do-silly-shit situation. I fumble for my phone and pull up my text messages with her brother, Marty.

Our last few exchanges are in a similar vein.

Hey, I wrote right after the Shelter Island party. Everything okay with Is? She's been on one lately.

He wrote back, Yeah, you know how she gets.

I left it at that back then, but now . . . I don't know. Something feels different.

Worried about her again. Maybe the pressure of the whole Legacy thing is getting to her? She doesn't seem to want to talk to me about it, but she's been getting shit-faced more than usual. A talk from her big bro might help?

Marty responds immediately. I'll make plans with her this week, he writes. You're a good friend, Bernie.

My stomach settles and I sit back down on the couch, closing my eyes for a second. Skyler slides into the seat next to mine and wraps his arm around my shoulder, letting a finger dangle down, dragging over the bare skin above my breast.

He whispers in my ear. "The guest room's just upstairs," he says. "Interested?"

I lean into him and close my eyes, inhaling him. He smells like the French body soap his mom puts in his shower. Like rosemary and cedar. "Yeah."

Skyler takes my hand and starts leading me toward the house, where I'm no longer so sure I want to go. But maybe . . . maybe this will help take my mind off everything, remind me how lucky I am to be here, to have these friends, this life. Mom will come back. Of course she will.

Skyler opens the back door, and we take the steps two at a time until we're at the second-floor landing, when he turns around with a questioning gaze.

"Hey," he asks. "How's your mom?"

"Fine," I say, the skin behind my neck prickling.

"Feeling better than yesterday?"

"Ish."

Skyler nods and something perks up in my brain. A wave of suspicion. Of confusion. "When did you start caring so much about my mom?" I ask, trying to make a joke.

Skyler shrugs. "Just curious, that's all. Haven't seen her in a minute. She's in town, right?"

All of a sudden, I want him to stop, and I want to rid my brain of all the questions I don't have answers to. So, I reach forward and take his chin with my thumb and forefinger and place my other hand at his waist, running my palm up the inside of his shirt.

"You ready to go upstairs now?"

Skyler's mouth curls into a smile and he leans his face toward mine, pressing his body against me so I can feel him beneath his pants. As his lips meet mine, I try to stay focused, to push everything else away—but all I can think about is what Skyler could know about my mom that I don't.

AFTER THE BALL

ONE BY ONE, *the guests are questioned.*

They are ushered into closets, behind doors, into the cavernous rooms decorated with mahogany furniture and heavy carpets. They answer politely, reminding the cops who they are, what they have accomplished. Anders Lowell requests a lawyer—and his publicist. A detective swoons and lets him go out a side exit but not without first requesting a photo.

The cops take notes. They write down pieces of information. They try to find a common thread. A story. The truth.

But what they don't realize is that they won't get the truth, not as they see it. They may learn some facts, key moments that led to the death. But they won't ever understand what really transpired inside the Club, because these people, the ones being questioned, they know how to construct their own truth in ways that benefit them and only them.

"They were roughhousing up there. It's obvious they fell."

"There's no way this was a homicide. Who do you think we are, gang members?"

Soon, the room has thinned. Students are sent home. Names are crossed off lists. Business cards exchange hands.

But a group of students remains, backs pressed against the wall, nerves like live wires.

Bernie Kaplan stands among them, eyes wide. Her green dress is stained dark near its hem, a rumpled tuxedo jacket draped around her shoulders. Her bright red hair is still set in waves, though knots and tangles are visible, even from across the room. Everyone says she's in shock, which is understandable, after all.

Someone reaches for her hand, but she won't take it. Can't. Because within her grasp is the biggest diamond necklace anyone in the room has ever seen. And she isn't letting go.

TWO DAYS
BEFORE THE BALL

Tori

THE WALLS OF the duplex are paper thin, so when my alarm goes off next to my bed, I try to stop it fast so the twins won't hear. George is quiet in the next room over, but Helen stirs in the bunk above me. I heave myself out of bed, tiptoeing toward the pile of clothes near the window, and pull on the pair of jean shorts I left on the floor when I got home last night. As I walk by the mirror, I get a quick look at myself, spotting dark circles under my eyes and my hair sticking out at an odd angle. I paste a smile on my face. *There. Better.*

I grab my phone and send Joss a text. Pancake day. You coming?

A smile tugs at my lips when she responds right away. On my way with iced coffees. Extra blueberries please!!

Joss and I both know that the easiest way to a pair of twelve-year-olds' hearts is through sweet, carby breakfasts, and today there will be big stacks of fluffy silver dollars on the table. Fortunately, my recipe, which was also my mom's recipe, is perfect.

I tie my hair up in a ponytail and glance at the framed photo triptych on my dresser, nudged into the corner of the room. One is of Helen and me, snuggled up together in matching pajamas on Christmas. The second is of my family—Mom, Dad, Helen, George, and me—on Mom and Dad's last anniversary, when we kids cooked them mediocre chicken parmesan and spaghetti.

And the third is an old photo I found of Mom after she died. It's of her when she was around my age, with her dark frizzy hair and an oversized T-shirt. In the photo, she's sitting next to another girl who looks around her age with auburn hair and a big toothy smile. They angle their heads toward each other, and they seem so comfortable, like best friends. Mom's laughing with her mouth wide open, and the other girl is looking at Mom with a mixture of wonder and delight. There's a bond between them. One I never knew about since she never talked much about her teenage years. All I know is that she grew up in Brooklyn Heights with a small family. Both of her parents died before I was born, and she didn't have siblings or cousins who lived near here. When she met my dad, she became a Tasso through and through, absorbed into the tight-knit family that celebrated every holiday and birthday with enough food to feed an army and a tradition of playing poker with pennies.

I found the photo hidden in a shoebox full of old Playbills and concert tickets she must have kept from childhood. There were no other images, no snapshots, and I loved this one, how she looked young and free. I wonder if she kept in touch with the girl in the photo, if they were friends for a long time, or if this was just a brief blip in her adolescence. I never got the chance to ask.

I slip out of the room, careful not to let the door slam, and soon I'm in the kitchen with the batter ready, old show tunes on the speaker. It only takes George and Helen thirty minutes to stumble down the steps and plop down in seats at the breakfast table.

"Morning," I say.

They grumble responses as they pour themselves orange juice and pull out their preferred mode of relaxation—an off-brand tablet loaded up with Tetris for Helen and a book about different kinds of plants for George.

Helen's basically my carbon copy, with the same dark hair and thick eyebrows, the chiseled nose we got from Mom's side of the family. George is softer, with lighter hair, narrow shoulders, and Dad's crooked smile. But whenever we walk down the street together, everyone knows we're the Tasso kids, third-generation Astorians, as native to the neighborhood as the fire hydrants or the fish market.

I heat up a pat of butter in a frying pan, and within seconds, I can sense everyone relax just a bit, thanks to the smell of melting fat.

The screen on the front door squeaks open, and my heart quickens. "In here!" I call to Joss as I drop my dish towel and head to the hallway where my extremely adorable girlfriend is stepping out of her tie-dyed Crocs and shaking out her long dark hair, cut in that trendy shag style that makes me want to run my hands through it. She's wearing a baggy old Backstreet Boys T-shirt she stole from her sister that hangs down to her thighs, obscuring bike shorts that I'm pretty sure are tie-dyed, too.

"Babe," she says, planting a big kiss right on my mouth in front of the twins.

"Get a room," George says without looking up from his book. Helen giggles.

"Do you even know what that means?" Joss says, ruffling his hair. She picks a blueberry off his plate and pops it into his mouth. If I tried to do that, George would throw a fit, but he and Helen have always adored Joss, thanks to the fact that she brings them little goodies from the independent bookstore her parents own a few blocks away. Today, she drops a few neon-colored pens on the table. "Little back-to-school something something for your homework."

The twins light up and grab at the pens, ripping the caps off and doodling on a stray receipt stuck to the table.

Laughing, I turn back to the griddle, where the first batch of pancakes is already burning.

"Shit," I say, rushing to flip them.

"Eh," Joss says, turning with me, and bumping her hip into mine. "First round is always trash, right?" She picks up the garbage can and holds it out to me. "Next."

I can't help but smile. Joss has always had a way of making me feel better, like no matter what, she'll be by my side. Especially after Mom. During that initial blur, right after she died, Joss was here every day after school, making sure the twins were doing their homework and getting to their clarinet lessons and their soccer practice. She'd bring over gallon bags full of frozen shrimp shumai her mom made and big stacks of books on how to deal with grief that her dad recommended from the store.

After she realized I hadn't washed my hair for about a week, she dragged me to the salon where her sister does cut-and-colors and made her give me the works. I told her nothing would make me feel better, but I had to admit that a clean, fresh head of hair actually *did* help. At least I felt alive again.

I spoon out a few more ladles of batter and watch the pancakes cook, little bubbles forming around the edges.

"So, how was yesterday?" Joss asks, grabbing another blueberry from the carton. "No surprise that after all these years those kids finally wanna hang out with you once you're a *nominee* or whatever."

I prickle at the notion, but I know she's right. None of them paid attention to me until this week, and I know they invited me over only because they wanted to size me up.

"I knew it."

"What?" I ask, flipping a pancake to find it perfectly golden.

"You hate them!" She laughs. "I told you wanting to join this elitist club was only going to make you feel bad. You don't need that shit, Tor."

"I don't *hate* them."

She snorts. "You do realize these are the same kids who've ignored you since freshman year? Did any of them even say *anything* about your mom when she died?"

Joss's words are a punch in the gut, mostly because the answer is *no*. I never really told anyone what happened, but word gets out in a small school like Excelsior. Dad informed the principal and the guidance counselor so they could watch out for any signs of major distress or depression, I guess, though obviously I experienced both. And soon, word got out that Tori Tasso from Queens was not only an outsider but also motherless.

The only person who said anything was Bernie. We had never spoken outside of class, but one day she came up to me at my locker and stopped, awkward, as if she didn't know what to say. When I looked up, I saw pity written all over her face, which made me want to run.

"I just wanted to say I'm sorry about your mom," she said.

I didn't know how to respond. *Thank you* seemed disingenuous, but *fuck off* felt rude. So, I just stood there and said nothing.

"I know we're not friends or anything," she said, which I appreciated. "But I just want to say that sucks and I hope you're okay."

I wanted to scream at her that I wasn't okay, that I would never be okay, but before I could say anything at all, she turned away and walked down the hall. It never occurred to me to ask how she found out. It's not like I told anyone, so I assumed she overheard the admins or a teacher talking about me.

"Oh shit, I think you might have burned that one," Joss says, pointing to a pancake that desperately needs to be flipped.

I hand her the spatula and let her finish up the bunch before plunking down a plate on the table in front of George and Helen. Together, Joss and I stand at the counter and watch them dive in, dunking their breakfast into a cereal bowl full of syrup.

"I'm sorry," Joss whispers. "That was mean."

"About my mom?" I ask. "Yeah. It was."

Joss wraps an arm around my shoulder. "I don't want to see them hurt you, that's all. You're putting so much into this and . . . I don't know. Sue me for not trusting some elite exclusive club that only started letting in women and people of color, like, a few decades ago. You gotta admit it kinda goes against basic ethics."

My skin flushes as I turn back to the stove.

"What's the point of all this, anyway? So you can get a key to some random building on the Upper East Side, which, I don't know if you've noticed, is *not* a cool place to hang out."

I grab a pancake and rip it in half, letting steam float up into the air. "It's more than that."

"Yeah, yeah. I've heard all about the network and connections and how it'll help you get into all those fancy colleges you want to go to, but babe, you go to Excelsior. You work your ass off and your grades show that. You can go *anywhere* you want."

I shake my head.

"What?" Joss crosses her arms over her chest and looks at me expectantly. "Come on, there's gotta be a good reason you're ditching me during the last week of summer before senior year to partake in what seems to be a glorified debutante ball."

Joss has known basically every single secret that I've ever had— how my mom caught me masturbating with my pillow in seventh grade, that I once left Helen outside in her stroller for ten minutes when I was eight, that my first crush was Elsa from *Frozen*.

But what I haven't told her is that money has been tight— and what I learned about the bills at the diner. It's not that she wouldn't understand. Her family's gone through tough times, like when the landlords at the bookshop raised the rent or her grandma had to move in with them after falling inside her own apartment. But admitting that we could lose everything feels like exposing something about my dad, like we can't get through this mess on our own.

"What?" Joss asks, suddenly serious. She lowers her head toward me so our foreheads touch. "You can tell me."

I inhale and fight the buzzing in my chest. "There's a cash prize," I say softly. "To the person who gets the most charity donations on Saturday."

"Huh," Joss says, taking a sip from my glass of orange juice. "How much?"

"Twenty-five K."

Joss starts coughing. "Are you serious?"

"Yup."

"Shit, girl. That'd make a big ol' dent in that college fund of yours."

Yep, college. I force a smile. "Exactly."

"Well, I'm just patiently waiting for you to send me your script so I can edit it for you." Joss puffs out her chest and bows down in front of me. "Future professional writer is here at your service."

Warmth blooms in my chest and I reach for her waist, pulling her to me. Her lips turn up in a smile, and I lean forward to kiss her softly on the lips, trying to ignore the creeping guilt that I didn't tell Joss the whole truth.

When Joss leans back, she grabs a pancake from the stack in front of George and Helen. "What's on tap for today, then?"

I pull out my phone and look at the Legacy Ball itinerary that was emailed to us after the luncheon, outlining the rest of the week's activities.

"Something called 'Acts of Service Day,'" I say, scanning the screen. "It's at Excelsior again."

Joss laughs. "Hopefully they won't have you do some bullshit community service thing that isn't really community service."

I keep reading the screen until I get to the part outlining what exactly will happen today. That's when my stomach sinks.

"It's all about the scholarships," I say, my mouth feeling sandy.

"Like the one you have?" Joss eats another hunk of pancake and mutters under her breath, "Well, that won't be awkward at all."

Bernie

THE APARTMENT IS cold and empty, the air-conditioning turned to a crisp sixty-seven, which is my dad's preferred temperature. Mom runs cold and keeps it at a balmy seventy-four. But the goose bumps on my skin are just another reminder that she's still missing.

I sip coffee at the kitchen island and fiddle with my phone, muscle memory taking over as I tap through the icons that might bring me closer to her.

Find My Friends shows me nothing.

Our text exchange is still all green—and one-sided.

My email has no new messages from her.

And my Google Alert for her name brings up nothing.

If she came back today, I could write this whole thing off as another eccentric Esther story, just as Dad said. It would be like the time she jumped in the pool wearing a silk Tom Ford suit in the Hamptons or when she dragged me to the show-tunes bar Marie's Crisis and belted out a song from *Wicked* at four p.m. on a Thursday when I was in seventh grade.

That's why she's so charming, so fun. The fact that she's playful and loving, forgetful and flaky. It was cute when I was a kid, when I was part of those spontaneous moments. At least once a school year, she'd pluck me out of class, feigning a doctor's appointment, and take me to the movies or the Botanical Garden or a matinee. But now . . . now it's just annoying.

I glance at the clock and see it's close to nine, so shit, I'm already sort of late for Acts of Service Day. Grabbing my purse and stepping into a pair of sandals, I head out the front door, my sunglasses high on my head.

On the street, the sun beats down with those final rays of summer and I hail a car, heading uptown to Excelsior. Nestled in the back seat, I turn to my phone, where I pull up the email from Mrs. Shalcross telling us what to expect.

Blah blah blah. I read down to the end where the rest of the nominating committee's names are listed. I pause, seeing my mom's.

Didn't Mrs. Shalcross mention that my mom texted her saying she was sick? That means that Mom *is* checking her inbox. Maybe . . . maybe, just maybe, she might respond.

The driver speeds up the FDR Drive, and with butterflies humming in my stomach, I tap over to my email and start typing. Then I adjust the settings so I'll be notified when she opens it. I give it one last read and, holding my breath, I hit Send.

Mom—If you come back today, we can forget all about this. But please . . . just tell me where you are. Come back. I need you.

† † †

Excelsior's auditorium is full of all the same kids from the luncheon, but now everyone's dressed a little more casually, in jeans and sundresses, knit polo shirts and boat shoes. Most everyone is huddled together with the other nominees from their school, and up on the stage, the nominating committee is chatting amongst themselves, clipboards in hands.

I walk down the red velvet stairs and make my way toward the Excelsior section, in the front row. I've always loved this building, where we have all-school assemblies and Monday morning meetings, and watch all the plays and band recitals. It's regal with balcony seating and velvet curtains embroidered with gold ribbon. It reminds me of the Broadway theaters in Midtown, but more modern with sleek finishes and a crystal chandelier that hangs from the fifty-foot ceilings, intricate molding surrounding its mount.

I spot Isobel first, looking better than she did yesterday, though I can't help but notice the splotchy look of her complexion, a few broken blood vessels around her mouth. Lee's got his arm wrapped around her shoulder like he's trying to protect her, and their feet are propped up against the seats in front of them. I feel the urge to tell them to sit up straight like some kind of narc-y college RA, but I bite my tongue as I get close. Tori and Kendall are sitting next to them, quiet, not talking to each other, but Skyler doesn't seem to be here yet.

When I reach their row, Isobel looks up first and her face brightens when she sees me. "Here," she calls, motioning to the open seat next to her. "Saved you one." My shoulders tense, and for a second I think about sitting in the open seat beside Kendall, far from Isobel. Maybe it's the way she's looking at me, so hopeful and eager, like she wants to prove to me that she's *fine*, that she's *normal*.

But I look at Isobel and see something shift in her face, the slight movement in her eyes that tells me she was just trying to do something nice, so I push Mom's voice out of my head.

I inch past Tori and Kendall and sit down next to Isobel, who untangles her limbs from Lee's and sits up straight.

"You okay?" I ask her softly.

She looks off toward the stage. "Yeah, of course."

"After yesterday . . ." I start, but she cuts me off.

"You know how it is. Too much fun."

I nod even though I *don't* know how it is. She's gotten wasted the past two days, something we might usually blow off. But there's been a bitterness to her drunken state. An urgent, accelerated quality. I hope Marty can talk some sense into her. At least get her to chill out a little.

"Where's Skyler?" I ask Lee, leaning over Isobel to change the subject.

Lee looks around the room and shrugs. "Late, I guess."

I lean back and cross my arms, trying not to be annoyed. I told Skyler a million times never to be late to one of these events. It looks bad, not just for him but for *me* and whoever nominated him, which may have been my mom. Though I guess she's really done caring about appearances, since she's not even here.

But finally, just as the crowd quiets and the rest of the students take their seats, I hear someone plop down behind me. When I spin around, I see Skyler, smiling at me, reaching a hand toward me to say hi.

"Hey, babe," he says, giving my shoulder a little squeeze. He's so close I can smell a whiff of his deodorant.

"You're late," I whisper.

He gives me that devilish smile, the one that has the ability to turn me into mush. It's this one, the crooked one that shows the one stubborn bottom tooth that never quite took to braces, that reminds me of what he was like as a little boy—single-minded and wild and always present. His white linen button-up is a little rumpled, like he forgot to iron it, and his hair is sticking out at odd angles, though on him, the whole look is a little more frazzled preppy than straight-up messy.

"Just a little," he whispers. "But you can't be mad." He reaches into his pocket and pulls out a small box the size of a deck of cards, nudging it into the wedge between my neck and shoulder. "Your favorite."

I reach around and take it, running my thumb over the raised logo of Ladurée, a Tribeca French bakery specializing in macarons.

"Chocolate and rose, just the kind you like."

I roll my eyes. "Fine," I say. "Not mad." I give him a smile and turn around, offering one to Isobel and popping the other into my mouth.

Isobel looks at the box. "He was in Tribeca?"

I shrug, and before she can say anything else, the lights in the theater go down and the assembly begins.

Isobel

THERE'S ONLY ONE reason Skyler could have been in Tribeca this morning, and that's to see Opal Kirk. I glance over at Kendall, who has a pissed-off expression on his face and has refused to make eye contact with me ever since we got here.

I press my hands against my stomach and wish I could melt into the chair. My hangover is violent, like every part of my body is rebelling against itself, pushing and pulling away from the other organs inside me. I don't remember much about what happened after I got back from getting ice with Kendall. All I know is that I woke up this morning in Lee's bed with a raging headache and a bandage on my forehead. Luckily Lee didn't make a big thing about it, and when I checked my wound, I realized it was nothing that a little Neosporin couldn't fix. An artfully placed bang covered the cut, and I pulled myself together with one of Lee's button-downs, cinched at the waist with a silk scarf I had in my bag.

But none of that can stop the fact that my nerves are on edge, wild and frayed, as my foot starts bobbing back and forth like it has a mind of its own. I'm fidgety. Agitated. I should have brought something with me to ease the hangover, make reentry into society a bit more manageable. Less shameful. But since I haven't been home, my stash has been depleted.

Fortunately, a few spotlights come up, illuminating five stuffed armchairs and one lectern. At least I can hide in the dark.

Mrs. Shalcross walks out on the stage, waving at the crowd.

"It's so lovely to see all of our nominees again for Acts of Service Day." She pauses for applause and a few kids in the back oblige. "Today, you'll hear from some recent alumni who received scholarships thanks to the Legacy Club's fund, and you'll get to hear why your work this week really has the chance to impact so many students."

She looks around the room eagerly, smiling. "And after that, we'll break up into groups based on which scholarship you have been assigned to present on. From there, we'll partake in some meaningful community service where you can learn more about your scholarships and do some *good* for the day."

Next to me, I sense Skyler's hand reaching forward to squeeze Bernie's shoulder. She leans into it, placing her hand on top of his, and my stomach flips, trying to ignore the gesture, the dishonesty behind it.

"Which one did you get?" Lee whispers to me under his breath. "I'm STEM."

"Fine Arts," I whisper back. "Thank god."

Lee squeezes my hand. "You'll kill it."

I squeeze back. "You too."

Though I can't say I've even started thinking about the presentation we have to give at the end of this week. All I'm focused on now is making sure we get through the week without blowing up our lives.

Tori

I'M NOT SURE I could have thought of anything worse than sitting through an assembly about the scholarship *I* was awarded with a bunch of kids who can't even fathom that perhaps one might need a scholarship to attend Excelsior, where the yearly tuition is more than that of most colleges.

But here I am, sitting next to Bernie Kaplan and Kendall Kirk, both of whom have Excelsior buildings bearing their last names, listening to former Intercollegiate League students talk about how much the scholarships meant to them—and how going to one of these schools changed their lives completely.

"I never really knew what I was missing until I started going to Gordon," says a short white woman with an unnaturally large headband and chunky clogs. "I saw the rest of the kids I grew up with struggle to find extracurriculars that stood out or workloads that challenged them. I was the first person in my family to go to college, and it was only because of Gordon that I got into all of my top choices. Gordon prepared me for the real world— to know how to network and focus and put my mind to things. No doubt it's the reason I got into Harvard Law and am now clerking for the New York State Court of Appeals." She pauses, looking all the way to the back of the room. "And it was because of the generosity of this group right here that I was able to make all of that happen."

My stomach cramps, and a sickly feeling takes over as I look around the room. Most of the other nominees seem bored or are sneakily checking their phones. They don't give a shit what this woman has to say, and frankly, it sounds like she's kissing every single ass on the planet, which makes me feel all sorts of fucked up, considering that the people in this room are all almost a decade younger than she is.

And for the first time since getting the nomination, I wonder if being part of this Club is a mistake. If even going to Excelsior was the wrong call completely.

Mom was the one who persuaded me to apply for the scholarship. She left the form on my desk one day, so I found it after school when I came home from soccer practice. I picked up the piece of paper and brought it downstairs, where she was browning chicken thighs in a Dutch oven, humming to herself while Helen did her homework at the kitchen table.

"You think I should apply?" I asked, a bubble of hope forming in my belly.

"I wouldn't have left it there if I didn't."

I looked down at the bright and shining faces in the pamphlet, staring intently at textbooks. The Excelsior buildings loomed large in the background, so different from the boxy, run-down middle school I attended a few blocks away. Mom let go of her wooden spoon and placed her hands on the counter.

"You might as well try," she said. "What do you have to lose?"

"But I like my school," I said. "I like my friends."

Mom shrugged. "They'll still be here. They'll still be your friends. But a place like that could change things for you. Open new doors."

I turned the pamphlet over where there was a list of colleges the seniors were heading off to—Yale, Harvard, Princeton, Stanford,

Penn, Dartmouth, Northwestern. Around here, most of the older kids I knew who had their sights set on college went off to state schools or City-funded colleges. When they came back, they were happy and healthy and full of wild stories. But that was the thing. They always came back. And I didn't know if I wanted to.

"I'll think about it," I told Mom.

She winked and went back to her chicken without saying anything else. But that was her way—supportive and direct without being overbearing. I thought about it for approximately five minutes and decided to fill out the application, writing and rewriting three different essays, leaving them on Mom's night table for feedback.

She and I went back and forth like that for two weeks, never speaking directly about Excelsior, just communicating through edits in the margins, little comments like, *Right on, baby girl* and *You can do better*.

Finally, one Wednesday night, she left the application on my desk with a sticky note. "Ready when you are."

I sent it in the next day.

She was elated when I got accepted with the Arts and Letters scholarship, which came with a three-page note from the Legacy Club, exclaiming their delight in offering me a full ride plus funds for textbooks, school supplies, and Excelsior class trips to places like Paris and Mexico City. The formality—the grandiosity—of it all only deepened my interest in the Club itself, its regal crest adorning every single piece of correspondence. It only took a little research to realize that nominations for membership went to rising seniors, picked out by a committee of devoted alumni.

In the few months between when I got into Excelsior and when school started, Mom and I spent a lot of time talking about the school, googling its alumni, and even visiting the grounds, peeking through the gates.

We talked about the school uniforms and how nice it would be to not have to think about what to wear every day, and how I could individualize the whole look by wearing my favorite leather loafers or an enamel pin from Joss's parents' bookstore.

She sent me off to school that first day with tears in her eyes and never stopped asking me for all the tiny details about everything that came with being an Excelsior kid. She was so proud, and she told me so every day.

Being at Excelsior meant that I was more aware of what I *didn't* have than ever before. But how could she have known that I would get weird looks for saying we spent winter break at home instead of in Aspen, or that people couldn't fathom that I shared a bedroom with my little sister? She would have had no idea that it would be impossible to make friends with kids who thought spending thirty-five dollars on lunch was normal, or that my peers weren't really interested in coming to Queens unless they were going to a box at Citi Field or an art opening at MoMA PS1. She had no idea that I would feel like I was an island in a sea of wealth. How could she have?

But now, I wonder what she'd think of all *this*—the fact that her daughter is now going to be part of the very community that offers the scholarships. I wonder if she'd still be proud of me or if she'd worry I would lose a part of myself by becoming one of them.

There's no way to know.

Up on the stage, Mrs. Shalcross heads back to the podium and leads the room in a round of applause. "Well, wasn't that just inspiring?" she asks, all perky and excited. "Before we close out for the day, I just wanted to acknowledge someone very special among this year's nominees."

The students all around me sit up a little straighter, stretch their legs just a tad.

"For the first time in the Legacy Club's storied history, we finally have a nominee who has actually received one of these scholarships."

Oh no. Please no.

"The nominating committee would love to acknowledge that wonderful student today. Tori Tasso, where are you?"

My face is on fire as thirty-five other students swivel their heads like rubberneckers. Mrs. Shalcross's eyes dart around the room until they find me and stay on me. She motions for me to stand up, but I can't move. I'm frozen in place.

Bernie nudges me and whispers in my ear. "It'll be easier if you just do it."

My stomach drops farther down into my gut, and with shaking legs, I stand hesitantly.

Mrs. Shalcross beams and leans closer to the mic. "Tori is a recipient of the Arts and Letters scholarship at Excelsior Prep," she says, as if I'm a cow up for auction at some rinky-dink state fair. "And we're so excited to hear her presentation on Saturday!"

The room claps and I take that as my cue to drop back into my seat, sinking as low as I can manage without sliding onto the floor. My heart beats fast and my fingers begin to shake, so I sit on my hands and close my eyes, waiting for the whole ordeal to be over at last.

Finally, after what feels like an eternity, Mrs. Shalcross closes the assembly and dismisses us to our group sessions. Before anyone else in the Excelsior row can say anything, I leap out of my seat and dart down the aisle, knocking knees with Kendall Kirk. I mumble excuses about how I have to use the bathroom as I wiggle past other students who pause to gawk—to look at me, Tori Tasso, the Legacy Scholarship kid.

When I get to the hallway, I make a break for the two-stall bathroom across from the band room and throw open the door. Fortunately, it's empty. I turn on the faucet, splashing water on my face before grasping the sides of the sink for dear life.

How could that woman think that was okay, singling me out as the only scholarship student? It's not like my status is a secret, but I don't go around advertising it. She shouldn't have either. The more I think about it, the more furious I get, a ball of rage building and boiling inside me until it wants to leap right out of my throat.

But then suddenly, the door swings open.

I jump and turn to see the woman from Gordon Academy who was on stage walk toward me and set her purse down on the counter. "Sorry, didn't mean to scare you."

"You didn't." I turn off the sink and dry my hands. My eyes sting and I blink, trying to swallow the lump forming in my throat.

The woman's quiet for a second, reapplying lipstick in the mirror. But then she turns to me, leaning her hip against the sink.

"So typical, huh?" I glance at her face as she rolls her eyes. "They trot us out every year like we're robots built to their specifications, making good on the promises of the scholarships."

A hitch catches in my throat, as I realize she's saying everything I've been feeling.

"Why . . ." I start. "Why do you keep coming back here? Speaking like that, praising them?"

"Them?" She smiles. "Don't you mean us? You're one of them now."

My mouth drops open a little bit.

"Nothing comes without a price. Not even these scholarships. We make nice, show up and say thank you, pretend like we could never accomplish what we did without them . . . and we stay in their good graces."

I stare at her, so confident and cynical and attuned to how the world works. "Do you regret being a part of this?"

She shakes her head vehemently. "Not for a second." But then she laughs. "I do have some advice, though."

"What?"

She leans in, a devilish look in her eyes. "I've come to enough of these assemblies to know that there's a cash prize that goes to the presentation winner. I've heard it's tradition for whoever gets it to donate it back to the Club. A gesture of goodwill and everything."

My stomach drops as the realization takes hold.

"If you win, don't give it back." She winks in my direction. "But you didn't hear that from me."

I nod slowly, trying to take it all in—wondering what I'll do if I win now that my whole plan just got absolutely fucked.

"I may never be a Legacy, or part of this world for real," she says. "But I can pretend, and pretty soon, so will you. You are, after all, the one scholarship recipient to get a nomination into the Club. That's gotta count for something."

"But . . . is that what you want? To be part of this?"

She shrugs. "Of course. It's just part of the game." She pats me on the shoulder softly and heads toward the door. "See you at the next one."

AFTER THE BALL

"LEE DUBEY." A *disheveled young man looks up, his eyes wide with fear. He's wearing a fitted tuxedo, his bow tie undone, hanging limp around his neck. Obedient and dazed, he follows the detective into the kitchen, where a laptop sits on a butcher block next to a recorder, its red light blinking.*

Lee licks his lips, wipes his sweaty palms on his wrinkled pants. He doesn't know why he's nervous. He doesn't have much to hide. At least he thinks *he doesn't.*

Except for the whole mess with Isobel the night before. He regrets the way he spoke to her. Really, he does. But it was for the best, wasn't it? His parents always told him that the most noble thing a person can be is honest. So, he was. To a fault. Even when the brutal truth hurt the people he loved. And he does love Isobel.

Did. He has to remember that. He did *love her.*

"Are you ready to answer a few questions?"

Lee swallows, his Adam's apple bobbing up and down.

"You're eighteen?"

"Yes," he whispers.

"How well did you know the deceased?"

Lee stands there, his arms hanging by his side like ropes.

"I take it the answer is well?"

Lee blinks, his eyes glossy and wet.

"I'm sorry." The cop hands Lee a paper towel, pulled from a stray roll near a baking tray full of mini blackberry tartlets that never made it out of the kitchen.

"Isobel . . . We had a fight," he whispers. "A big one."

The cop leans in. "What happened?"

Lee sniffles, his breath catching in his throat. "She lied to everyone." He looks up then, tears in his eyes. "Do you think that's why this happened? That the fight could have . . . People are saying it was a jump. On purpose."

The cop checks the recorder to make sure it's doing its job. This kid . . . He doesn't seem as jaded as the others, as performative. If the detective was a betting man, he'd guess that this kid is showing real, actual remorse—and that he had nothing to do with tonight's tragedy.

But he's been surprised on more than one occasion. He knows not to jump to conclusions, not to take all tears as truth. This Lee kid could be playing him, just like the rest of the snot-nosed preppies. Maybe he's just a better actor than the others.

The cop clears his throat, stays on task. He knows how to endear Lee to him. He extends a gruff, meaty hand and pats Lee's shoulder awkwardly.

"You are only responsible for your own actions, son."

Lee looks down, unconvinced. "Did they do any tests?" he asks. "Like, for . . . you know."

The cop pauses. No one's mentioned drugs yet. "Tox report won't come back for a few days. But you think there may be evidence of that?"

"Yeah," Lee says. "I do."

Bernie

I FOLLOW THE poster-board signs to the French wing, where the rest of the nominees assigned to the Arts and Letters scholarship are supposed to gather, and as we all climb the marble staircase, I look around for Tori.

She's trailing the group, her face red and turned down. I hang back a little until she catches up to where I'm standing and start walking in time with her.

"You okay?" I ask, trying to keep my voice low.

She bites her lip but keeps looking ahead.

"That was fucked up," I say, which is true. I've never even thought about who might be on scholarship at Excelsior—never crossed my mind to care—but based on the way Mrs. Shalcross blurted out Tori's name, like she was exceptional for becoming a Legacy while *also* being on scholarship, the whole thing felt wrong. Shouldn't that have been Tori's information to share? "I just—"

Tori shakes her head, cutting me off. "I don't want to talk about it."

"Okay," I say, and together we walk in silence behind the rest of the nominees heading in the same direction.

We all file into one of the classrooms where the chairs are arranged in a circle, and Tori finds her own seat on the opposite side of the room as Mrs. Gellar comes in and perches on the teacher's desk at the front of the room.

She claps her hands together. "Ready for some community service?"

Heads nod eagerly, and I steal a glance at Tori, who's looking out the window.

Mrs. Gellar picks up her clipboard and reads a prewritten script about the Arts and Letters scholarship and how it's given to students who have excelled at subjects like language, history, and English. Around the room, I see people steal glances at Tori, whose eyes are glued to the paper in front of her. I wonder if they're looking at her differently now . . . if I am, too.

For a moment, I feel protective over her, like I want to tell everyone else to fuck right off and stop staring. I want to tell them that Tori has the highest GPA in our class, and that her ninth-grade essay on Homer's *Iliad* won a national prize in literature usually given to college-level students. Maybe they'd stop staring if they realized that she is probably going to get into one of the best universities in the country *without* help from parents or family friends—something few of us, including me, can say.

But then I realize that I've never considered Tori in this way, that she might be someone worth being friends with. I've never even considered her at all.

Like everyone else, I stay quiet and listen as Mrs. Gellar moves on to the instructions for our community service project, how we'll spend the next two hours packing up bags of school supplies to be shipped to women's shelters around the city. As soon as she stops talking, the vibe in the room is jocular and laid-back. No one's thinking about those women, their families, the kids who will use these products—just about what the next few days will bring. It's all predictable, a little icky. By the way Tori's squirming in her seat, I bet she thinks so, too.

As Mrs. Gellar hands out the canvas totes we're supposed to

stuff, I slip out my phone and refresh my email to see the most recent messages. My stomach flips as it loads, as I will a response from my mom to arrive, to finally reveal where she has been, what's going on.

Finally, my most recent messages appear, and there at the top of my inbox is an automated response, letting me know that my mom opened my email an hour ago. My heart skips a beat. She's seen it. But when I pull down my inbox again, refreshing to see what's new, there's no message from her. No response. No flare. No nothing.

I drop my phone into my bag and try to deepen my shallow breathing, try to make myself calm. But there's no use, because what lies ahead is now clear—Mom's not coming back, and I still have no idea why.

Isobel

BLANK CANVAS. LOUD music. The smell of turpentine.

Finally, I'm home.

Here, in the shed we built at the back of our brownstone's garden, is my makeshift studio, where I've spent my whole life drawing, painting, and even sculpting during that one winter when I thought molding clay might calm my brain. It did, for a while.

But nothing compares to the thrill I get when I have a piece of charcoal or a wooden brush held just right between my thumb and forefinger. Today, I prop up a small canvas on my easel and turn up the speaker, which is blasting Bonnie Raitt so loud I can barely hear myself think. Exactly the way I like it.

I cover all the windows with black construction paper and change into my uniform—one of my dad's old crew-neck tees from medical school that's now so stained it's impossible to tell its original color. Then I get to work mixing colors on a thick plastic palette and outline my next steps. I know I should be working on my presentation for Saturday, but I've learned that when I get the itch, there's no way to relieve it, no way for me to focus on anything else besides the image in my brain, until I've gotten it out into the world. And today—right now—I can't think about anything else besides the crashing waves, a dark storm. A monsoon.

First comes a sea of blue, a violent burst of darkness onto the canvas. I bop my head along to the music, dripping paint all over the floor.

My process has always been this way—one that exists in short, furious bursts that cannot stop until I've wrung myself out completely. When I started painting, Dad expressed concerns that my work was aggressive. Grotesque. That there *had* to be something wrong with me. But Mom told him to back off and let me be creative.

It wasn't that I was drawing violence in the traditional sense. No beheaded people or bloody corpses. No acts of rage or cruelty. But my work—my interests—have always veered toward darkness, the ways in which we deceive one another. But always through nature, through wilderness. I don't paint people, only the nude figures I'm forced to in class, and even then, they always morph into something else. The curve of a hip becomes the California coastline. A dip in the pelvis, a volcano erupting.

Moments go by. Minutes, an hour, and I lose myself in the thing I love, the thing that keeps me motivated, that propels me forward, until a loud knocking sound against the door makes me jump.

I set down my brush and turn down the music. The air is oily, and I feel light-headed from the turpentine, but I yell out, "One second, Mom!"

The door swings open, letting dusky summer light inside, and I realize I've been in here for hours longer than I thought.

"Sorry," I say. "Finishing up soon."

But when I turn to the entrance, I don't see Mom. Instead, Skyler's leaning up against the doorframe, looking around, and for a second, I feel like he's got me splayed open, raw and naked, looking at the most intimate parts of me. He needs to get out of here.

I push toward him, forcing him to back up into the garden, and close the door behind me. I wipe my sweaty hands on my smock.

"Nice shit you got going on."

I shake my head. "What are you doing here?"

Skyler sighs and plops down in a hammock my brother, Marty, installed when we were kids. He kicks his legs back and forth, swinging.

"We need to have a little talk."

My stomach flips and I cross my arms over my chest. "About what?"

Skyler looks at me like I'm playing him. "Kendall. He knows."

Shit. Did Kendall confront him? Tell him that he already told me? If he did, that means I'm fucked—that Skyler's here to double down on me keeping his secret.

"Opal told him," Skyler says with little concern in his voice. He drags his feet on the ground and cocks his head. "So, what are we going to do about it?"

I blink, still trying to assess if he knows that Kendall confided in me yesterday, if it would be a smart move to let him know I told Kendall to forget about it.

"I don't know." I shake my head. "Nothing?"

"Ken's only going to stay quiet for so long. You know him." He waves his hand, amused. "All do-goodery and shit. I need a plan. *We* need a plan."

Rage rises in my throat, and all of a sudden, I feel a burst of protectiveness over Kendall. I have to try to divert Skyler. "If you actually don't want Bernie to find out, maybe you shouldn't visit Opal hours before a Legacy event. Macarons from Tribeca? You're asking to get caught."

Skyler rolls his eyes. "It's not like they said 'I just fucked Opal Kirk' on them."

"They might as well have," I mumble. But then I turn to him.

"Opal isn't as weak as you think, either, you know. She could tell Bernie, too."

Skyler grins at me and all of his teeth show, which makes me step back. Flinch.

"She's not going to tell Bernie."

"What makes you so sure?" I ask, though as soon as I speak the words, I don't think I want to know the answer.

"I have something on her."

"Tell me it's not a video."

"Oh please, I'm not a *monster*."

"Then what is it?"

Skyler smiles. "Opal loves me," he says.

A pit forms in my stomach and I know he's right.

Skyler's eyebrows shoot up, and suddenly, I get the urge to rush toward him and punch him in the throat. To take my paintbrush and stab him in the stomach, to make him understand what it means to be helpless for once.

But I don't do that. Instead, I ask, "Why the hell did you come all the way to Brooklyn to tell me this?"

He looks around, taking in my backyard, the studio, me covered in paint. "I wanted to see where the magic happens." His voice has a condescending tone, full of jest and vitriol. "Nah, just kidding." He takes a step forward so the space between us shrinks, and I can smell his breath, sour. He reaches into the chest pocket of his button-down shirt and pulls out a slim clear baggie, a few small pills visible inside.

I clench my paintbrush tighter, the splintered wood digging into my palms.

"Just got a refill. Figured it wouldn't hurt to leave you with a little reminder of how I can help you."

I want to smack him, shove my palms into his chest and direct him toward the street. But everything in my body rejects that, and instead, I feel my hand reaching toward him, snatching the bag.

Skyler nods, pleased, because we both know that I'm not about to let his secret out. And then, finally, he turns on his heel and leaves as if he was never here at all.

As soon as I see him disappear, I rush back inside my studio. My safe place. But when I see the painting, the one I spent all afternoon crafting, I can't look at it. My nerves on fire, I grab it from the easel and toss it across the room, where it lands on a coatrack, puncturing the middle. Something inside my chest cracks right open and I get on my knees, reaching under the couch in the corner, until my hand finds what I'm looking for.

I pull out the glass bottle and open it, the pungent smell of warm alcohol filling the room. I take a sip and slip one of Skyler's gifts under my tongue. I chug the rest until things start to feel hazy. Bearable.

Finally. Finally, I can rest.

AFTER THE BALL

IT'S GETTING LATE. *That strange window of time in New York City when the night owls—those who moved here to take advantage of that old adage, the one that says the city never sleeps—claim forbidden blocks as their own for an hour or two.*

They walk casually, bawdily through the warm August air with no clear destination in mind. Perhaps an apartment for one more drink. Or a late-night slice of pizza. Maybe the dive bar on the corner that stays open until dawn.

But those who saunter by the white brick building that is usually quiet and demure slow to a stop when they see the flashing red lights, New York's finest jotting down notes in little leather books. They stare, wondering what could possibly have taken place in a building like this, one that gleams against the streetlights.

"Think somebody got whacked?" asks a man, slurring his words. A red wine stain deepens on his collar.

"Here?" says his date, a short woman wobbling on chunky heels. "What is this place?"

The man shrugs. "Dunno."

They look up at the Legacy Club, at the illuminated windows, the shadows moving from room to room inside.

Just then, a yellow cab pulls to a halt in front of the building, and a young woman throws open the door, with wide eyes and heaving sobs, hysterical and uncontained. She's wearing pajamas—a matching lavender set with dark purple piping on the collar. She looks like a child woken from a bad dream.

"You okay?" the man asks her.

But the girl doesn't seem to hear him. "My brother," she wails. "Kendall Kirk. He's not picking up. I heard . . ."

The couple exchange glances, worried and unsure, but what could they say to comfort such a girl? The front door of the club opens with a bang, and a young man in glasses and a rumpled tuxedo comes barreling down the stairs. The couple crane their necks to look in behind him, catching slivers of the glass chandelier, the yellow caution tape, the warm glow of opulence. But then it shuts hard, a reminder that this place is not for them.

"Opal," the boy cries, rushing to his sister. He wraps his arms tightly around her shoulders, but he can't contain his fury, his anger. "What are you doing here?"

She sobs, a moment of relief. "I thought you . . ."

He shakes his head and hugs her harder. "It wasn't me," he whispers. "I'm fine. I'm okay."

She heaves a sigh of relief. "Who?" she asks. But before Kendall can respond, a detective rushes through the door of the Club, waving her hand at the Kirk siblings. "Hey!" she calls. "You haven't been dismissed yet."

Kendall turns to face her, but just as he does, Opal inhales sharply, her chest heaving up and down. Kendall steps back and watches, terrified, as Opal's eyes roll into the back of her head, and suddenly, as if she were a feather or a piece of silk, her whole body floats to the ground, hitting the street with a tender little thud.

ONE DAY
BEFORE THE BALL

Tori

BY THE TIME I get to the diner for the morning shift, the early risers are all but gone and there's a steady trickle of regular brunchers coming in. Always the Kleinmans, who walk over from Beit HaShalom after Shabbat services; the retired Hartley grandparents, who scarf down egg-white omelets after Zumba at the Y; and the Reeses, who just had a baby named Kyle and come every Saturday because they know Marina will jump at the chance to hold that little kiddo for an hour so they don't have to.

Looking around the diner, I feel a sense of ease set in, of comfort knowing this is exactly where I should be, far, far away from the Legacy Club and all those people I'm supposed to impress. I swap my denim jacket for an apron, but when I get close to the servers' stand, Dad holds up his hand to stop me.

"You're not on the schedule today."

I roll my eyes. "Come on, Dad."

Dad stands firm. "Don't you have a presentation to finish?"

"I was up until two working on it," I say, which is the truth. It was harder than I thought it would be to write down a sanitized version of why these people should put their money behind me. *I'm the only one here who needs that cash—who would actually keep it* may be the truth, but the sentiment won't win anyone over. I fell asleep with my laptop on my chest, boring phrases repeating over and over in my brain.

"All the more reason you should be resting," Dad says.

Marina appears, snuggling baby Kyle against her hip. "Put her behind the pastry counter," she says, swiping a kiss on his cheek as he wriggles in her arms. "Fiona had to run to a doctor's appointment. It's slow now anyway."

Dad throws up his hands and waves toward the cake counter near the breakfast bar. I mouth the words *thank you* to Marina and she gives me a wink.

I perch on one of the leather stools behind the glass case full of cakes, cookies, baklava, doughnuts, halva, and bear claws. It's a mismatched smattering of random, buttery goodness that Dad curates specifically to his own liking—cookies from Winner in Park Slope and doughnuts from Fan-Fan in Bed-Stuy—and whatever the regulars request.

There was a while when Lori Reese was trying to be gluten-free, and he ordered some special croissants so she wouldn't take their business to the fancy coffee shop next door. Not that she ever would. But nice gestures like that are in my dad's nature. Everyone thinks he passed that gene down to me. But that's just because I'm an observer, someone who sucks in information with the intention of using it to my advantage later.

At least that's what I thought I was doing with Skyler.

I pull out my laptop to look at my presentation script, but a pit forms in my stomach as soon as my fingers hit the keyboard. What I wrote last night was empty, void of any meaning. What is there to say about the scholarship—about why people should support *me*—when I can't help but feel like I didn't earn this nomination, that I shouldn't be here?

If people knew the truth about why I'm a part of this now, I don't think anyone would want to help me, let alone let me into the Club.

And besides, maybe I don't want to be part of this group anyway—one that was built on bigoted, outdated beliefs and still doesn't seem to give a shit about the people they say they're helping.

Maybe . . . maybe I should quit.

But then I think about all those late notices on Dad's desk. The bills. The worried look on his face when he realized I knew the truth. How his face went ghastly when I joked about suing the lawyers who still haven't paid us.

I can't quit. Not when I have the chance to help keep the diner.

But all of a sudden, my vision goes dark and I feel someone's hands against my face, covering my eyes.

A smile tugs at the corners of my lips as I rest my palms against the warm skin on my face.

"Hi, Joss."

"Damn, I thought I'd get you one of these days." She releases her palms and gives me a quick kiss on the cheek before hopping up on the stool next to me, her shoulder right up against mine. She leans down to squint at my computer.

"'The Arts and Letters scholarship is an exciting opportunity . . .' Come on, Tor, I think you can do better than *this*."

My cheeks redden and I slam my computer shut.

Joss's face contorts into a frown. "Too harsh?"

I shake my head. "I can't do it. Get up there and talk about this scholarship knowing *they* all know that I'm the one who received it."

Joss shrugs. "So? Ditch the whole thing."

I shake my head, unable to admit I was thinking the same thing. "I can't."

Her jaw tenses, a sign she's holding back, that she wants to say more.

"What?"

Her shoulders melt down her back, and for a second it looks like she's debating whether to say whatever it is that's on the tip of her tongue or stay silent. But Joss has never been one to hold back. It's like passive aggression doesn't run in her blood.

Joss and I gravitated toward each other because we didn't have to pull that crap. I could always tell her when she was bothering me with her loud chewing or sighing, or when I wanted to be alone and read. She'd never get mad or upset, or whisper about me behind my back. Instead, she'd throw it back at me, too, unafraid to confront me if I was being too stubborn or insensitive. So, I'm not surprised when she goes off.

"It's pretty hard to support you in all of this," she says, her words coming out slowly, like she's making sure every single one is right. "I can't help but feel like you're setting aside all your morals to join some ridiculous old club because there's a cash prize, which, sure, I can understand. But then you tell me that you don't want to be part of it for all the reasons I've been saying but insist that you have to do it anyway because what will your life be like without it." Joss shrugs, almost embarrassed for me. "It's all a little self-absorbed. You're not even considering how it makes *me* feel to hear you freak out about this club that I'll never even get the opportunity to be part of for a million and one reasons."

She shakes her head and bites the inside of her cheek. "Make a decision," she says. "And stick to it. Because otherwise, I don't think I can handle this waffling back and forth anymore. I don't have time for this, and neither do you."

Her words cut through the air, piercing, and I realize they hurt so much because I know she's right.

I didn't endure yesterday's humiliation or the barbaric practice of standing up and being judged on my appearance by some committee of adults to *not* go through with tomorrow.

Joss looks at me, her eyes wide and sad. "What are you not telling me?"

I inhale sharply, running down a list of all the secrets I'm keeping, the ones I said I'd never tell. The one about how I got the nomination—that's one I'm not willing to share. Not yet. Not now. But the other one . . .

"Dad could lose the diner," I say. "Missed mortgage payments." I shake my head. "We're still waiting for the money from the lawsuit. We need something to hold us over."

"Shit. I'm so sorry, babe." She reaches for my hand and takes it in hers, squeezing it in a way that lets me know she understands how painful that would be. Her eyes drift to the framed photos next to the entrance, the ones that have hung there for decades. But I don't have to look too closely to know she's set on the one of my mom manning the grill with a big smile on her face and a grease-stained Tasso's T-shirt rolled at the sleeves. Joss sighs and holds my hand tighter. "You know this isn't your problem to fix, though? You're not in charge here."

The tears are coming hot and fast, and there's nothing I can do to stop them. I nod, knowing she's right. "But I can try," I eke out. "I can try to win."

Joss envelops me, pulling me close to her chest, and rests her head on top of mine. I know she doesn't get it, doesn't fully support what I'm doing, but she stays quiet, holding me to her, knowing somehow that's all I need for now.

Bernie

THE MORNING SUN streams through the blinds in the kitchen as I'm spooning avocado on top of toast, violently mashing the green bits down into the sourdough until the bread becomes flatter than I had anticipated. I can't stop thinking about the simple fact that Mom read my email and didn't respond. She knows I'm looking for her—that I'm worried—and she doesn't care to set my mind at ease, give me the kind of comfort she knows I'm craving.

All of this fills me with an undeniable ball of fire in my stomach, one that crackles and causes all of my muscles to tense, my jaw to clench. This whole week, I've felt anxious, desperate for answers. But for the first time since Mom disappeared, I realize I am utterly, undeniably *furious*.

I slam my spoon down on the counter and decide I need to *do* something. I need to act. Or else I'll just be stuck in this hellish loop with no control. I wipe my hands on my cotton pajama boxers and head down the hall to Mom's office, where I haven't been.

It's not that I'm not allowed in here; it's just that there's no reason for anyone to be in here, really. Mom hasn't held a job since she married my dad, but she uses this room to do all of her "correspondence," as she says, and as a retreat from the rest of the house. A few years ago, she redecorated it with floral hand-painted wallpaper from England and reupholstered velvet chairs in a dark burgundy color, so the whole space feels regal and rich, which I guess was Mom's point.

The door pops open with ease, and as soon as I enter, I'm immediately hit with the smell of Mom—her perfume, which seems to have permeated everything. The thick curtains, the plush carpet, even the Italian leather swivel chair, pushed under her desk, with one of her silk scarves hanging off the back.

I pull out the seat and plunk down, spinning around and around, taking in her world. The wall is lined with framed photos of our family at various important life events over the years—my baby naming, my graduation from Excelsior elementary school, the time I was a flower girl for my aunt Hilda, my bat mitzvah. There's one of her and Dad at their wedding, too, stiff and formally posed in the lobby of the Plaza Hotel.

Along the bookshelves across the room, I spot all of her Excelsior yearbooks, their navy-blue fabric spines fading into the darkness against gold writing. In front of them is a framed photo of Mom at a young age—maybe seventeen—laughing with another one of her Excelsior friends, looking so carefree. So alive. She looks the same, with fiery red hair like mine, and a wide, symmetrical smile, also like mine. It was the early nineties, and Mom idolized the celebrities who wore dark lipstick, with sleek, volumized bobs. She was radiant, even then, with her arms around another girl with dark, frizzy hair and a wide smile in the shape of a laugh. It was obvious they were close, tight-knit. Mom always said this one was taken only a few months before the Ball.

I spin around and around in the chair, my socked feet dragging on the carpeted floor. But then my elbow bumps the wireless mouse sitting on the desk, which makes the screen on her desktop blink alive.

I press my feet to the ground, stopping to check out the

computer. It's a blank home screen, a bunch of icons lined up in neat little rows with folders labeled things like FAMILY PHOTOS and HOME DOCUMENTS. But when I look closer, I see there are nearly a dozen windows that were minimized, sitting at the bottom of her screen.

Tentatively I click on one, bringing up a browser page that looks to be the order form for Madame Trillian's. Ah, I guess that means she nominated Isobel instead of Skyler. I squint at the details but can't deduce much. It's just a confirmation that a dress was purchased. No name. No size. No description of the gown.

I scroll down and see a handwritten note from Madame Trillian that was inscribed on the bill:

Dear Esther, How fabulous is Bernie's dress?! She will be the belle of the Ball indeed. You and her nominator have great taste, but everyone knew that already. Can't wait for the big day.

I hadn't really ever thought about *who* would nominate me for the Ball. Receiving entry was always such a given. It depended on whose year it was to nominate. Maybe Lulu Hawkins, who got a nomination this year, or another one of Mom's longtime friends like Iris Frankel, from Central Synagogue's choir, or Marvin Rutledge, who plays mixed doubles with Mom once a month. Jeanine Shalcross, until she approached me at brunch last year and pouted that she wished she could nominate me, but sadly, she wasn't due for a pick for another year. Women she's known for decades, who circle one another at benefits and society functions and, while obviously competitive with one another, would stab someone in the eye with an oyster shucker to keep the circle of power contained to themselves and their offspring.

The last time Mom was able to nominate someone, she chose Iris's son, Kevin, and after that was revealed, Iris sent her a full set of Baccarat crystal barware as a thank-you. Kevin turned out to be a bit of a shit, landing himself in a cheating scandal at a small liberal arts college in Vermont, but one of the board members there was a Legacy and he graduated unscathed with an internship at J.P. Morgan. So, perhaps Iris returned the favor this year.

I close out of the PDF and pull up another window from her dock. It's her email inbox. A warm, nervous feeling fills my chest. Mom's always had access to my social media, texts, or emails when she asked to see them. I even let her read my diary when I was ten because sharing things with her made me feel closer to her, like no one else had a mother-daughter bond the way we did. She liked to say that she made an effort to be my best friend because she never had that close-knit bond with her mother before she died.

But I'm starting to think that closeness never went the other way. Sure, she told me when she and Dad had a fight or when she thought Jeanine Shalcross's outfit was tacky, but what if she never let me in on the real her? What if her email was about to tell me?

I take a deep breath and rest my hand on the mouse, not knowing where to start. It says she has 53,458 unread emails, which is enough to give me heart palpitations since I'm very much an inbox zero type of girl. And from the looks of it, most of them are generic emails from brands or newsletters hyping up new products or a shopping experience.

When I scroll farther down, I see my email, marked as read

but ignored. And then I stop on an unopened email from Mrs. Shalcross, sent only an hour ago. I click to read it before I can think better.

Subject Line: Tonight???

E: It's been days since I've heard from you and I'm starting to get worried. You're coming to Reveal Night, right??? We've missed you at all the events this week and to be frank, I'm a bit concerned that if you don't show up tomorrow for the Ball, we will be in a pickle with your nominee. As you know, we were all a bit concerned about your choice but supported you, as we always do. (You do know that, right? That shrimp at the luncheon thing was the old guard's preference, not mine.) Anyway, what a surprise it would be if they won tomorrow, though as you know, both nominee and nominator need to be present for that to happen. I believe you wrote that into the bylaws last year—a good addition for sure!

At the risk of sounding too desperate, I would love to hear from you before tonight, Esther. And, obviously, if you are somehow indisposed or you need anything at all—you know where to find me.

Jeanine

My stomach hardens. If she's not getting in touch with Mrs. Shalcross anymore, then *where* could she be? My mind races, horrifying scenarios playing out in my head: kidnapping, blackmail, murder.

I keep scrolling past a bunch of emails about the Bergdorf's VIP shopping experience, and the new line of Gucci winter coats, until I find a message with a subject line that makes me pause: *Hawkins Kaplan Lawsuit*.

I tap it open and am immediately greeted by a block of text written in a small font. I lean in closer to see what it says.

Dear Esther,

As you know, the lawsuit that is soon to be filed against Hawkins Kaplan, Rafe, Lulu, and their team of attorneys will undoubtedly bring more attention to not just the firm but also to your families, specifically recent lavish spending habits and who has been using what money to fund vacations, clothing, home renovations, etc. All of your recent actions and transactions will be put under a microscope. Do not assume Bernie is in the clear either. Her spending, funded by the firm's pursuits, will be scrutinized as well.

While we will remain firm in our stance that you had and continue to have NO knowledge about the actions alleged in the lawsuit, we are formally advising you to distance yourself from Rafe, Lulu, and the entire firm. Permanently.

Per our conversation, we have drawn up the divorce motion and are attaching it here for your review. Once you confirm, we are prepared to serve Rafe. Please advise on how to proceed, but note that the lawsuit is set to be filed imminently. The plaintiff is eager. Desperate, even. Time is of the essence.

Sincerely,

Lisa Taggart

Partner, Lionel, Prospect, and Associates

When I finally finish reading, my heart is pounding hard in my chest and my fingers are trembling against the mouse. The email says it was sent on Tuesday, the day Mom disappeared. The day all of the Legacy events began.

Divorce.

The word lands on my chest like an anvil. Even though her relationship with Dad is nothing I'd ever hope to emulate, she always demurred when I asked if their issues might be fatal. Sure, they've slept in separate bedrooms since before I can remember, and "date night" means going out with Dad's clients or co-workers, or attending a black-tie function to support a charity they're involved with.

But they don't fight, not like you see in the movies where adults scream at one another and throw things made of glass against walls. Instead, they prefer to coexist pleasantly and with little overlap. They call themselves partners, which sometimes sounds transactional but most of the time just seems practical.

I thought the D-word was out of the question since back in fourth grade, while they were going through a particularly chilly phase, and I asked Mom point-blank if they were going to get divorced. All she did was laugh uproariously, almost until she had tears in her eyes.

"What?" I asked, confused.

"Oh, honey," she said. "There's too much at stake here."

She left it at that and over the years I realized what she meant: that she and Dad, together, were more powerful than they were apart. She had her money and he had the legal clout. He was indebted to her for funding his career in the beginning, for introducing him to the right people. And she needed him to maintain a sense of seriousness, that she wasn't just a party girl. There was love there, too, I knew it. But a different kind of love than you might see with some of my other friends' parents who make out in public.

But now . . . what could have changed? I scan the email again, and this time other words jump out at me. *Lawsuit. Lavish spending habits. Bernie.*

My insides freeze, and it's like the air around me has gone still. What the hell has been going on at Hawkins Kaplan?

But then I hear footsteps in the hall. "Bernie?" Dad calls.

I pop up from the seat and tiptoe over to the door, shimmying into the hallway, where I move farther down toward my room so it doesn't seem like I was poking around in Mom's office. My heart pounds hard in my chest, and for a second, I imagine saying something to my dad.

Did Mom serve you with divorce papers?

Are you and Lulu doing something illegal?

Why am I wrapped up in this, too?

But what if Dad doesn't know? What if he has no idea Mom is thinking about divorce? What if he doesn't even know anything about a lawsuit?

"Bernie, you down there?"

I duck into the powder room and then lean my head out so it looks like I was just finishing up in the bathroom. "I'm here," I call.

Dad's footsteps grow louder as he gets closer until he appears in the doorway, wearing sweats, a damp stain around the collar.

"Gym?" I ask.

Dad looks confused but nods. "Sure," he says.

He still has bags under his eyes, and the frown lines around his mouth seem to have deepened. He looks like he hasn't slept in days. "Are you okay?"

"Fine." He clears his throat and stands up a little straighter, like the dad I'm used to. "I have to get back to my calls." But something doesn't sit right.

"Have you heard from Mom?"

Dad sighs, exasperated, and rubs one hand against the back of his neck, like he's trying to massage all of my questions away. "She'll be back, Bernie. Before the Ball, of course she will."

"Not tonight?" I ask. "Not for Reveals?"

Dad pats my shoulder. "I stopped trying to predict your mother's actions years ago."

"But she's okay? She's coming back, right?"

I expect him to push back with what he said the other day, that she disappears and always returns, that she's just Esther, flighty and free. But his mouth betrays him, tense.

His phone starts buzzing in his pocket and once he takes a peek at the screen, he answers. "Go for Rafe."

He waves at me and starts down the hall, back toward the door, away from me and all my fears.

"She has to come back," I say to no one, my voice hovering above a whisper.

Isobel

I TURN THE water as hot as it will go, until the tender skin on my chest starts to burn, but I don't change the temperature, not yet. I give it another second, then another, until finally, I grit my teeth and reach toward the shower handle and yank it all the way to cold, shocking my system with a stream of icy water. I count to five and then shut off the water, my brain buzzing, and reach for a towel.

For a second, I feel last night coming up in my throat—all the vodka I drank after Skyler left—but I swallow it, tasting the sick as it descends into my stomach. I try to push the memory of him away as I step out of the shower and reach for my phone, swiping at the screen, clouded by steam.

There's a text from my brother, Marty: Lunch in Fort Greene Park? Noon? I'll bring the grub.

A sense of warmth blooms in my chest and I send him a thumbs-up. It's almost eleven, so I hustle to throw on a pair of black jeans and open-toed clogs, a loose muscle tank, ripped near the armpit. I shake my wet hair so it starts to form a curl and head downstairs, where the smell of coffee is calling to me like a siren.

"She lives!" Mom says, sitting at the kitchen table with her laptop and a steaming mug. She's wearing workout clothes, but has a full face of makeup on, her hair blown out in waves.

"Press hits?" I ask, pouring oat milk into my coffee.

Mom sighs. "ABC then NBC, then heading to a talent meeting at DUMBO House in an hour."

"Living the dream."

Mom laughs and keeps her eyes on me. "You've stayed out a lot this week," she says. A statement, not a question.

My stomach cramps and I feel the familiar sense of wanting to flee, to avoid all questions. Usually I'm good at dodging them, able to anticipate her curiosity. But I'm rusty this week. "I texted you," I say, turning away from her. "I was at Bernie's. Then Lee's." I take a sip of coffee. "I was here last night."

Mom's quiet, and I know she'd rather I not sleep over at my boyfriend's house, but ever since we had *the talk* and I got an IUD, she stopped fighting it. Part of me suspects that she doesn't mind so much because it means that I'm probably spending time with Arti, too, which Mom views as networking.

"Were you working on your Yale application with Arti?" she asks. "Last time I saw him, he said you were a shoo-in, especially with that Brooklyn Museum show on your résumé."

She glances up at me and my limbs tense. I still haven't told her about my dream to take a year off, mostly because I know she'd laugh right in my face and probably submit the Yale application on my behalf anyway. "There's still a few months before it's due."

Mom nods. "Of course, but the earlier the better, you know? It shows your interest. Besides, if the whole art thing doesn't work out, you'll still have a Yale education." She reaches for her reading glasses and smiles at me.

I clench my fists. "What do you mean, 'doesn't work out?'"

"You're not cut out to be a starving artist, Isobel. You need a fallback. And I'd say Yale is a pretty excellent one."

"Mom—" I start.

She holds up her hand and turns her attention toward the

screen, putting in an earbud. "Sorry, sweetie. Meeting starting." Then she looks back at me and pauses. "You know," she says. "I wanted to be a poet when I was a kid. I told your grandparents and they laughed and laughed, and told me to study English all I wanted, but to find something where I could actually make *money*, *do* something. And you know what?" She throws up her hands. "I did." Mom smiles, satisfied, and then points her finger at me. "Now it's your turn to learn that even artists need a backup plan."

I open my mouth, a retort hot on my tongue, but then Mom turns intently to the screen in front of her.

"Jeff, hello!" she says. "Yes, continue."

I slam the coffee cup on the counter and make a break for the front door, rushing down the steps of the brownstone as I dart down the tree-lined street, past the kids scootering by, their helmets askew on their heads.

Mom may think she knows what's best for me, but all I heard was that she doesn't believe I'm good enough to chart my own path as an artist, that I need to follow whatever path has been prescribed to me by being an Excelsior student, a Legacy.

I make a hard left turn and walk quickly toward Fort Greene Park. It's tiny compared with the big boys—Central and Prospect—but to me, it's perfect, intimate and full of Pratt students having picnics on woven blankets, first-birthday parties gathered by the wooden tables, and amateur tennis players popping balls back and forth across the net. If I get here early enough for off-leash hours, I can watch the dogs run and tussle and be free within the wild walls of the city.

But now I realize I'm almost late to meet Marty. I enter the park on Dekalb Avenue and weave past a dad pushing a double stroller while also leading a massive poodle mix to the playground, and it takes me only a few seconds to spot Marty sitting on a bench making kissy faces at a French bulldog. When he sees me, he jumps to stand.

My brother's six foot three, and despite the fact that I'm a full foot shorter, people always know we're related. Probably because we have the same thick dark hair, tan complexions, and saucer-sized eyes that a first-grade classmate once called "freaky."

Marty never went to Excelsior. Instead, he attended a hippie-dippie private school in Brooklyn until eighth grade, when he then tested into New York City's most sought-after public school, the kind that has a smaller acceptance rate than Harvard. Now he's followed in Mom's journalism footsteps by landing a fellowship at the *New York Times* that seems to consume his every waking hour. I bet she never told him to find a backup career.

I look up and see Marty barreling toward me, cheeks pink, hair unwashed and flopping in a sort of sleepy manner, and I feel a wave of affection for my brother, who's always known my secrets. Most of them, anyway.

He *is* the one who slipped me a Vyvanse when I needed to study for a bio exam in eighth grade, showed me how it could be fun to take half an Adderall and chase it with a shot of vodka. But Marty didn't have whatever need I do to feel something different, to light my insides on fire. He was obsessed with history and journalism, preferring to go deep in the Brooklyn Library archives rather than waste an entire day enjoying a grade-A, euphoria-induced adventure. I prefer not to tell him when I'm having *fun* anymore.

"Reveal night coming up. I see your primping hasn't started

yet," he says, wrapping one arm around me and squeezing my whole body toward him. He wiggles his eyebrows at me, almost menacing.

Without meaning to, my shoulders hunch, shame burrowing in my chest. Marty would never buy into the Legacy scene, and being with him makes me wonder if I should have ditched the nomination all together, though I'm not even sure that's an option.

Bristling, I change the subject. "What's for lunch?" I nod down to the big plastic bag he's holding in his hand.

"Sahadi's," he says, a big smile forming on his face.

I clasp my hands together and feign a prayer. "Bless you."

Marty leads us over to a grassy patch on the hill by the tennis courts, and I lay out a blanket while he unpacks the goods from our favorite Middle Eastern grocer: a package of homemade pita, a tub of hummus, crisp cucumber salad, a plastic baggie full of dried apricots, a container of white beans marinated in some sort of spicy oil, and a big block of feta.

"You hero," I say, tearing into the pita bread.

Marty smiles and together we dig in without saying much, listening to the final sounds of summer vacation—of little kids climbing rocks and tennis balls thwapping in the air.

For the first time since all the Legacy events started, I finally feel calm, like my limbs can relax and I can breathe.

"Mom was being so annoying this morning . . ." I start. But when I turn to Marty, I see him looking at me intently. "What?" I ask.

"Aren't you going to ask me why I wanted to hang out?"

I shrug. "Can't a girl take what she can get from her brother who is usually too busy for her?"

Marty smiles but stops short of laughing, and it's clear there's something going on. I swallow my pita. "Is everything okay?"

He nods, stabbing a bean with a plastic fork. "Yeah, I mean . . . sorta."

"Sorta?"

He sighs. "I wanted to talk to you about something."

My stomach flips, and all of a sudden, the pita bread feels like sandpaper in my hand. Instinctively, I slip my fingers into my pocket and feel around for the little baggie of pills. To my surprise, I can feel only one left. One to get me through the day. *Don't panic.*

I try to focus on Marty's face, the one that looks so much like mine.

"About what?" I manage.

He sets down his plastic fork and wipes his hands on the edges of the blanket. "How have you been feeling lately?"

"Fine."

Marty's face is still as stone, serious and concerned. "Really?" he asks.

"Yes."

"That's not what Bernie told me."

My whole body tenses, my fingers flexing by my side. "Bernie?" I ask. "What are you talking about?"

Marty sighs. "She texted me earlier this week, saying she's been worried about you. That you've been taking things kind of . . . next level lately. I know how this whole Ball thing can make people go a little wonky. I just want to make sure you're handling it okay."

I blink a few times, feeling a little dizzy. Finally, I find the words. "I'm fine."

"Izzy, I've seen the shit you're working on. That ripped-up canvas yesterday? You're not fine."

"You went into my studio?" My skin is on fire, rage pooling in my middle.

Marty sighs, exasperated. "Yeah, and I found you passed out in last night's clothes with an empty bottle of vodka." He leans in closer. "You're lucky I brought you inside before Mom and Dad got home, though it's not like you're being stealth about anything." Marty shakes his head. "Dad asked me point-blank if you had been on a bender. I told him you just passed out after working hard in the studio, but . . ." Marty trails off, and he's looking at me in a way that tells me he thinks it might be true.

I blink back tears. "This is absurd," I say, standing up, letting my pita drop to the blanket. "No one knows what they're talking about. It's like I can't even let loose *once*." I shake my head. "What more do you all want from me?"

Marty stands, too, towering over me. "We just want you to be happy. I want you to be okay."

"No, you don't or you wouldn't be accusing me of being some sort of . . ." I pause. "Why do you care, anyway? You're never around. You never call me and now you're bombarding me with a fucking intervention? Because Bernie's too uptight to realize when someone's having a little bit of fun?"

Marty steps toward me but I reach out and push him hard, so he steps back, his arms in the air.

"Fuck you!" I yell, before turning around, running back home, tears stinging my eyes and blocking my vision as I curse Marty, my parents, and Bernie over and over and over again, mostly because I know they're right.

† † †

The house is quiet when I get home and I tear through the first floor, up the staircase, and into my room. I scan the furniture I've had since I was a kid—a black iron canopy bed, the matching slim black desk pushed up against the window, and my favorite, a farmhouse dresser we found at an antique store upstate. It's got six big sections where I keep all my clothes, but along the top, it has a dozen tiny drawers, lined up neatly with little wooden knobs. When I was younger, I used to keep different trinkets in each one. Buttons in the one farthest to the left, colored paper clips in another, balled up pieces of fabric in an end drawer.

Now, I move fast with deliberate focus, locking the door behind me and lunging toward the dresser where secrets lie in three of the tiny drawers. I reach toward one and yank it open, hooking my pinkie under a piece of felt I laid down last year. But there's nothing there. I move to the second one, a slight wave of panic pulling at my chest, and find it similarly empty.

The rest of my stash must be in the third drawer, the use-in-case-of-emergencies drawer. I could have sworn I put the rest of what Skyler gave me in here. But as I lift the final piece of felt, my stomach drops. Frantically, I move my palm, hoping to feel a sign of little lumps, waiting for me. But . . . nothing.

My parents know. That's it. That's the only solution. They came in here and found my evidence, and finally, after all this time, the consequences will come.

But suddenly, my pinkie latches onto something plastic—the remainder of a baggie that had become wedged between the wood.

Relief.

My stomach settles as I pull out Skyler's bag and then another, half-full of rainbow pills floating inside. I count each one and feel a sense of ease. A release.

The front door closes downstairs, and my heart starts to race. I hear someone padding around the kitchen, swinging open the fridge, turning on the electric kettle.

There's something loud and unsettling in the air. An impulse. An urge. When I sink to the fuzzy carpet on the floor, I realize it's me, breathing heavy, gasping for air.

I know what's coming and where my hands are going before they make their moves. It's as if they're not part of me, as if I'm levitating above myself. I'm not here. I'm nowhere.

A Xanax sits on the tip of my tongue, sweet and comforting, until I reach for a water bottle and throw my head back, swallowing it at once.

I am calm. I am here. I am alive.

AFTER THE BALL

THE STREET IS *quiet until Kendall Kirk drops to his knees beside his sister and lets out a scream that spreads through the night.*

"Help!" he calls, cradling Opal's head in his hands. "Can someone help?"

The detective rushes over and leans her ear against Opal's mouth. "She's breathing," she says. "She's okay."

Opal's eyes flutter open, and a confused look appears on her face. "What happened?" she whispers.

"You fainted," the detective says. "Let's get you up. Some water?" She moves back to the Club, but Opal shakes her head.

"I can't go in there," she says, dazed. "Members only." The detective tries to protest, but Opal doesn't move.

Kendall wraps an arm around her shoulder and pulls out his phone. "I'll take you home." He tries to hide his shaking hands, the terror in his voice. He doesn't want Opal to know how scared he is, how grateful he is to see her, to know that after everything that happened tonight, she's okay. Because if she did know the truth about what happened, he's not sure she'd recover.

The detective clears her throat. "Sir, you haven't been dismissed yet. And you . . ." She looks at Opal, so young she could be a cherub. "I think you both should come inside now for some questions."

Opal glances at her brother, waiting for permission or guidance, and Kendall nods curtly. He's always been good with adults, the kind of kid who asks about their work, their hobbies, the paths that led them to success. An undiscerning parent might be charmed by his excellent eye contact, his genuine enthusiasm. But Kendall is often playing a game, too, just like the others.

He knows he's smart—brilliant, maybe—but he doesn't only want to be seen as a Kirk. He wants to be known in his own right. He wants to be excellent in spite of his privilege, not because of it.

But tonight . . . tonight everything has changed, and he doesn't care about putting on a good face or hobnobbing or having the right people learn his name. All he wants to do right now is take care of his little sister.

Kendall looks directly at the detective and hardens his voice. "Are either one of us under arrest?"

"No."

"Then we're leaving," he says, punching at the screen of his phone. "Come on, Opal."

Opal doesn't protest, and she lets her brother help her up, leaning against his side. Perhaps she knows that she's not ready to learn the truth about what happened tonight. Maybe she realizes that one more night of comfort in knowing that her brother is okay is worth more than learning the facts. At least right now.

A black car pulls up, and Kendall leads her into the back seat without turning back to the Club, without knowing how this all will end.

The detective watches them leave, knowing she should force them to stay. But there's nothing she can do. The boy was right. They were not under arrest. Kendall's alibi was rock solid, anyway. There are time-stamped photos of him posing with his nominator in front of the Club's ballroom at the exact time the deceased landed on the patio.

So, the detective turns back to the Club and heads inside, where answers await. Where Bernie Kaplan still stands at the window, smiling, grateful that Opal Kirk is safe.

Tori

THE DRESS CODE for Reveal Night said "semiformal," which meant absolutely nothing to me until I punted the decision over to Joss, who, even though she was still frustrated with me after the brush-up at the diner, lent me a black A-line dress, embellished with small beads that form flowers around the skirt and insisted I pair it with her chunky gold hoops and gold platform sandals.

The whole thing made me miss my mom, though. It's not that she would have found me a new dress. Most of her wardrobe consisted of jeans and old band tees that she always said she was saving for me. They're still in a cardboard box in my closet that I can't bear to open. But she loved the act of preparation, the excitement of picking out an outfit to wear somewhere special. When she and Dad had date night, she'd let me hang out in her room while she did her makeup, blasting Billy Joel, spinning around the room to "Uptown Girl."

But maybe Joss knew this. Maybe that's why she told me to come over and gave me a blowout with some soft curls and did my makeup, too, carefully dabbing eyeshadow on my lids, a hint of blush on my cheeks.

After an hour of sitting on the subway with my thighs sticking to the plastic bench, I say a silent thank-you that she chose long-lasting mascara so my face doesn't melt in the heat. We're in the final days of summer now, the ones where the air is so heavy it feels claustrophobic, like the weight of the atmosphere is pressing down on your chest so hard, it's tough to breathe.

It's the same kind of heat that followed me around at that Shelter Island party, that pressed up on me as I wandered around Lee's house, trying to get those boys' voices out of my head, the ones that told me, *You'll never be one of us.*

But a solution came to me when Opal dashed out of the room, pulling on a sweatshirt, Skyler bounding down the stairs.

Opal saw me there in the hallway and whispered, so small I wanted to hug her, "Please don't tell."

I nodded and watched her gather her things, taking the stairs two at a time. I planned to keep my promise to her, but as she ran off, I realized for the first time in my entire existence at Excelsior that I had power—the kind that could bend Skyler Hawkins to my will. All I had to do was use it.

I stayed frozen, weighing my options when Skyler came up the steps again, furious, his hair sticking out at all angles. He looked around for Opal, throwing open doors, clenching his fists. But she wasn't there, and instead, I was, waiting in that hallway, prepared words dancing on my lips.

Skyler looked around frantically, his bare torso slick with sweat, without giving me a second glance.

"Opal left," I said as calmly as I could. "She's gone."

Skyler turned around, slowly at first, but spinning hard on his heel. It took him a minute to place me; I could tell based on the way he looked me up and down like he was trying to find recognition. Worth.

"She took off after Isobel walked in on you," I said, trying my best to keep my voice steady. I crossed my arms against my chest, standing firmly in place, gaining confidence with each passing moment.

Skyler sneered at me, an awful laugh escaping his lips. We didn't know each other, not in the way that we do now. Sure, we had a few classes together. Were paired together for a handful of group projects. But nothing about this interaction showed me that Skyler saw me as anything more than window trim. A throw pillow. Something to underestimate.

"Big imagination, huh," Skyler said.

At that I had to laugh. "I saw the whole thing."

Skyler shut his mouth then.

I took a step forward, weighing my next move. I swallowed my nerves and inhaled a mouthful of hot air, sticky with beer, and in one whoosh of breath, I changed everything. "I could tell Bernie, you know."

He shook his head. "Why would Bernie believe you?"

I shrug. "Willing to risk it?"

Skyler sighed, almost bored, which caused a ball of rage to form in my stomach.

"You don't think I'll do it, do you?" I opened my phone and pulled up the Excelsior class chat, where everyone's numbers were public. I tapped Bernie's name and started composing a message, making a big dramatic deal about it until Skyler exhaled sharply.

"What do you want?" he asked.

I looked up then, smiled, and put my phone back in my pocket. "The Legacy Club," I said, the words feeling precise, exact. "I want a nomination."

Skyler took a step back and shook his head. "Those things are like fucking lottery tickets. I can't get you into Legacy. I barely know if I'll get in myself."

I was scared then that I was fucking it up. That he'd call my bluff and I'd have to tell Bernie, embroiling myself in some of Excelsior's most dramatic gossip. But then I remembered Joss's tactic for speaking with sources while reporting for the newspaper. She told me that people hate empty silences, so they work hard to fill them, talking when they shouldn't. All I had to do was stay quiet. So, I did.

Skyler took the bait.

He ran a hand through his hair, that perfect coiffed mop that people obsess over. "I guess I could try to get my mom to do it. It's her year to nominate someone. Or my brother. It's his first year as a nominator, I think."

I nodded.

He looked me dead in the eye. "Nominations are due next week. You know that, right?"

I nodded again even though I had no idea when nominations were due—or how they were decided, nothing. I was so naïve.

Skyler licked his lips, his eyes wide and nervous. "You'll keep quiet until then? Stay quiet if you get a nomination?"

"Yes," I said, my heart pounding in my ears.

Skyler seemed to think it over, and then a smile crept across his face. "Deal." He extended his hand toward mine, warm and sticky with the humidity passing through the house.

"Deal."

We shook, and as our palms touched, something electric and biting passed between us. Something that made me never want to feel his skin against mine ever again. I knew what I was gaining in that moment—entrée into a society I'd only heard whispers about—but I also knew what I was giving up. From then on, Skyler Hawkins would have this over me. He'd know how I earned my nomination. For the rest of my life, I would live with this fact. Long after he and Bernie Kaplan were happily married, when old high school trysts were distant memories no one cared about even if they were exposed, I would still know that membership in this Club was mine only because of Skyler. Because of what I saw.

But if tomorrow's Ball goes according to plan, it will all be worth it.

I stop short, realizing I've arrived at the restaurant where Reveal Night will take place. It's an upscale Italian place, different from the red sauce spots Joss and I love to go to on date nights, where the tablecloths are made of checkered plastic and the chicken parm is the size of my head. I reach for the door, but before I can open it, a security guard swings it open for me.

"Legacy Club private event?" he asks.

"Yes."

"Right this way."

I inhale and take a step inside, knowing that soon enough, I'll know which member of the Hawkins family Skyler begged and pleaded with to change my life to keep his intact.

And I'm ready as hell to find out.

AFTER THE BALL

INSIDE THE CLUB, *agitation takes hold. The remaining partygoers are losing patience. It's not that there are babies to check on or dogs to walk—no, they have help who take care of those tasks. But these people want answers. And they're not used to waiting for them.*

A boy in a tuxedo, still somehow ironed straight, taps a detective on the shoulder. "Chase Killingsworth," he says, with the cadence of someone much older. "When can we leave?"

The detective spins around and sizes him up, taking in his straight bow tie, his neatly parted hair. "You been questioned yet?" The boy shakes his head and the detective leans in. "Tell me this, then. What do you know about Tori Tasso?"

Chase considers the question, that name, and ducks his head down low. "Why are you asking about Tori?"

"Why don't you tell me?"

Chase nods, as if this is a fair assessment, because if Chase is being honest with himself, he's had misgivings about that girl from the orientation luncheon, when he realized he was seated next to an anonymous nominee instead of someone known. Someone like Bernie Kaplan or Skyler Hawkins. Someone whose name means something.

"Tori wasn't really part of the group," Chase says. "I recognized most of the kids from the beginning. Not her." He shakes his head. "My sister told me it's rare for random nominees to get through the process. They're usually vetted out." He looks around. "Freshman year I could have told you the six kids from my class who would get in. I was spot-on. I kept

*wondering what she did to get a nomination." Chase crosses his arms
and laughs, as if surprised by his own observations. "Seems ridiculous
now."*

The detective scribbles on the notepad held close to his chest. "Why?"

"Oh, because it's obvious."

The detective arches an eyebrow, looking for more.

*Chase realizes this, and smirks like he's not going to give up any
information without getting something in return. That's the thing with
these kids—they understand the power they wield.*

"How'd Tori get picked, then?"

"Can I go home after I answer?"

"If I like what I hear."

*Chase smiles like the answer is right in front of him. Finally, after a
moment too long, he leans in. "She got in just like the rest of us."*

The detective cocks his head, curious.

"She knew the right people."

Bernie

HERE, IN THE back garden of some random Italian restaurant, I try to settle my nerves by walking around the perimeter of the space, taking in the setup. There are massive floral bundles, in all sorts of muted colors, and café lights twinkling from the arched tent. I know I should be making small talk with the others, but I can't stop thinking about my mom's email, the fact that she's left me here with all these questions and not a single answer. I tap my foot against the floor, clench my fists into little balls by my side. With one eye toward the door, I keep expecting her to walk right in and tell me this whole week has been one big prank. A misunderstanding.

But then I spot Isobel coming through the entryway, her makeup a little too heavy, the thin straps of her slip dress sliding off her shoulders.

"There you are," I say, leaning in to hug her. But Isobel is stiff under my touch, and I pull away. "You okay?"

She's looking at me with fury in her eyes. "I'm fine," she says, barely looking at me. The air between us is like ice.

"Are you sure? You seem off."

"Yup," she says, crossing her arms, unconvincing.

We stand together in silence, watching the others, and I open my mouth, wanting to say something. To acknowledge the tension.

"What did you get up to today?" I ask, worried to hear the answer.

Isobel turns to me, her lipstick smudged. "I had an enlightening lunch with my brother. But you probably knew that already, huh?"

"What are you talking about?" I cock my head, curious, but then I remember what I texted him yesterday—how I wanted him to talk to Isobel about her drinking. *Shit.* Maybe that was the wrong move. "Isobel—" I start, but she sidesteps me.

"I'm going to the bathroom," she mumbles, dipping away quickly.

Panic rises in my throat, and I feel like my face is on fire. I should have confronted her myself. But that didn't go so well at the Shelter Island party. I handled the whole thing like an immature baby. Shame fills my chest as I recall how I spoke to her, calling her a "fucked-up fool," telling her that she was embarrassing not only herself but also Lee, Skyler, and me. But that didn't give Isobel the right to talk to me the way she did—to put my greatest insecurities on display.

It dawned on me then that perhaps Isobel *did* have something resembling a problem. It wasn't something I had considered before. I thought she was just wild. Free. Constantly in search of a good time. The person who pulled me out of my homebody tendencies. Uproariously *fun*.

I try to turn my focus back to the tented garden, the night ahead. Most of the nominees seem to have arrived, milling around in their cocktail attire, munching on skewered meatballs and hunks of parmesan, passed on silver platters, standing awkwardly with soft drinks in hand.

The only adults invited tonight are the nominators, so it's an even mix of students and adults, all wearing dorky-looking name tags proclaiming our schools and the scholarships we're supposed to represent tomorrow. And yet, Mom is still nowhere to be found. I grasp my glass a little tighter.

In the corner, I notice two big, burly men in all-black standing in front of the door, their hands crossed in front of them, and I wonder who they're trying to keep out. Or in.

Mrs. Shalcross appears in the middle of the crowd, wearing a poofy shirtdress belted at her midsection. She smiles widely and taps a knife to her wineglass until everyone quiets down.

"We are so thrilled to have you all here for my favorite part of Legacy Week," she says, her cheeks rosy red. "As you know, tonight you will find out which club member nominated you." She drops her voice as if to make a point. "This is when you will receive a key, which lets you into the Legacy Club on Sixty-First Street, a key that every single other member has, a key that binds us together. When you are nominated by a member, you become not only part of the Club but part of their lineage—a group that consists of every person that member has nominated, but also who nominated them."

Her eyes are wide like saucers, and something about the whole spiel makes me uneasy, like whatever's coming next is . . . not right. Almost sinister.

"But we know you are all eagerly awaiting your nominators, so without further ado, let's get this party started, shall we?" She pauses, waiting for applause or cheering, and it comes, quietly at first and then with an uproarious rush.

"We'd like you all to take your seats at the tables that have been assigned to your schools." She motions for us to get to our places, and through the movement of the crowd, I find myself sitting between Tori and Skyler at a small round table covered in a soft black cloth. Isobel slides into her seat across the table, nuzzling into Lee but not really looking at anyone else. The act of ignoring me feels deliberate.

I smile politely to Tori, who looks like she's trying to hold her composure. She wedges her hands under her thighs.

The rest of the garden is on edge, a tension shooting through the air like we're all holding one collective breath, waiting to exhale, to let it all out, to scream, to see which adult deemed us worthy.

Though I know the truth. None of us are *worthy*. We're all here for a reason, one predetermined and predestined, set into motion by our parents or grandparents or the powers that surround our very beings. None of us are better or more skilled or more special than the other. We're all here because of who we *know*, and what those closest to us feel that we are owed.

But the truth hits me suddenly and with such force: I did nothing to earn this.

The very thought turns my stomach, and I push away the plate in front of me.

Mrs. Shalcross begins then, drawing a name out of a giant glass bowl. "Lydia Yen," she says. A tall girl with cropped hair at the Gordon Academy table stands and walks to the podium, her cheeks glowing red. She stands with her arms by her side, looking around expectantly until a slight, short, elderly man with an angular face approaches her.

No one answers, but then the man starts speaking. "For those of you I haven't met, I'm Todd Ulbright," he says, "chair of the donations committee. I am delighted to nominate this stellar young woman, who is not only one of the best soccer players in the Intercollegiate League but has also been recruited by my alma mater, Stanford, to play for the fighting Cardinals." A smattering of applause breaks out, and for a moment, I'm surprised that Lydia was plucked from the group as an unknown, chosen for her talent.

Mr. Ulbright continues. "I first met Lydia through her parents at the Bronxville Country Club . . ."

Annnd there it is.

Lydia shakes Todd's hand and takes a small velvet box from his hands, running her fingers over the surface, before heading back to her table, where the rest of the Gordon Academy kids lean in, touching the box that holds the Legacy key before they get their own.

Mrs. Shalcross continues the ritual, pulling names, matching students with nominators, relishing in the excitement, the anticipation. Each reach into the bowl makes me draw my breath, tense for a moment.

Kendall is the first Excelsior student called, nominated by a young alum who worked for Kendall's dad's tech company before launching his own app. Now he speaks about how he had been following Kendall's coding education and was impressed by his submission for a New York City–based start-up incubator. Kendall looks down, embarrassed, but is clearly pleased with the presentation.

Skyler leans in toward me. "Hey, where's your mom?"

"Still sick," I whisper. "But she'll be here tomorrow."

Skyler looks surprised. "Really?"

I nod. "Wouldn't miss it."

He smiles and rests a hand on my knee before turning back to the front of the room. I fight a shiver.

Mrs. Shalcross pulls a name out of the bowl and stops, her mouth curling into a smile. "Bernadette Kaplan." She looks right at me and motions for me to come stand by her. My heart beats fast, and as if I'm being lured, I make my way through the mess of tables until I am standing in front of my peers and the nominators, feeling like a calf up for slaughter.

The garden is quiet, and I can hear noise coming from the main restaurant, voices and laughter, but here, it's silent.

Until finally, in the back of the garden, Lulu Hawkins rises from her seat. She smiles widely at me and shrugs, winking at me as she approaches. Skyler's looking up at me, surprise written on his face.

Being nominated by Lulu should put me at ease. It should be a relief. A form of comfort. I've known this woman my entire life. She always likes to say that she watched other people change my diapers—since she never changed any of her own. But as she makes her way to me, I can only think about my mom's email.

We are formally advising you to distance yourself from Rafe, Lulu, and the entire firm.

Lulu wraps an arm around me and presses her mouth to my ear. "Too bad your mother isn't here to see this. She would have loved it."

A chill shoots up my spine, but just as quickly as she says it, Lulu releases me and turns to address the group. "I've known little Bern-Bern here for her entire life, having been best friends with the Kaplans since long before Bernie was even a twinkle in her parents' eye. It brings me great pleasure to welcome her into the Club that's been a cornerstone of my life." She turns to me and reaches for my hand. "Many know Bernie as an excellent leader, a focal point at Excelsior. But to me, she'll always be the little girl who bossed my son Skyler around on the beach as they made sandcastles. She still does, thank god!" A laugh breaks out, and I eke out a thin smile. "I have no doubt she'll be an asset to this Club for decades to come."

The group applauds and it sounds like nails against a chalkboard, ringing in my ears. I want to run, to hide, to leave this place for good. But instead, I go through the motions of hugging Lulu, saying thank you in my most earnest voice, and taking the key box from her hand before heading back to my seat, where Skyler wraps his arm around me, pulling my body to his.

I run my fingers over the box and hold onto its sides before flipping the top up to reveal a thick gold skeleton key. I pick it up, feeling its weight heavy in my hands, and flick the key chain, the letters *L* and *C* engraved into the metal.

"Knew it," Skyler mutters, his breath warm against my ear.

But I can't shake what his mother said, that she wished my mom were here. Was her voice as menacing as I remember it? Was she implying that she knows where my mother is? Why she isn't here?

We applaud politely as Mrs. Shalcross reads the rest of the names. As we suspected, Lee gets nominated by a little old lady named Gertie, who knows his parents from the art world and praises Lee's individuality and humor. Skyler's brother stands up and speaks about a kid from Tucker who was his summer intern at City Hall.

Finally, after what feels like an eternity, they call Skyler's name. I sit up straight as he walks toward the front of the room. Mrs. Shalcross doesn't move, though, and I expect her to make some announcement that sadly, Skyler's nominator isn't here because she's sick, but instead, she beams bright and wide and addresses the crowd. "It's me!" she says proudly, launching into a little monologue about how the Hawkins family have been dedicated stewards of the Club's goals and dreams over the past thirty years and she's delighted to welcome Skyler into this year's class.

Skyler plops back down beside me and shrugs. "Who do you think picked Isobel?" He nods in her direction, and for the first time since we took our seats, I look hard at my best friend. She's fidgety and nervous, tapping her fingers against the table, squirming uncomfortably in her seat, until finally Mrs. Shalcross calls her name.

Isobel moves slowly through the crowd until she's standing at Mrs. Shalcross's hip, looking right at me. My heart beats fast as no one stands, and I worry that my mom *did* end up nominating Isobel and that she's about to be left all alone in front of the room, wondering why the hell she couldn't show up.

But then, improbably, a sleek, gray-haired woman wearing a boxy, modern art–inspired tunic walks toward Isobel and gives her air kisses on both of her cheeks.

"Rachel Breathwaite," she says. "Excelsior class of '77. Isobel is one of the greatest artists of your generation," she says to the rest of us, her voice completely serious. "As a curator at the Brooklyn Museum, I've been honored to showcase her work and know this is just the beginning of a bright career ahead." She turns to Isobel and nods at her sternly, to which Isobel blushes hard, clearly surprised by the praise, the authenticity of being nominated by someone who saw her not for her name or status but for her work and talent.

Isobel makes her way back to the table, and I want to stand up and hug her, to whisper, *Don't you know how special that was?*

But she doesn't look at me, and so I avert my eyes and ignore the prickly feeling coursing up my spine.

Mrs. Shalcross reads a few more names, and as the list dwindles, I wonder if Mom maybe didn't nominate anyone. Perhaps the invoice from Madame Trillian was a mistake. Perhaps she knew all along that she would never show up. Maybe she didn't want to let anyone else down besides me.

Tori

AM I ACTUALLY going to be the last name pulled out of that ridiculous bowl? All around me, people are beaming with pride, taking delicate bites of their chocolate mousse cakes, their free hand wrapped around their key box, and whispering with one another about their lineages, their legacies. Everyone except me.

I try to find the nominator in the crowd who hasn't gotten up from their seat yet, the sole adult who will lay a claim to me. But I can't find a single person who has yet to select their student.

I steal a glance at Skyler and wonder, for the first time, if he set me up. Maybe I wasn't meant to be here at all. Maybe it was all a joke, and right now I'm going to be exposed for not having received a nomination at all. But then Mrs. Shalcross clears her throat.

"Tori Tasso."

I'm not sure if I am relieved or terrified, but my legs feel like Jell-O as I walk toward the center of the floor, so unnatural in my dress and heels. Mrs. Shalcross doesn't move from her place, and instead, she smiles at me, a little nervous.

"Hi dear," she says, louder than a whisper.

I nod politely and look out at the room, at all of those eyes staring at me. Are they wondering why I'm here? Who among them would have thought to choose *me*?

But no one stands. No one walks toward me. A pit forms in my stomach and I look at Mrs. Shalcross, who's looking down at her phone, frowning. But then, as if realizing, she looks up and out at the crowd.

"Sadly, Tori's nominator could not be with us today because of an illness," she says, punctuating the last word with an affect of disbelief. "But she sent me a little something to read on her behalf."

The pit deepens as I look around the room. I try to lock eyes with Skyler, but he seems to look right through me.

Mrs. Shalcross clears her throat. "'Throughout her time at Excelsior, Tori has demonstrated that she is a determined and tenacious student who has excelled in all academic arenas. Having witnessed Tori's academic prowess and admired her grit from afar, I am honored to nominate Tori Tasso.'" Mrs. Shalcross looks up. "Signed, Esther Kaplan."

"Oh." Mrs. Shalcross picks up the blue velvet box, the key to my future, and thrusts it toward me. It's heavier than I expected, weighty in my grasp. Holding it, I only feel relief. The room claps politely, but I can't take my eyes away from my table, the one where Skyler's head is off to one side, and Bernie sits there, her eyes wide and surprised, her mouth forming the shape of an O.

Mrs. Shalcross leans over. "You can sit down now," she says, behind her hair.

Embarrassed, I head back to my table, where the rest of the group is staring at me as the room gets louder, talking amongst themselves, the final moment of pomp and circumstance before the night ends.

"What?" I ask, suddenly annoyed at all of them for being surprised that someone like Esther could have picked me, even though I know *why* and *how* my name came to her attention.

Lee speaks first. "That's so cool, Tori," he says enthusiastically.

"How do you know Esther?" Then he turns to Bernie. "Good on you for keeping that secret!"

Bernie shakes her head, her gaze never leaving my face. "I had no idea."

She looks at me, shocked and curious, almost a little impressed, and suddenly I feel like I can't breathe—like everything inside my body is rebelling against these people, this place. It's like I can't remember all the reasons I wanted entry into this world and all I'm left with are these surprised stares, the ones that assure me *You'll never be one of us. We'll always doubt you.* Even Lee's question— *How do you know Esther?*—implies that there was a connection, a healthy bout of elbow rubbing and vying.

Which, of course, is easier to swallow than the actual truth.

"Excuse me," I say, pushing my chair back noisily. People at other tables turn to look, but I rush off down the hall and out the front door of the restaurant. People whiz by me, talking into their headphones, humming to the music. The sounds of sirens and honking calm me, reminds me that this is my city, too, that it doesn't belong just to those people in there. Out here, with everyone else, I can breathe—like even in a sea of people, I am finally, blissfully alone. I inhale deeply until my breathing slows, until I can feel my heart rate steady, my hands stop shaking.

You're okay, I tell myself. *You're okay.*

I make my way back inside, finally calm, and head back to the garden. But before I can reach the entrance, I spot Skyler waiting for the bathroom. I grab his elbow and yank him off to the side.

"Esther Kaplan?" I ask. "Don't you think that's a little suspicious?"

"I don't know what you mean."

"Bullshit," I say. "Did you see Bernie? She was extremely weirded out. How the hell did you get her to pick me? There's no way in hell she even knows I exists."

"You got your nomination. You got what you wanted. Let's just drop it, okay?"

"Don't tell me you blackmailed her, too." I laugh, crossing my arms over my chest. "Did *she* also catch you fucking someone else?"

But then Skyler looks behind me over my shoulder and his face drops, his skin growing pale. "What?" I ask, but as I go to turn around, I already know what I'm going to find. *Who* I'm going to find.

Bernie.

AFTER THE BALL

LYDIA YEN, ONE *of the nominees still left at the Club, slumps back against the armchair in the lounge. "So, you want to know who was on the roof?"*

This girl. She's just like the others. Poised and powerful with an athlete's confidence, the unwavering eye contact that comes only with practice. She thinks she holds all the answers. Maybe she does.

The detective plays along. "Yes, we're looking for any sort of information that might help."

Lydia leans in. "My guess is Bernie Kaplan. And obviously Skyler, Tori, and Isobel."

"Obviously?"

Lydia nods. "All anyone was talking about the night before was that Skyler had hooked up with Opal Kirk, which I'm guessing you already know. I heard she showed up here a little while ago." She shakes her head. "Poor girl."

"And when did everyone find out about this little . . . dalliance?"

Lydia cracks her knuckles, thinking it over. "I first heard about it last night after Reveals," she says. "But I go to Gordon. So, I wasn't in the middle of it or anything."

"And is there a lot of mingling between schools?"

Lydia thinks this over, pondering the question for the first time. She grew up summering out east, going to day camps with Skyler and Bernie, spending weekends at the Bronxville Country Club, frequenting Lee's mom's gallery with her father, a prominent investment banker with a penchant for collecting modern art. But she wouldn't call their interactions "mingling." What these kids do together is more deliberate than that. Intentional. Always with an eye toward what they can offer one another in the future.

"Most of us know each other," she says.

"Was there anyone you didn't know? Whose presence surprised you?"

"Tori, of course," she says. "No one knew her."

"But you think she was on the roof?"

Lydia crosses her arms over her chest. "Well, yeah. She was at the center of the whole Skyler–Opal thing."

The detective narrows his eyes.

"I mean . . . she's the one who told Bernie." Lydia says.

"Huh."

Lydia scoffs. "No one knew who she was before this week. The fact that she had the power to break up Skyler and Bernie? Legendary." Then she leans in. "But get this. It wasn't just Tori who knew. Isobel, Bernie's best friend, turned out to be the biggest traitor of them all."

Isobel

"WHERE DID EVERYONE go?" I ask Lee. The only people left at our table are the two of us and Kendall, and I haven't seen Tori or Skyler in what feels like forever.

Lee looks around and shrugs. "I have no idea."

The rest of the garden is starting to empty out, and I lean back in my chair, hearing the Manhattan Friends kids talk about heading down to someone's loft in SoHo. "Should we leave?" I ask.

Lee shrugs. "Sure, why not?" He turns to Kendall. "Wanna come?"

Kendall looks at me, his disgust apparent. "I don't think so."

Lee, ever agreeable, shrugs again and turns back to me. "Let's find the others."

We get up from our seats and Lee grabs my hand, leading me inside the restaurant. That's when I see them all there—Tori, Skyler, and Bernie. I pick up my pace, but as we get closer, I hear snippets of conversation.

"You *did what*?" Bernie asks, her voice getting louder and higher.

I turn away but Skyler spots me, fire in his eyes.

"Isobel," he says. "Get over here. Now."

I stop mid-step and Lee shoots up his eyebrows.

Bernie turns to look at me, rage filled and furious. "He cheated," she says, pointing directly at Skyler. "With Kendall's *sister*." Bernie shakes her head, tears forming in the corners of her eyes. "And *she*"—Bernie points directly at Tori—"knew all about it. Blackmailed Skyler into getting a nomination to this Club." She turns back to both of them now. "And you roped my goddamn *mother* into this? What is wrong with you? Both of you?"

Tori looks like she wants to melt right into the floor, and Skyler's mouth is a tight, firm line. I can sense it, the hiding and lying I've done for the past few months, all about to unravel. Skyler's planning his attack, a way to distract Bernie from *him*.

I get closer, my stomach spasming, knowing what's about to happen. But like a train wreck, I can't stop it.

"Isobel knew all about it," Skyler says, the words coming out fast and hot. "She walked in on us in Shelter Island. After she said those horrible things about you."

Lee lets out a surprised gasp beside me, and as I turn my head, I see Kendall's coming up right behind us, hearing every single thing Skyler's saying.

"That's right," Skyler says. "Isobel saw everything in Shelter Island and kept it all a secret from you. She's been covering for me for months."

Bernie looks me right in the eyes, her face searching. "He's wrong," she says, her voice trembling. "He has to be wrong."

I shake my head. What can I say? That I stayed quiet because Skyler was plying me? That I didn't tell her because I was afraid she wouldn't believe me, that she would choose Skyler over me, leaving me on an island alone? That I doubted her, even after she forgave me that horrific night?

But maybe it doesn't matter. She did, after all, betray me, too, by going to my brother behind my back. I know she'll say it was because of her good intentions, but bullshit. She has no idea what I need. She never has. All she cares about is maintaining her perfect image, her perfect relationship, her perfect friend. But now she might finally realize that none of it is perfect.

"Why?" Bernie sounds like a little kid then, her voice small and scared.

"I didn't . . ." I start, but Skyler scoffs behind me.

"She never cared about you," he says to Bernie. "All she cared about were the pills I was feeding her and a good time. She had no problem hearing about me and Opal, staying quiet when she could tell you at any point. All that shit she said at the party? Guess it was real."

Bernie looks at me, tears in her eyes, and for a second, I think she's going to start sobbing, but in a moment of complete surprise, she reels her hand back behind her and brings it forward, smacking me straight across the face with an open palm.

No one does anything. No one says a word.

No one except Bernie, who's standing there, suddenly calm and composed. She looks me dead in the eyes and tilts her chin up before walking right out the door, away from all of us, from this.

From me.

Tori

"BERNIE, WAIT!"

I don't know if it's because her mom chose me and is nowhere to be found or that I actually *do* feel guilty about the fact that everyone in Bernie's life was keeping this big secret from her, but for whatever reason I'm the only one from the group who takes off running after her.

I reach the sidewalk and swivel my head back and forth, searching for her in the crowd. It takes a second, but then I see her standing on the corner, backed up against the brick wall of a bodega. When I get closer, I see tears are streaming down her face, which stays still, gazing out at the street.

"Hey," I say, approaching her. I reach to rest a hand on her arm, but she pulls it away, almost violently.

"Don't touch me."

I take a step back, trying to catch my breath. Bernie's hair is windswept, her skin red. She looks at me with narrowed eyes, her face hard. "I'm sorry," I say. "I know you—"

But then Bernie shakes her head, blowing air out her nostrils. "You don't know me." She steps toward me slowly, her fists shaking by her side.

For a moment, it dawns on me how strange it is to see the most put-together girl in your school slowly come undone, her perfectly sewn seams ripping apart, her nerves fraying. All because of some fucking *boy*.

But no, that's not it. It's not just because of Skyler.

It's because of Isobel and the secret she kept.

Bernie says it one more time, punctuating each word so it hangs in the air. "You don't know me." But as she steps toward me, I shake my head, the words coming out before I can think to stop them. "Of course I know you. Everyone knows you."

Bernie jerks her head back.

"You are Bernadette Kaplan. Daughter to Rafe and Esther Kaplan, of the Upper East Side. You go to Excelsior Prep, where you've been a student your *entire* life. There's a wing at school with your name on it, and you've already secured a spot at Cornell, even though applications aren't due for another few weeks, because your grandfather went and, conveniently, there is a full wing with your family's name on it." I pause, but only briefly, to grab a sip of air. "You play field hockey but hate it. Dr. Jung is your favorite teacher even though he was tough on you in AP US History. Isobel Rothcroft is your best friend. Or maybe I should say *was*. And Skyler Hawkins is your boyfriend, even though everyone on the planet knows he's a grade-A scumbag. You summer in the Hamptons and enjoy matcha iced lattes and Pilates. You shop at—"

Bernie slams her hands against her head. "Stop," she says so loudly that people on the street stare. "Just stop."

I shut my mouth then, almost not believing my own gall, but then again, maybe I do. This ragged sense of urgency, of impulsiveness has always been inside me. I've just been suppressing it ever since I got to Excelsior, and now that I've opened the gates, I can't stop.

"Everyone in the world knows these things about you because you're Bernie Kaplan. It's impossible to ignore you. If you go to Excelsior—you *know* Bernie Kaplan. People treat you differently because of that. So, I'm sorry for not telling you, a girl who has never really given a shit about me, that her dumbass boyfriend was cheating on her."

Finally, then, I stop, almost out of breath, and when I look at Bernie, I see, improbably, that a smile has spread on her lips.

But then she looks behind me and her face grows stormy. I spin around and see Isobel, Lee, and Skyler walking toward us, a shell-shocked vision on the crowded street.

Bernie grabs my hand and hails a cab, which halts at the corner, nearly running over a few tourists. She swings the door open and pushes me inside, climbing in after me.

"Go, go, go," she urges the driver, who slams his foot on the pedal, so we cruise right on by Skyler, Isobel and Lee, running after us.

"Where to?" he says after we get to the red light on the next block.

Bernie looks at me, her mouth agape.

I clear my throat and lean my head between the seats up against the Plexiglas divider. "Queens."

Bernie

THE CAB PULLS to a stop in front of a small, sweet-looking row house that's painted bright blue with white trim all along the windows. There's a welcome mat at the top of the front steps, and the upstairs windows are aglow, dressed with lacy curtains.

I pay the cabbie and follow Tori out onto the street, where I realize I have no idea what I'm doing here or why. It seemed like a good idea back in Manhattan, where all I wanted to do was flee. But now that I'm here, I realize I'm stuck in an outer borough with a girl I barely know who has been keeping a secret from me—and is now, for whatever reason, tied to my mom for the rest of eternity.

Tori ascends the front steps and unlocks the door.

"This was a mistake. I think I'm going to head home," I say, staying put on the street. "It's getting late and . . . you know."

Tori opens the door, and the smell of something sweet and buttery wafts down toward me.

"You sure?" she says, motioning inside. "Seems like Dad baked a pie. Want some?"

I look up at this house, one in which a parent *bakes*, and all of a sudden, the only thing I want to do is climb those steps and sit inside, and pretend for once that I'm someone else.

"Okay," I say. "Just for a few minutes."

I follow Tori inside the house, where she kicks off her shoes and throws her bag down on a bench. Before she can say something, a cute Asian girl wearing an oversized T-shirt and jean shorts barrels toward her and nearly tackles her in a hug, planting a kiss on her mouth.

"Babe," she says to Tori. "I've been *dying* to hear what happened. Who the hell nominated you?"

But when she pulls back and sees me, she lets Tori go, confused.

Tori smiles and motions to me. "Bernie," she says. "This is my girlfriend, Joss."

A look of recognition comes over Joss's face, and I wonder what Tori has told her about me—about all of us. Based on her sour expression, nothing good.

"Hi," I say.

Joss gives me a once-over but doesn't show any signs of warmth. "Helen and George are about to devour your dad's cherry pie if you don't get in there *fast*," she says. "So, I'd say time is of the essence."

Tori shrugs in my direction, and I trail behind her and Joss as they head into the kitchen, so unlike mine. The chipped counters are covered with bowls full of bananas and lemons, a few stray apples, and some onions. Artwork clearly drawn by children is tacked to the fridge, and framed family photos crowd the walls. Above the sink, a retro metal sign that looks like it belongs in the eighties and says TASSO'S DINER is nailed to the wall. Small dessert plates with stray crumbs are stacked in the sink, and on the Formica island sits a half-eaten pie with a spoon dug into the middle.

"Thanks for babysitting," Tori says, grabbing a knife to slice us up pieces.

Joss hops up on the counter and shrugs. "Gave me time to edit your presentation, which is *bomb*, by the way." She gives me a glare, then wraps her legs around Tori's middle and brings her in for a hug, resting her elbows on Tori's shoulders. Tori smiles and leans her cheek against Joss, a moment that makes me want to look away for how intimate it is, how tender. Skyler and I are never like that, so open with our affection.

Everything's a performance. A foregone conclusion.

And suddenly, I realize . . . just like my parents.

Maybe that's why he cheated. Why he realized before I did that maybe, just maybe our lives aren't meant to be paired together forever.

"Can I use your bathroom?" I ask, suddenly desperate to have a moment alone for the first time since all these revelations piled up.

Tori points to the staircase with her forkful of pie. "Up the stairs, down the hall. First door on the right."

Joss eats the bite off her fork, and Tori laughs as I slink away, retreating from them, the thing I thought I had. But never did.

I take the steps slowly, taking in all the photos on the wall of Tori and her family. The twin siblings who look cut from a catalog, her loving parents, whose arms are around all the kids in each image. Solo shots of a familiar-looking woman with big hair manning the grill at a diner. A prickling sensation comes over me. That must be her mother.

Tori never said much about her, and I only learned about her death because my mom mentioned it one morning before school.

"Are you friends with a girl named Tori Tasso?" she said as we bit into flaky cheese-filled bourekas at the Middle Eastern café near our apartment.

I shook my head. "Not really." I knew Tori in the way that you know every kid in a class of ninety-three. You know what they look like, what subjects they excel in, what sports they suck at, how they dress, who they sit with at lunch. I knew she lived in Queens and never gave her much thought, because unlike so many of our peers, she just seemed to appear out of thin air during freshman orientation, a random student in a sea of people I'd grown up knowing.

Mom nodded then, a worried look on her face.

"What about her?"

Mom swallowed a bite and dabbed her lips with a paper napkin. "Her mother passed."

"Oh," I said. "That's so sad."

Mom looked out the window at the bustling street, commuters descending into the subway entrance at the corner. "It is."

That was all she said before changing the subject to discuss our upcoming spring break vacation to the Maldives, and we spent the rest of breakfast talking about different caftans we would pack, how clear the water would be, and which spa treatments we would get.

But when I got to school and saw Tori standing at her locker, a sallow, lonely look on her face, I walked up to her and fumbled for words of condolence. I don't remember what I said, but I do remember her shocked expression, the one that told me she was surprised I had found out. A little mad, even.

Now, in her house, I wonder how Mom knew. If she had somehow met Tori's mom at one of the PTA events over the past few years. A cruel thought enters my head. Maybe it wasn't just Skyler who convinced mom to nominate her; maybe she nominated Tori because she knew what it was like to lose a mother so young and felt bad for her.

I reach the top of the steps and start down the hall but pretty soon I realize I've made a wrong turn, and instead of a bathroom, I'm standing in the doorframe to what is obviously Tori and her sister's room.

I can't help it. I take a step inside.

A bunk bed is pushed against the wall, the top mattress messy and pink with unicorn-printed pillowcases while the bottom is neatly made, a pretty purple bedspread tucked into the corners, with a few simple throw pillows arranged up against the headboard. There's a small white desk next to the bed, and the wall behind it is decorated with a framed black-and-white photo of Tasso's Diner, clearly taken years ago, since it features the sign hanging in her kitchen. Twinkle lights hang from the ceiling, giving the room a soft glow.

I approach a wooden dresser shoved between the door and the closet and run my hand along the top of it, clocking a photo of Tori and her mini-me, who must be her little sister, and a picture of Tori kissing Joss. But when I reach the end of the surface, there's a framed image that makes me stop, my heart rate pick up.

I lift the frame and bring it close to my face. An image I've seen before of two best friends, caught mid-laughter as if they're sharing a secret.

"What are you doing?"

Tori's voice makes me jump and I drop the frame, hearing the glass shatter against the floor. She runs toward me, but I can't move. I shake my head, confusion and fear rising in my throat. Finally, I speak.

"Why do you have a photo of my mom?"

AFTER THE BALL

PERHAPS NO ONE *at the Legacy Club is as infuriated as Jeanine Shalcross. After nearly a year spent obsessing over every single detail involved in this week's programming with Esther Kaplan breathing down her neck, the entire evening—no, the entire group—is collapsing around her.*

She stands in a corner of the room, arms crossed, high heel tapping against the marble floor. Her lips are pursed, and she ignores the other Club members asking her questions, demanding answers. Why does she *have to be the one to respond? And where the hell is Esther? That's what she's wanted to know for days: why the woman who says she's most loyal to the Club was absent during the most consequential week of the year. Why was Jeanine put in charge of the nomination events? Reveal Night? The presentation schedule? This was* not *what they agreed upon when Esther begged Jeanine to join the nominating committee last year.*

But Jeanine knows better than to question Esther. After all these years, bowing down to the queen bee of their little group had been a given. It'd been this way since they were kids, Jeanine knows that. Back then, when Esther told them to vote for her for Excelsior class president, they did. When Esther told her which sorority to join at Cornell, she did. And when Esther told her to run with that awful rumor, the one that ruined that poor girl—well, she's not keen to admit it, but Jeanine did that, too. They all did.

And now, as cops—the horror!—crowd the Legacy Ball and trek grimy footprints through their beautiful Club, of all places, Jeanine can't help but feel the creeping suspicion that if Esther Kaplan hadn't nominated Tori, they would never be in this situation at all.

Jeanine should have pushed back when Esther said she wanted to pick Audra's daughter. She should have said no. Vetoed the nomination. Thrown a fit. Instead, she stepped aside and tried to forget how this whole mess started and what exactly Esther was trying to prove by inviting the Tasso girl into their world.

But who was Jeanine kidding? If she'd really thought long and hard, she could have guessed that Esther Kaplan would nominate Tori Tasso from the day that girl entered Excelsior Prep. Her fate was sealed years before. Jeanine knew that. But there's no way Tori did.

Isobel

YOU CAN'T SEE stars for shit anywhere in New York City, but that doesn't stop me from trying. Tonight, I'm sprawled on a lounger up on the roof deck of our brownstone, staring up at the sky, clutching a water bottle filled with white wine.

Ever since I got back from the dinner, I haven't been able to stop replaying the events of the night over and over in my head. Bernie's smack. The horrified expression on Lee's face. The way she looked right at me as she sped off in the car with Tori. As if I shouldn't be mad at *her* for calling Marty on me. As if I deserved it.

I take another gulp of wine, which starts to make the memory disappear. Almost.

Things are beginning to blur and finally, finally, I can relax, sink back into the memories of the *before*, when Bernie and I were so in sync with each other, back in the beginning of the summer.

We started the season with a weekend out east, at her house in the Hamptons, fresh off our finals and AP tests, but before we started our summer internships, planning for the future. It was a Tuesday night, and Esther suggested Bernie and I go to the Clam Bar for dinner while she stayed in, and handed us two hundred-dollar bills and the keys to the topless Jeep Wrangler they drove only at the beach.

We sped down the dusty, sandy road right before sunset, blasting old Paramore as the wind tangled our hair. Once we arrived, we sat across from each other at a picnic table and ordered oysters, lobster rolls, paper cups of clam chowder, and greasy French fries served over parchment in a red plastic basket. Bernie sweet-talked the waiter into bringing me a can of rosé, and I gulped at it greedily as the salty air stuck to our skin.

Bernie looked so happy then, so alive. That was what summer did to her—it changed her persona, her outlook. Made her breezier and lighter, as if the sun and the sand and the salty ocean air allowed her to release the tension and the stress of school years in the city. Mom always says we're too young to be stressed, but she didn't grow up here, didn't go to a school like Excelsior. Stress is just another name for survival.

But that night, we had none of that, just freedom in the form of car keys and a slight buzz that made me feel invincible. Lee and I had already been in the process of redefining our relationship, morphing whatever our friendship was into something more. So, when he texted me and she saw his name flash across the screen, Bernie drummed her fingers on the table. "What did he say?" she asked, leaning toward me, her eyes twinkling.

I looked down at the screen and flipped it around to show her.

I'm at Skyler's tonight. You at Bernie's?

Bernie practically squealed. "I've been waiting for this double date to happen my whole life. Tell him we'll be there in twenty."

I flushed when I saw Lee's response. I was hoping you'd say that.

It was a straight shot to Skyler's house from the Clam Bar, and once we got there, Bernie led me around the back, through a door made of driftwood that opened onto a private stretch of beach. Sandpipers hopped along the dunes as the sky turned a hazy mix of purples, blues, and oranges, the sun making its descent. Lee and Skyler were propped up on their elbows, lying in the sand, wearing hoodies and long pants, their faces alive and electric with that sweet summer glow.

As far as I knew, Skyler was about to start spending the summer out here under the guise of interning for a local real estate developer—but was really playing golf with a former PGA pro four days a week. Lee's place in Shelter Island was a quick ferry ride away, and he said it was easy to cruise back and forth from his job working on a farm up in the North Fork, where he was learning about sustainable agriculture practices. Lee was always into environmental engineering, but the job made sense once I realized there was a massive modern art museum out there that owned the farm, and that they housed one of Arti Dubey's most famed works.

This's how summers go for Excelsior kids. We become full of sand and sun and half-assed but impressive-sounding jobs that pad résumés and open doors. Even I had one, interning in the art department at a home goods magazine run by one of Mom's friends, a few days a week.

When I told Mom the gig was a prime example of nepotism, she looked at me and laughed. "What isn't?"

On that beach, on that June evening, we weren't thinking about the menial tasks that were about to be asked of us or what lay ahead when school started three months later, when we were supposed to start filling out college applications and sucking up to the admissions officers. We weren't thinking about the Legacy Club, about who would nominate whom or what the next few months would bring us.

All we were focused on was one another and the waves and the Bluetooth speaker Skyler streamed rap music from, as we sat around a struggling bonfire, a foursome with the world stretched out before us.

At one point, Bernie whispered something into Skyler's ear and then turned back to us. "We'll be back," she said with a mischievous smile, as if they were doing us a favor by heading back to the deck. She winked at me as she skipped away.

Lee looked at me with hope, and a nervous smile danced on his lips, causing my stomach to tumble and flip-flop over and over.

"I was waiting for them to take a hint," he said, wrapping an arm around my shoulder. He smelled like mint and seaweed, and his fingers were cold.

I leaned in halfway, my eyes open, and after sharing a breath, a wish, he closed the space between us for the first time.

A rolling sensation of desire coursed through me, and in that moment, it didn't matter who his parents were or if they liked my art. I didn't care that I had never had a deep conversation with Lee the entire time I'd known him or that I didn't know his favorite foods or movies. All that mattered was how his lips felt on mine, how his palm pressed lightly against the skin below my ear, how his hair was thick between my fingers.

That memory sends a lightning bolt through my spine. My eyes open wide.

Lee. At least I still have Lee.

After the dinner, he rushed out of there quickly, barely saying goodbye. But that was hours ago. An eternity.

I fumble for my phone, which I find on the fake grass below me, and speak into the microphone. "FaceTime Lee."

It rings a few times until finally his face fills the screen. He's wearing a simple white T-shirt and he's in bed, his linen bedspread rumpled around his middle. He squints and throws one arm over his face.

"There you are," I say, smiling and sinking back into the seat. "I wish you were here."

"It's two o'clock in the morning."

I let out a laugh and drop my phone into my lap. "No, it's not."

Lee rolls over, muffling his camera for a second, and then I see the blurry numbers at the top of my screen. *Shit*. He's right.

"Oops, sorry," I say, lowering my voice.

"You're drunk," Lee says, all judgmental.

My stomach tenses, and I resist the urge to reach for the bottle of wine sitting at my feet. "Come on, give me a break after tonight. That was so fucked up."

Lee groans and leans back against his pillows. "Go to bed, Is."

"Don't you want to come over?" I pout into the camera.

"No," he says a little too harshly.

I can't stop myself though. "Why not?"

"Because you're wasted." He sighs and looks right into the camera. "And honestly? I'm pretty pissed off at you right now."

"What?" I ask. "You're pissed at *me*?"

"I mean, yeah. You walked in on Skyler hooking up with Opal Kirk and didn't tell me? You didn't tell *Bernie*? Your best friend in the world? Even if you said all that shit about her, that's inexcusable."

I shake my head. "Skyler never told you about Opal?"

"Nope. And if he had, I would have told him to tell Bernie or I would have. She's my friend, too, you know."

I never thought of Bernie and Lee as allies—just joined together by their.devotion to Skyler. But now that he says it . . .

"I know I was wrong," I say. "I just . . ."

"You were only looking out for yourself, Is. She would have believed you."

Agreeing with him feels like a trap, but I shrug because I fear he's right. Did I keep Skyler's secret because I was afraid of not having a backup stash? Because I was greedy and selfish and so focused on my own needs? Because I really, truly didn't care about Bernie?

"I thought you'd have my back." The tears are coming hot and fast, and I blink, wanting to stop them. "But you're siding with Bernie in all of this. I said some fucked-up things, but come on."

Lee looks away. "I don't want to do this right now."

"Do what?"

"Fight."

"We're not fighting." I'm pleading now. Desperate. "Please," I say. "Just come over. We can talk about this."

Lee shakes his head. "I gotta be honest. I'm pretty sick of your bullshit. Getting so fucked up all the time, going behind your best friend's back like this. I don't know if this is what I signed up for."

"What about Skyler? He's your best friend and you're fine with what he did?" I rack my brain for something to say, for something to get him back on my side.

"Isobel," he says, my full name hard and callous on his lips. "You need to stop."

In an instant, I feel all of my organs sinking into a cavern in my stomach, threatening to swallow me whole. I know where he's going. I know where this is headed. "No," I whisper. "Lee, no."

But it's as if those words only confirm his realization that this . . . this is it.

"I think we need a break. At least for a little while."

"You don't mean that." My lungs are on fire, and my chest is about to explode.

"I do, Is. At least for now. Until you get it together."

"Wait," I say.

"It's late," he says. "And we have the Ball tomorrow."

"Lee," I sputter.

"I'm sorry," he says. "I really am."

The screen goes blank, and I'm left here on the roof in a sea of light, flooding from the neighbors, the city, the bars down below. Sirens wail and music blasts through speakers, the sign of a Brooklyn night, warm and pulsing and alive.

But not here. Not on this patio, where suddenly the reality is crashing down on me. I kept Skyler's secret because I worried about what might happen if I didn't—I feared that Bernie would be done with me for good, that I might lose Lee, that I would end up all alone. And now? Now that's happened anyway because of what I've done. But I can't deny who put this series of actions into motion.

Skyler.

I clench my phone with a tight grasp and then without a second thought, hurl it across the deck so it smashes into pieces, the screen cracking against a concrete pot holding a plant.

Good, I think as I reach for the wine beneath my seat.

I drink it all, feeling the calm wash over me as it descends into my stomach, filling me up, whole. For once. For now. Until everything around me disappears and finally, after what feels like forever, the night goes black and complete and utter darkness falls.

Tori

"THAT'S YOUR MOTHER?" I pick up the photo, careful not to cut my fingers on the broken glass, and stare at the image I know so well I can see it with my eyes closed. Of course, I've seen Esther Kaplan with her tall build and bright, shiny red hair, impossibly elegant and always dressed like she's on her way to a celebration. But the girl in the photo looks totally different, with splashes of acne and curly, wild hair and a big, open smile. Could Esther have changed *that* much since high school?

Bernie whips out her phone and taps until she stops and turns it around so I can see the screen. On it are these same two girls—my mom and hers, apparently—sitting in the same outfits they're wearing in my photo, posing in the exact same way.

"Where did you get this?" I ask, my voice warbling.

"This has been in my mom's office forever," Bernie says calmly.

I grab her phone and stare at the photo, looking at the two images side by side.

"Why do you have this?" Bernie asks, but her shaky voice betrays her. She knows why.

I point to the other woman, the one who looks like me, with her dark frizzy hair and big brown eyes. "That," I say, "is my mom."

We stare at the improbable images, so quiet I can hear Joss humming to herself from the kitchen below.

"I didn't know your mom went to Excelsior, too."

I snap my head up. "She didn't."

Bernie cocks her head. "My mom always told me this was her best friend from high school."

"That's not possible."

"That's what she said."

I shake my head and sit down on the edge of my bed, the wood frame digging into my thighs.

Bernie's still standing, but she grabs her phone and taps until she turns it back to me.

"Excelsior yearbook," she says. "In the digital archives."

My stomach seizes as I thumb through the pages, past photos of the school, which is so familiar with its marble entryway, its red-brick buildings. Finally, I come to the pages that list every student in alphabetical order, their faces smiling back at me.

Bernie's looking over the screen and points at an image. "There's my mom," she says.

Esther Baum, looking exactly as she does in the photo I've been looking at for months.

Fear churns in my stomach as I continue on, looking for my mom even though I know it would be ludicrous to find her here. Unbelievable.

But then against the odds, only a little bit farther down the page, there's an image of a joyful girl with dark, frizzy hair and a heart-shaped face. Her lips are pink and her smile shows all her teeth. She looks, unbelievably, like me.

Under the photo, her name is printed, clear as any other word in the English language: Audra Baros.

"I—I don't understand."

Bernie sinks down beside me. "She never told you she went to Excelsior?"

I shake my head, confusion washing over me like a tidal wave. Since Mom died, there have been so many things I've wanted to ask her, things I never did when she was alive: *What were you like at my age? Did you always want to work in food service or did you just wind up at the diner? What made you fall in love with Dad? How will I ever survive without you?*

But one thing I never thought about was her high school experience—where she went and why. It never occurred to me to care. Now, though . . . it seems like the only thing that matters. Why did she keep this a secret? Especially when she knew how I struggled at Excelsior, how I never found my people, my place?

But maybe . . . maybe Esther would know.

"Your mom said this girl was her best friend?"

Bernie nods.

The idea is coming fast, rushing through me, and I jump to my feet, adrenaline kicking in. "I need to talk to your mom now. Can you take me to her?"

Bernie doesn't move, blinking up at me. "No," she says.

"What do you mean, no? I know you're mad about the whole Skyler thing, but come on. My mom's *dead*. Your mom's just sick with a cough or something. Can't you at least—"

But Bernie cuts me off. "I have no idea where she is."

Bernie

TORI'S LOOKING AT me with her eyes bugging out of her head, and I want to put up all my defenses, but then I remember that she just realized her mom kept a huge part of her life a secret and I try to stay calm, slow my breathing.

"What do you *mean* you have no idea where she is? The Ball is tomorrow and she's my nominator. Doesn't she *need* to be there for me to be considered to win?"

My whole body tenses and I know I could keep lying—making up excuses for my mom. But what good would that do me here, with Tori, someone who might actually lose more than I could if Mom doesn't show up tomorrow? In one breath, I decide to tell the truth. "She's been missing all week."

"All week?" Tori's practically screaming now. "You have to find her. I can't show up without her."

I cross my arms over my chest, which feels like it's going to explode from how fast my heart is beating. "Don't you think I've been trying to find her?"

Tori groans. "So, what? You think she's just going to bail?"

I open my mouth and try to find something to say, but I can't find the words. I never really thought I would be confronted with this question. I guess I assumed—hoped—that Mom would come back before tomorrow. But it's the night before the Ball and she's nowhere to be found.

I avert my eyes from Tori and reach around grasping for something to hold onto, to keep me upright. My hand lands on the open lip of one of the dresser drawers.

"Are you okay?" Tori asks.

My throat is dry and feels like it's closing up, but I nod. "Yes," I whisper. I have to be okay. I *have* to get through the next twenty-four hours. I leverage my weight against the drawer to keep me upright, but when I push against it, it opens farther and I can see deeper inside.

Sitting there is a small velvet box, red with gold detailing around the edges. It looks so familiar, like something I've seen my whole life. But . . . that would be ridiculous.

Still, I can't help myself. I reach inside the drawer and pull it out, feeling its weight in my hand, the familiar contours filling my palm. I pop the top, and a small piece of paper falls to the floor. I reach for it and see it says something in Mom's quick scrawl. I glance at it—TRINITY—followed by some other words I can't quite make out. She must have left some note to herself in here by accident. I reach inside, pinching a silver chain between two fingers. I hold it up, and in my grasp, I see my grandmother's diamond necklace, catching the light as it dangles from my hand.

I turn it over to find the platinum setting, the same one I've looked at dozens of times over the years in my mother's dressing room. The one with five prongs and my grandmother's initials engraved on the back.

"Why do you have this?" I ask, my voice shaky.

Tori must sense something's strange, because she pulls the necklace back, out of my reach. "Mrs. Shalcross gave it to me at the fitting," she says. "She said it was from my nominator. Your mom."

It takes everything in my power not to yank the thing out of her hands and put it around my neck where I was told my whole life it belongs.

"What?" Tori asks.

"It was my grandmother's. The only thing *her* grandmother took with her when fleeing the pogroms."

"Shit," Tori says. She thrusts it back toward me. "I can't have this."

But something inside me shifts. If my mom gave it to her, it must have been for a reason. And now, in addition to finding her, I need to know why.

I shake my head. "We need to find my mom."

Tori nods and we're both quiet, full of so many questions and no answers, all of which surround our mothers, who may or may not be exactly who we thought they were for the past seventeen years.

"Helloooo," Joss calls from the hallway. "It's been, like, a million years. What's going on?"

Tori and I look at each other and there's an ocean of conversation between us, silence filling the air. I glance at the clock and see it's already after two a.m.

"I should head home."

Tori looks at me, her eyes wide and concerned. "You sure?" she asks softly. "We have an air mattress. You could stay here."

Joss gives her a death stare, and even though the idea of curling up here in this cozy house with Tori, whom I should hate based on everything that's happened today, seems like it might actually be a pleasant experience, the weight of the day and its revelations suddenly come crashing down on me all at once.

"I need my own bed," I say, heading for the stairs. But before leaving I turn around and look at Tori, confused and scared, still holding that diamond. "Tomorrow," I say. "We'll find her tomorrow. Together."

She looks up then, determined, and nods. "Okay."

AFTER THE BALL

ALL ACROSS THE *city, news has started to spread that something has happened at the Legacy Club. A death. A tragedy. Group texts have gone out. A tweet questioning the cop cars that line the streets. A frantic middle-of-the-night message sent to a stringer for the* New York Post, *and now, in the depths of night, a small crowd has started to form outside the Club, bringing the worst: a spotlight.*

Inside the building, Jeanine Shalcross peeks out the window, a pit forming her in stomach. After all this time, she and the others have tried to keep the Club's privacy. Not just for the future members, but for themselves. And now . . . one death may ruin it all.

Someone taps her shoulder lightly, one finger pressed to her lace-covered skin. Jeanine spins around to find Yasmin Gellar standing there, a concerned look on her face.

"What is it, Yas?" Jeanine asks. She knows her nerves must be on display. Where the hell is Esther? Did she tell—after all these years? "Does Tori know?" Jeanine's stomach drops. The idea of that girl knowing what happened . . . It's so shameful. Then she looks around—at the caution tape, the cops, the broken glass, the hints of blood staining the stone. "Do you think . . . ?"

Yasmin shakes her head vehemently. "No, no. She doesn't know."

Jeanine wishes she had her confidence, her optimism. Because

Jeanine's not so sure. She had a sneaking suspicion all those years back when they betrayed Audra that their actions would come back to bite them, that karma was indeed real, that they—and the Club—deserved to be punished for their wrongdoings.

She just didn't think it would happen tonight.

THE DAY OF
THE BALL

Isobel

AS SOON AS I wake up, I'm blinded. My vision is gone, a black pin-point in the middle of brightness, until finally my eyes adjust and I realize where I am: on our townhouse's roof deck, wearing last night's clothes, an empty bottle next to me.

I fumble around for my phone until the memory of last night comes rushing back, thick and heavy. The shattering of glass. My destroyed phone. Bernie's slap. How I betrayed her. Lee's disappointed face. His final words. The end of my life as I once knew it.

I roll over on the cushion, damp with morning dew, and scream long and loud into the canvas, muffling my voice. Pigeons flap their wings around me, taking flight into the early morning sky, deserting me like everyone else.

But then I feel something small and subtle, pressing against my thigh, and a bubble of relief forms in my chest. I reach down into my pocket and retrieve two Xanax, swallowing them dry before I can think better. Calm washes over me and I resign myself to staying here forever, avoiding the Ball, senior year, college, every-thing. No one will care anyway.

That's the thought that lingers with me as the door swings open loudly, banging against the roof wall.

"Isobel? Are you up here?"

The voice is male and frantic, but too young to be my dad and definitely not my brother. "Lee?" I whisper, but I keep my eyes shut.

Someone comes close to me; I can feel them getting nearer, and even though I want to see who it is, I stay still.

"Jesus Christ," the voice says. "Are you okay?"

"Mm-hmm," I mumble, but apparently that's not good enough because within seconds, I'm jolted upright by a wave of cold water splashing all over me, dampening my clothes.

I sputter, propping myself up as much as I can until I open my eyes and see who's standing right in front me. "Kendall," I say, his name garbled on my lips.

He looks furious, his arms crossed over his chest. "Get up," he says. "And get changed."

I lean back in the chair. "You're not in charge of me," I say like a child.

"Fine," he says, heading back to the door. "But if you don't, I'm taking this." He reaches down and picks up my little baggie. It must have slipped from my pocket, but now I see a few pills floating inside.

Panic comes over me, and I force myself to stand and follow Kendall down the stairs into the top floor of the townhouse, where Mom set up a little den a few years back as a place where Marty and his friends could play video games. Kendall plops down on the couch and runs his hands over his face, exhausted.

"Why are you here?" I ask.

He drops his hands and looks at me, cocking his head. "I was worried about you," he says. "After last night . . . it didn't look good. I tried calling you but you didn't pick up."

"Smashed my phone."

He holds up the bits and pieces. "Saw that." He lets them drop onto the coffee table, a heap of metal and glass. "Plus, I heard Lee broke up with you."

I wince. "Damn. That was fast."

Kendall shrugs. "If it makes you feel better, I don't think people know whether to talk about *that* or the fact that Skyler blew up his relationship."

"Shit. How's Opal?"

"A mess. I'm going to kill Skyler," Kendall says, venomous.

"Yeah, well, you and everyone else." I pause. "Why are you here?"

"I didn't want you to be alone."

A warmth blooms in my chest and for a second, I want to hug Kendall, this boy I've known for almost my entire life, whom I cast aside years ago because he wasn't what I thought my life needed. I didn't deem him worthy. Important. But now . . . he's the only one who's here.

"You've changed so much since we were kids," he says. "It's like I barely know you."

I nod, swallowing the lump in my throat. "I know."

"But maybe . . . maybe this is an opportunity for you to remember who you really are. Get back to that person."

"Maybe," I say, wishing he was right.

"Do you even want to be friends with those people? Skyler, who blackmailed you? Bernie, who you screwed over?" He shakes his head.

"It's not that easy," I say, bristling. But what I really want to say is this: If I'm not Bernie's best friend, I have no idea who I am— and that's scarier than anything else in this world.

"Explain it to me, then, because your friends have basically ruined not only your life but my little sister's, too. How can you not see how toxic they are? Aren't you *mad* at them?"

"What do you want from me?" I ask, my voice rising. "To kick and scream and call them names? To draw blood and become *violent*?"

Kendall's face drops. "I just want you to stand up for yourself. For Opal. You've been in Bernie's shadow. And she's just been a pawn of Skyler's. How can you not see that?"

And for the first time in a long time, suddenly everything is clear. Maybe Kendall is right. Maybe . . . maybe the way out of this mess is by teaching them a lesson once and for all.

Tori

TRYING TO SLEEP was a useless pursuit. I tossed and turned for hours, trying to figure out why my mom never told me that she also went to Excelsior, even after she was the one who convinced me to apply. I try to replay every situation in my head—how elated she was when I got in but never came to all-parent meetings. How she wanted to know all about my teachers but never betrayed any moment of recognition that we had shared the same experiences. It was as if she wanted to live vicariously through me . . . but never admitted that she had really, truly lived them, too.

I rack my brain to remember if she ever asked about Bernie Kaplan or anyone named Esther, but nothing comes to mind.

Giving up, I throw back the covers and tiptoe out of bed, careful not to wake Joss, who's conked out beside me, spooning a pillow, or Helen in the bunk above. I make my way down to the kitchen and start a pot of coffee, and then someone coughs behind me, causing me to jump.

I spin around and see Dad standing there, rubbing his eyes with the back of his hands. "It's six thirty in the morning. What are you doing up?"

"Couldn't sleep." I nod to his pajamas. "No diner shift this morning?"

He shakes his head.

There's an eerie silence between us and I know I should ask him about Mom—about Esther—but how do I find the words?

It's as if admitting that Mom lied to me means I might admit that everything that transpired between us was a lie, too.

But Dad can see right through me.

"Come on," he coaxes. "What is it?" He opens a cupboard and pulls down a mug that has a printed photo of Mom and him at their wedding on it. It's faded now, their faces nearly gone, but I can still make out Dad's beard, Mom's veil. Their smiles. He fills it with coffee and a splash of half-and-half, and starts making himself toast, like this is any other morning.

I swallow the lump in my throat. "Why didn't Mom ever tell me that she went to Excelsior?"

Dad stops, the comforting, concerned look falling from his face, and in an instant, I realize that he knew, too. That he lied just as much as she did. And that's a thought that's almost too much to bear. But I must, because right now I need answers.

"Why? Why did you keep this from me? You knew how hard it was for me those first few years, how much hearing from Mom could have helped me." Tears are stinging my eyes and I take a sip of air, desperate to breathe.

Dad slides onto a stool behind the counter and rests his head in his hands. "She had a terrible time at that school," he says quietly. "She didn't want you to know."

"Then why did she have me apply for the scholarship? Why did she want me to go there?"

Dad sighs. "She saw what it could do for people, how it lifted them up and changed their lives," he says. "She thought it might for you."

I shake my head. It's not like Mom grew up to found some start-up that was worth a billion dollars or become a politician. "It didn't change *her* life."

"Your mother didn't graduate from Excelsior," he says, looking up at me with a fallen face. "She was expelled."

"What?" I sink into a stool next to Dad. That's unimaginable. The same mom who banned screen time during the week except when it was for homework—the woman who wouldn't let me go out past ten even when everyone else on the block stayed out until eleven. I can't imagine her doing anything that would get her in trouble, let alone expelled from a school like Excelsior.

"I don't know the whole story. She always said it was too painful to talk about." Dad shrugs. "All I know is that the lawyers seemed to know about it, for whatever reason."

I crane my neck up. "The lawyers?"

Dad nods. "Yeah, with the malpractice settlement. They mentioned it when they were gathering background information on your mom. It was odd. It never even crossed my mind that would come up."

We're both quiet for a beat, so many questions still unanswered, until another piece of the puzzle clicks into place, causing my heart rate to pick up, a nervous energy to creep through my body.

"The law firm that handled her case, what's their name?"

Dad sips his coffee, his mug almost empty. When he sets it down, he looks right at me. "Hawkins Kaplan."

Bernie

MY PHONE RINGS, breaking through the chatter of the coffee shop a block from my apartment. I came here to think and munch on a croissant while I try to figure out where the hell to go from here—how to get through the day.

The screen says it's an unknown caller, but it's a New York area code so I pick up.

"Mom?" I say, hopeful.

"It's Tori." Her voice is high and urgent through the phone.

"Oh," I say. "How—"

"Did you know Hawkins Kaplan was representing my family?"

"Excuse me?" I tuck my phone between my shoulder and my ear and hustle out of the café, dumping my trash in the garbage. "What are you talking about?"

"My mom. There's a case against the hospital where she died, and it's all settled and everything, but the law firm who represented us has been holding on to the money for months."

My heart races as I shake my head, trying to understand how all of these pieces fit together. "A Hawkins Kaplan suit."

"Yup," Tori says, a tinge of anger in her voice.

"I had no idea."

"Yeah, well, me neither. Doesn't that seem a little odd, considering we now know our mothers knew each other well? Like *best friends* well?"

"I guess, yeah, a little," I say, walking quickly back toward home.

"What's also weird is that my dad told me this morning that my mom was *expelled* from Excelsior and that's why she never told me she went there."

I stop in my tracks. "What did she do?"

"He doesn't know," she says, frustrated. "Says she never talked about it."

We're both quiet, the awkwardness palpable across the river that divides us.

She breaks first. "We need to find your mom. They both kept that photo for a reason. I need to know why."

"Maybe they were still best friends," I say, reaching.

"That neither one of us knew about?"

I open my mouth but I'm at a loss for words. I hear something sizzle in the background, and I wonder if she's back in that warm kitchen, flipping pancakes or maybe slices of French toast for those cute twins.

"Where is she?" Tori asks.

"I don't know," I say, my voice breaking. But suddenly the reality of it all catches up to me and for the first time since Mom disappeared, I can't fight the tears, the stinging in my eyes. I pause and lean back against a brick building, steadying myself as I swallow a sob. "I'm trying to find her."

"Not hard enough." Tori pauses. "Think. Where could she be? Did she leave you any clues? Any emails or secret messages?"

I let out a snot-laden laugh. "What, like a spy movie?"

Tori groans into the phone.

I wipe my cheeks with the back of my sleeve and pull up Find My Friends, hoping I'll get lucky. There's nothing there, only an image of Isobel somewhere in Brooklyn and my mom's icon listed as not found. Her last known address was the Trinity Hotel.

But then, something clicks into place.

"Go upstairs," I say.

"Excuse me?"

"Into your dresser, that velvet bag that came with the necklace."

I hear her walking, feet hitting steps as she climbs to the second floor. A door closes and a wood drawer creaks open. She's riffling through something, clothes or underwear or scarves, until finally she stops.

"What am I looking for?"

"A piece of paper," I say. "When I took it out of the box, there were some letters and numbers."

Tori sighs. "Nope, just the necklace."

"Shit, I must have dropped it. Look on the floor."

I hear the sounds of movement, of bumping around, until finally it's quiet again. "Okay," she says. "Found it."

"What does it say?"

"Trinity." She stops. "Hold on, the rest is in chicken scratch." But then I hear a confused sigh. "It just says Audra."

My heart beats fast like it's going to leap into my throat. "She's at the Trinity Hotel. I went there earlier this week because my mom must have turned on location sharing for a second, but they said no Esther had checked in—Kaplan or Baum." My mind is racing now, and I feel like I'm on the brink of an explosion. "But I didn't ask them for someone named Audra."

Tori inhales sharply. "You think she's using my mom's name as a cover?"

"We might as well try. How fast can you be at the Trinity?"

I ask, but before she can speak, I pull up my ride-sharing app. "Never mind, I'm sending you a car."

Tori breathes heavily like she's trying to catch her breath. "We only have a few hours before the Ball. You better be right."

Tori

I RUSH OUT of the cab, clutching my purse, the one that has the necklace safely inside, and am greeted by a doorman wearing a blazer with a coat of arms embroidered on the chest.

"Welcome to the Trinity," he says, ushering me inside.

It's an imposing hotel straight out of *Eloise* with sky-high ceilings and gold-plated steps, elegant glass chandeliers. I let myself get taken with it all for just a moment before I run straight into Bernie, who's pacing back and forth in the lobby.

"There you are," she says, grabbing my elbow. "Come on."

Together, we approach the front desk, where Bernie looks like she's about to rip this concierge's face right off.

"Show them your ID," she says forcefully.

"Excuse me?"

"Your license, come on. I asked if Audra Baros was here, and they said they needed to see a very specific person's ID, and I'm gonna assume it's you."

I fumble for my wallet and pull out my license, handing it to the woman across the counter. She looks at it, then at my face, and smiles. "Right this way, Tori."

Bernie throws up her hands. "I'm going to kill my mother."

My stomach begins to fizzle as we trail behind the hotel staff, who deposits us in front of an elevator. "Seventeenth floor," she says, handing us a room key.

Bernie snatches it from her hand. "Unbelievable."

We step into the elevator and I hit the button, and together we ride in anxious silence for a few floors. "It's pretty fucked up your mom checked into a hotel under my dead mom's name."

Bernie's face is red, and she stares straight ahead. "It's pretty fucked up I barely know who she is anymore."

"That makes two of us. With moms, I mean."

The doors come to a halt and open on the seventeenth floor, and together we step out into the hallway. Bernie leads the way, making rights and lefts through the mazelike hotel until finally she stops in front of Room 1733 and takes a big breath.

She raises her fist, and my heart feels like it's about to leap right into my throat. But before she can knock against the door, it swings wide open to reveal a woman who looks just like Bernie—with her bright red hair and curvy hips—but with a few fine lines around her mouth, a more refined jaw, cheekbones just a touch higher. She's wearing a set of matching silk pajamas in a cool minty color, and she's looking at both of us with an expression of resignation, like she's been caught during a game of hide-and-seek.

Her gaze moves from Bernie to me, then back to Bernie. She looks like she wants to say something to her, but instead, her gaze lands back on my face.

"Tori Tasso," she says. "You look just like your mother."

Bernie

THE FIRST THING I want to do when I see my mother is throw my arms around her and hug her tight, weep into her shoulder, and let the relief wash over me that after all this time worrying, she is totally, improbably fine. I want to curl up in her arms and tell her about everything that's happened this week—how Skyler and Isobel both betrayed me and how I have no idea whom to trust.

But that's not what I do, because I can't ignore the fact that perhaps her betrayal was worst of all. Mom moves away from the door, and Tori and I follow her inside. She's clearly made herself at home here: A box from our favorite bakery sits on the desk, and I can see through the mini-fridge's glass door that it's stocked with her specified brand of watermelon seltzer and the skin serums she gets shipped over from France. A clothing rack stands in the corner, and I spy some of her favorite dresses standing still on velvet hangers, a few hats draped on hooks.

Mom sits down on the chaise and tucks her feet up under her, and I wonder if she's waiting for me to say something—to speak first—but luckily, I don't have to.

"Where should I begin?" Mom asks, worry in her voice. She's looking at me like I'm fragile, like I might break if she makes a wrong move, and honestly, she might be right.

"What have you been *doing*?" I ask. But at the same time, Tori speaks, too.

"Why didn't my mom tell me she went to Excelsior?"

Tori's face is pleading as she bites her bottom lip, and suddenly, I realize my mom may be the only link Tori has to Audra, to her own past. At least that brief time period that leaves her with so many questions.

"Answer her first," I say, sitting down on the neatly made bed. "She deserves to know."

Mom clenches her fists but acquiesces, turning to Tori in her chair. "I take it you've gathered that your mother and I were quite close in high school. She was one of my best friends," she says carefully. "Inseparable freshman through junior year. But . . ." Mom pauses. "Everything changed the summer before senior year."

Tori leans in, her brow narrowed. "What happened?"

Mom furrows her brow. "It was all very upsetting." She starts to pace around the room. "Your mother was so smart. Brilliant, really. But she was awful at math. Just dreadful. Unlike you." She smiles at Tori, who's looking at my mom with a stoic face. "At the end of junior year, we had this big calculus exam, and she wasn't proud of this, but she stole the answer key."

Tori looks up, stunned. We both know Excelsior has a no-cheating policy and breaking it is one of the only ways kids can get expelled. "My mom would never do that."

Mom pouts. "She was desperate. It was junior spring. The most important semester, even back then. She needed that A. But, well, over the summer, one of the admins was cleaning out the lockers to get ready for the new school year and found the answer key in hers. A horrible mistake. She must have left it in there."

I cock my head, confused. Locker cleanout day is a time-honored tradition at Excelsior—one of the final days of school where we have no classes and just dump everything into garbage pails in the halls. To forget something like a stolen answer key would be impossible.

Mom sighs. "Once the school found out, they told the Legacy Club, and she lost not only her spot at school but her nomination to the Club."

Tori looks up. "Wait. My mom was a Legacy?"

Mom winces. "She would have been. This all came out during nominations week."

"They just kicked her out?" I say, horrified.

"It spread like wildfire and it became . . ." Mom shakes her head, as if remembering a bad dream. "It followed her everywhere. When she was applying to college, she had to explain the expulsion—why no one at Excelsior would refer her. It ruined everything."

Tori and I are both stunned into silence, a sharp crackling spreading through the air.

Mom reaches forward and rests a hand on Tori's chin. "The silver lining of all this, though, is that if she hadn't left Excelsior, she never would have met your father," she says. "You wouldn't exist."

Tori stares, stunned, and backs away. "I don't understand. Why didn't she ever tell me?"

Mom sighs. "I don't know. We lost touch after that. I reached out a few times, but I think the shame was too much for her. So, we never really reconnected." Mom rubs her temple. "When I heard that her daughter had won the Arts and Letters scholarship and would be in Bernie's grade, I tried to see her again." Mom shakes her head. "She said she wanted nothing to do with me, that she didn't want to relive that time. She just wanted *you* to have the best education, to experience what she missed out on."

"Why would she want to send me there if it brought her so much trauma?" Tori asks.

Mom pauses. "She saw what happened to the rest of us—all her other classmates. She wanted that for you, even if she hadn't been able to have it herself."

Tori shakes her head, stunned.

Mom sighs. "I never stopped trying to make amends. Not until I heard about what happened."

Tori looks up then. "You," she says. "You sent Hawkins Kaplan to us."

Mom nods. "I saw a story in the Metro section about her death and how Big Apple Hospitals was known for neglect. I implored Rafe and Lulu to take it on."

Tori's face grows cloudy. "We still don't have that money."

Mom sighs. "These things take time. Even fast settlements."

But then Tori's mouth drops open, a look of realization taking over her face. "So, that's why you nominated me for the Club. Out of guilt. Not because I deserved it or because Skyler pressured you to?"

Mom looks up, a look of surprise on her face. "Skyler?" She holds Tori's gaze. "I nominated you because your mother made one mistake and it ruined things for her. I wanted you to have what she didn't. You deserve this."

Tori shakes her head, tears glinting in her eyes. She reaches into her bag and pulls out the velvet bag that holds my grandmother's necklace and sets it down on the desk next to my mom. "I can't participate in this charade," she says. "I'm not joining this club."

Mom glances down, running a finger over the velvet. She's

calm. Too calm for what's transpiring. She looks up at Tori and smiles softly. "This Club can give you a future. We look out for our own. It's what your mother would have wanted."

Tori stands, looking Mom right in the eye. "You have no idea what my mother would have wanted." She grabs her things and heads for the door, slamming it behind her, and I'm left with my mother, the person I thought I knew best in the whole wide world, who now looks to me like a total stranger.

There's a silence pulsing through the room until I swallow hard and find the words I've been looking for. "How could you leave me?" It comes out a whisper.

She turns to me, her eyes pleading. "I'm sorry, Bernie."

"Have you been here this whole time? At the Trinity?"

Mom nods, a look of resignation on her face.

"Why?" I ask, my voice a whisper. "Because you asked for a divorce?"

Mom's eyebrows inch up, and she moves toward the bed so she's sitting right beside me. "Yes," she says, reaching for my hand. "Your father and I need to be apart right now. I know that's difficult to hear, but it's for the best, even if it means I'm not at home with you right now."

I shake my head. It's not possible. The mom who held my hand when I had the flu, who gossiped with me over green juices and whitefish would never do this. But when I look at her, I realize she would. Because that mom was still, always, Esther Kaplan, a woman who knows to look out for herself, and only herself. I should know because that's how she's made me, and right now I have no idea what to say or if she's ever coming back to the lives she built for us.

I'm furious, so mad that rage boils inside my stomach like hot lava and black stones, but all of a sudden, the only feeling that washes over me is exhaustion. The kind that, as a child, led me to curl up in my mother's bed and let her hold me until I fell asleep.

So, despite my better instincts—despite what I just learned about the woman who made me in her image so completely we are mistaken for each other even now, I rest my head on her lap and let her stroke my hair until finally, all at once, I feel like I can breathe.

Isobel

KENDALL'S VOICE BLARES in my head as I walk into Madame Trillian's atelier. His words bleat over and over again: *Your friends have basically ruined your life. How can you not see how toxic they are?*

He's right. And I'm finally ready to do something about it.

I barely hear the security guard telling me where to go, but it doesn't matter. I just follow the shrieks of other Ball-goers pulling on their dresses, stuffing their feet into too-tight shoes. The back dressing room has been outfitted with individual glam stations, and our gowns and accessories are set up next to each of them—all with our names on them.

When I approach mine, I see it's right next to Bernie's. *Shit.*

At least she's not here yet.

I slump down in my seat and close my eyes, gripping the side of the vanity so hard my knuckles turn white. When I finally get the courage, I open my eyes and look at myself in the mirror. What I see shocks me.

The girl there has big dark circles hanging down beneath her eyes, and her face is swollen and puffy. Even though I took a shower, my short bob looks dry and brittle, beyond help from the hair and makeup teams scattering around the room to find their charges. The girl there, she is raw. A live wire.

"All right, everyone!" Mrs. Shalcross calls. I turn to see her walking through the dressing room in a black ball gown with matching gloves that go up to her elbows. Her hair is tied in an updo at the base of her skull, which could look elegant, but really just looks like she's trying to knock off Audrey Hepburn. "Thirty minutes until we have to leave. Act accordingly!"

All around me, there's a frenetic, excited energy in the air as zippers are pulled, buttons are closed, lipstick is refreshed. The sound of giggles and whispers and full-on *joy* permeates the room, and I can't help but think, *That should be me.* I should be here with Bernie, relishing every single moment of this day, even though I think it's silly and juvenile—even though I never wanted to be here in the first place. Bernie would have convinced me to be excited, that this would be the best night of our lives. But Bernie's not here, and suddenly I don't know why I am, either.

The door is so close. I could just slip out. Leave. Not give my presentation.

No one would even care.

But then I realize that would just prove everyone right—that I'm nothing without Bernie by my side. That I gave up, chickened out. But what everyone failed to recognize yesterday was that I *did* earn my spot here. I was chosen because of my talent, my artistic skill. I wasn't nominated by Esther or Lulu or someone who works with my parents. I didn't nepo-baby my way into this club. I deserve to be here, and I'm not going to let anyone take that away from me.

I grip the arms of my chair and tilt my chin up just as a peppy-looking man with a bouffant comes over and shrugs his shoulders.

"Confidence," he says. "I love it!" He introduces himself as Perry, my glam artist, and starts spritzing my hair with something that smells sweet and crisp. He pats my face with some serums, spreads moisturizer on my skin, and cups my chin in his hands. "What are we going for today? Moody? Natural? Sparkly?"

I look around the room at all the other girls in their beachy waves, their sparkly eyeshadow. They all look like pageant queens or debutantes, preppy starlets ready to cross over into adulthood. Last week, I might have wanted to be like them, to blend in. Or to let Bernie pick out my hair and makeup.

But tonight . . . I want something bold. Something different. Something me.

I look at Perry with such intensity that he flinches.

"Powerful," I tell him. "Make me look powerful."

Perry releases me and steps back, crossing his arms over his chest. He nods. "That," he says, "I can do."

AFTER THE BALL

BERNIE GROWS MORE *anxious by the minute. She lifts a manicured hand to her mouth and begins to nibble at her thumbnail, but when she looks down and sees it flecked with blood, she has to use every muscle in her body to hold back vomit.*

She looks around the room, wishing for an ally, for someone else who understands what transpired this evening. But all she sees are potential threats. Land mines. People she now has to lie to.

None of this was part of the plan. It all came together swiftly after Tori left the Trinity Hotel, after it was just her and her mother together in that big hotel room, the truth about Esther and Audra sinking in.

Bernie suggested the idea, that perhaps they could give Tori a leg up at the presentation. Help her in that room full of vultures. All they had to do was make sure she actually returned to the Ball and accepted her nomination.

Esther was eager and willing, desperate to make sure Tori's experience was different than Audra's. That was how Bernie persuaded Esther to come to the Ball in the first place, to text Rafe and let him know she was all right, she was here.

But now, standing inside the enormous, regal entryway to the Club, the place that was always intended for her, Bernie knows that all the events that led her to this moment were built on lies. Mistakes.

She glances at the cops manning their stations. No one has come to question her yet, and she has not deigned to make herself available.

Instead, she has watched as others—Lee Dubey, Lydia Yen, Chase Killingsworth—have spoken to officers in hushed tones, with bowed heads. She wonders what they said. What they knew.

But now she may be running out of time. She may soon have to tell the truth. Unless she can fight her way out of it.

Tori

I'M WALKING AROUND the Upper East Side aimlessly, trying to figure out my next move, when my phone rings, alerting me that Bernie is calling me for the fifth time in the last twenty minutes.

Finally, after sending her to voice mail over and over, I decide to pick up and tell her to leave me the fuck alone.

"What?" I ask. My throat burns after trying not to cry since I left that horrible hotel room, since I learned the truth about how Bernie and I are tied together by our mothers.

"You need to come to the Ball," Bernie says. She sounds breathless, like she's running, and I wonder where she is, if she's on her way to Madame Trillian's to get all dolled up and smile and wave just like she always intended to.

I shake my head even though she can't see me. "No."

"You have every right to be mad."

"Mad?" I scream. "You think I'm *mad*? I'm fucking furious. I—"

"Okay, sorry. Wrong choice of words, but look. I know I can't make up for what happened to your mother."

I snort.

"But my mom *did* nominate you."

"So?" I say.

"The way I see it, you can view this nomination in one of two ways," Bernie says, determined. "First option: You throw it all away and go on living as you always did, keeping your life contained and small."

"If this is you trying to be nice, you are failing spectacularly," I say, offended.

Bernie ignores me. "Or you can use my mom's nomination and seize this opportunity. You can *win* tonight. Change everything."

I let her words sink in. What if Bernie is playing me now, too? What if she and her mom have something planned? What if . . .

But suddenly I find myself outside Madame Trillian's studio, those big glass doors staring at me. Past them are all the others, getting their hair and makeup done, zipping up their dresses, trading whispers with their friends, preparing for the night that could change their lives.

Why can't this one change mine, too?

I'm about to say something when I hear someone approach from behind me. I turn around and see Bernie standing there, her phone pressed to her ear. She hangs it up and smiles.

"Come on," she says. "You're here, aren't you?"

I look at her—this girl I knew of for three whole years but only began to understand this week. She could be a stranger, someone I withheld gossip from because I wanted something from her life. But she's not. Because whether we like it or not, our connection was predetermined by the women who came before us, who kept secrets from us, who made us.

I think of my mom, what she would say if she knew what had happened—that Esther Kaplan was trying to make amends by giving me this gift. There's no way to know, but I can only take a guess. And when I think about it, really, I know what she would want me to do.

"I'm here," I say. "And I'm going to win."

Tori

WE ARE ALL lined up on Sixty-Second Street, a block or so away from the Legacy Club. There's a nervous energy permeating our little cohort as passersby walk around us, gawking at the dozens of teenagers wearing red-carpet-worthy outfits.

"Straighten up, please!" Mrs. Shalcross calls from the front of the line, her voice full of stress and anticipation.

All around me, people are lifting their shoulders, sucking in their stomachs, rearranging themselves to be as prepared as possible, but somehow, I end up in between Isobel and Bernie, and both of them are silent and still. Isobel's wearing stunning, dark makeup that makes her look like a model out for revenge, not a high school senior preparing to mingle with some fancy adults. Bernie's her opposite, with girlish pink cheeks and mermaid waves. Neither one of them seems to acknowledge the other, making the whole thing extremely awkward.

I think of saying something to both of them just to break the tension, but then I remember that there's a lot of history between them—the kind one betrayal might be able to ruin—and I let them be. I don't need to fix them. I need to save myself tonight. Prove myself. I need to win. All of a sudden, the line starts to move forward and we're all walking single file toward the door, our future.

As we get closer, I catch my breath and send up a silent prayer for this night to go as planned—for me to use the Club as best I can. *Nail the presentation. Win the prize money. Keep it.*

No one dares speak as we make our way to the entrance, and finally it's my turn to see the Club head-on. It's a nondescript white brick townhouse that ascends six stories into the air. Sitting on a double-wide lot, it's twice as big as the rest of the homes on the block, which is the only thing that differentiates it from the other stately buildings. Well, that and the small gold plaque that says LEGACY CLUB, MEMBERS ONLY nailed to the door.

Right at the entrance, thick, navy velvet drapes shield us from what's on the inside, what the place actually looks like, and above Bernie's head, I see students pull their skeleton keys from their boxes and use them to enter the Club one at a time.

Butterflies hum in my stomach as I take a step forward, getting closer and closer to my future. Mrs. Shalcross is waiting for us, standing just inside the entrance, her chrome clipboard in her gloved hand. I wrap my fingers around the gold metal, feeling the key ring dig into my palm. Finally, it's Bernie's turn to enter and she disappears through the door, locked shut behind her.

Mrs. Shalcross turns to me and looks down at her clipboard, then up at me. "Are you ready, Tori?" I gulp and slide my key into the door and turn it hard, hearing a satisfying click as the deadbolt unlocks, and I step forward, my stomach flipping one, two, three times over.

Velvet curtains hang heavy inside the door, and before I can push them aside, the door closes behind me and I'm standing still in the darkness, a midway point between my past and my present. I tilt my chin up and grasp the key tighter. I think of my mom and let out an exhale. I'm ready.

The curtains part as I step forward into the Club, my heels clicking against the marble floor. When I look up, I see a grand staircase adorned in gold, and dozens of Club members dressed in black tie, sipping from crystal flutes. Waiters wearing bow ties and white gloves hold out silver platters full of canapes and drinks, and enormous bouquets of flowers line every tabletop.

All along the walls are banquet tables full of food—a meat carving station serving filet mignon and pork tenderloin, a made-to-order sushi station where a chef pinches rice right in front of you, a mountainous raw bar overflowing with juicy oysters and slick cracked crab claws, and a dim sum setup where a server unveils perfect, round dumplings sitting inside bamboo steamer baskets. Along the bar, I spot thick glass bowls full of slim matchbooks emblazoned with the discreet Legacy Club logo, elegant martini glasses lined up and ready to be filled.

I gaze up at a sparkling chandelier that shimmers as the light peeks in from the floor-to-ceiling windows along the back of the first floor. Standing on my tiptoes, I see that they lead to a garden out back, where the party continues and a string quartet plucks classical music from their perch.

My feet seem to be stuck in place as I take it all in, watching my peers and club members waltz around the room, plucking pieces of crudité and blocks of cheese off a mountain of food, as if all of this is normal—expected.

But it's not. None of this is normal *or* expected. It is, however, a game that if played correctly could change the rest of my life. And that's all I need to focus on now.

Isobel

I FELT SO confident up until this moment when I enter the Club for the very first time, taking in the sheer scale of the building, the beauty in its details. I glance down to see the floor is constructed of honed green marble, and when I look up, I have to take a moment to catch my breath. The walls are lined with ornate frames holding up works of art I instantly recognize. A Hilma af Klint next to a Mark Rothko, beside a Wassily Kandinsky. I let out a long, slow breath of air, humbled by what's in front of me. Even though I never wanted to be here in the first place—even if I thought I never needed this place—I have to admit how spectacular it is to be among these greats, standing in front of them only a few feet away, free from the hordes that gather in a museum.

It takes me a moment to catch my breath, and when I do, I finally take in the rest of the room. This isn't just a regular function, like the rest of the events that took place this week. Tonight is something different, something special. There is a heightened frenzy in the air, a popping and a fizzing that makes me want to hide with these paintings. Everyone is dressed up as I knew they would be, but seeing all of the members and nominees in their gowns and tuxedos, their formal gestures and how-do-you-dos makes me feel like I don't belong here.

Especially because the first person I see having a grand old time is Lee.

Over by the bar, he's mingling with Gertie, who nominated

him, and a few other students from Lipman and Tucker Day. He smiles wide, laughing, and slaps one of the guys on the back. But when he stands upright, his gaze flits around the room and lands on me, standing still in the middle of the foyer.

His face falls as our eyes meet. I take a step toward him, my heart rate picking up. I wonder if he thinks last night was a mistake, a bad dream. What if he walks right over and tells me he was wrong? But as soon as that thought enters my head, I feel a wave of dread, one that shocks me. I stand up straighter and avert my eyes. Perhaps I was ready to be done with Lee, too. Maybe it was time for us to end, for me to realize that it was a relationship borne out of convenience, that I really *was* more enamored with his family than him, and that I, too, was the bad guy in this situation.

I throw my shoulders back and try to right myself.

I wish I had a fucking drink.

"Guess we're in the same boat." I turn to see Skyler has sidled up to me in his tuxedo, his hair slicked to one side and his bow tie slightly askew.

"Fuck off," I say.

Skyler smiles. "Here," he says. "I'm repaying the favor." He extends his fist toward me and, like it's the most natural thing in the world, I open my palm as he drops a small white pill onto my skin. "An upper. You'll like it."

A little jolt zaps my stomach and I pop it into my mouth, swallowing it dry. I don't think about anything else, just the adrenaline that's coursing through my veins, more from taking something than the actual pill itself.

"No 'thank you'?"

"Again," I say. "Fuck off."

Skyler feigns a pout, but looks away, off at Bernie. "Don't worry. I'll get her back."

I let out a laugh. "You're joking, right?"

A grin spreads across his face. "Once she realizes what she might lose, I think I'll be able to convince her."

"And what could she possibly lose that might convince her of that?"

Skyler looks surprised by the question, but he turns around and says with all certainty, "Me."

Bernie

MRS. SHALCROSS USHERS all of us up the marble staircase and into a different section of the Club, and while I'm standing on top of the landing, I realize Mom still isn't here. Before I left her at the hotel, she promised she would show up, despite everything. She promised she'd be here for Tori. But now? Now I'm second-guessing everything.

I'm pushed forward in the sea of people until we're all deposited in an elegant ballroom with massive windows that overlook the garden downstairs and a stage set up in the front of the room. Scattered throughout the room are dozens of round tables set for a formal dinner, and enormous, overflowing vases full of flowers adorn each one. Behind the stage, images of Legacy Balls past are projected on a screen, and I look around as the alumni stop to look at them with nostalgia as their youth passes them by, flashed up there for all of us to see.

The image changes, and I'm greeted by a larger-than-life photo of my mom, looking exactly as she did in the photo with Tori's mother. She's posing with teenage versions of Jeanine Shalcross and Lulu Hawkins. The three of them are carefree and caught in the middle of a laugh, Mom's hand resting gently on Lulu's arm.

"They were cute, huh?"

I spin around to see Skyler standing there, his arms crossed over his chest, looking up at the photos of our mothers.

I step away from him, hoping to ignore him, to not make a

scene. But Skyler's hand finds my elbow and jerks me back to him. Hard.

I see a few eyes turn toward us and Skyler must, too, because he drops his grasp.

"Sorry," he mumbles.

"For putting your hands on me just now or for cheating?" I ask. "Or for blackmailing my best friend? Oh, or for promising to get someone a nomination if they shut up about your little activities?" I throw up my hands. "The possibilities are endless."

Skyler opens his mouth to speak, but before he can say anything, I turn away and head to find my place. But when I get there, I realize we're all seated with the other nominees from our schools—and our nominators. In what must be Mrs. Shalcross's idea of a good time, I'm seated between Lulu Hawkins and my mother.

I swallow hard and sit down, clenching my fingers together under the table. It doesn't take long for the rest of the room to fill up, for excited chatter to fill the air, and finally, even though my mother's seat is still empty next to me, the lights go down.

Tori, who's seated on the other side of Mom, leans over to whisper, "Where is she?"

I open my mouth to say something but just shake my head. *I'm sorry.*

Just then, a spotlight appears on the stage, where a podium has been set up. The crowd hushes, waiting for what's to come, and before I can see who appears, the room erupts in applause, loud and thunderous as everyone clambers to stand.

I rush to my feet and stand on my tiptoes to get a good look, and when I see who's there, relief fills my chest.

Standing on the stage, waving at the crowd, is my mother,

wearing a custom royal-blue one-shoulder gown. Her bright red hair cascades over her shoulders, and she's got huge sapphire stud earrings in each lobe. She looks regal. Flawless. Like she was born to run this club.

She smiles wide and motions for everyone to sit down. Tori glances my way, and I can see she's relieved, too. Her nominator is here. She can still win.

Mom beams out at the crowd as the remaining people sit down and the room goes quiet. She leans forward into the microphone. "Welcome to the annual Legacy Ball!" The room erupts again, and for once, I let the energy of the space, these people, wash over me. I'm finally here, with my mother, in the place I've known I belonged for my entire life.

I am with them, one of them, clapping as hard as I can. Maybe, just maybe, this night will end up okay.

"It's such an honor to celebrate this evening with you. Every Club member can remember the first time they stepped foot inside this magical, special place. They can tell you exactly what they wore, what charity they supported, who nominated them. But they can also tell you how it felt to finally realize you were among your peers." She pauses and looks around, her eyes wet with emotion. "This has always been a special place for me, and now it's about to become even *more* special." Her eyes roam around the room before landing on our table, on me.

"Tonight, I'll welcome my own daughter, Bernadette, into the fold." My cheeks redden, but I can hear people clapping around the room. "As Ball co-chair, I am honored to usher her in this year of all years." She smiles at me, but then her gaze softens, flits around the space. "But I am also excited to get to know each and every one of our nominees. So, without further ado . . ." She motions offstage, and Mrs. Shalcross appears to a more muted round of applause. "Let's begin the presentations!"

Mom backs away from the podium and gives Mrs. Shalcross a kiss on each cheek before exiting the stage. As she leaves, Mrs. Shalcross starts explaining how the night will go, but I'm not listening. I'm just tracking Mom to see where she'll go next. I see her walking down the side of the stage and out into the room, air-kissing acquaintances and waving hellos before she approaches our table with a sense of calm and resolve, as if nothing strange has happened at all this past week.

A waiter appears and pulls her seat out for her. Mom slips in, placing her napkin onto her lap. She reaches for my hand and squeezes it. "It's all going to be fine," she whispers, before taking Tori's hand on her other side, too.

I expect Tori to recoil, to pull away and flee. But instead, she leans closer to my mom. A brief moment passes between them, and for a second, a flare of jealousy rises in my chest, one I can't contain.

AFTER THE BALL

WHILE THE REMAINING *Legacy Club members mill about the first floor, two women have crept up the stairs and into the games room, which has always been their special hiding place during events here at the Club.*

Jeanine Shalcross clucks her tongue at Yasmin Gellar. "None of this would have happened if she hadn't insisted on giving Tori a nomination."

Yasmin sighs. "You know how Esther is. No one could have stood up to her." She looks pointedly at Jeanine.

"What?" Jeanine huffs. "You could have said something, too."

The women look at one another, so many years of secrets and tears and friendship between them. And yet after all this time, there is still the incident with Audra that they don't dare talk about. Have never talked about. Until now.

"It was a mistake to let Audra's daughter in," Jeanine says, rubbing her fingers to her temple. "I still don't know why Esther wanted to."

Yasmin takes one step closer to Jeanine. "Do you really believe what Esther told us all those years back? That Audra called us sluts after that party?"

Jeanine frowns. "What, you think Esther lied?"

Yasmin looks over her shoulder to make sure no one's in the doorway. "You never doubted it?" She shakes her head. "She told us right after she found out that the three of us had a sleepover without her. I always suspected she was jealous of Audra. She worried we liked her more."

Jeanine waves a hand. "How much have you had to drink tonight, Yas?"

Yasmin lowers her voice. "I'm serious," she says. "Audra was never one to talk shit. But we just believed Esther." Her voice cracks, desperate. "We wouldn't have put that answer key in her locker if Esther didn't tell us to, if she didn't tell us all those horrible things Audra said about us."

Jeanine turns up her nose. "'Try-hard bitch who would sleep with a dog if it looked at her.' Never could forget that one."

Yasmin's eyes grow big. "That's what Esther said Audra said about you."

Both women are quiet, their lips pursed, their minds spinning. Could it have been true? Could a young Esther have lied all those years ago to keep these two in line? To hold control over her friends with a tight grasp, one that could not be broken by the sweet, bubbly girl everyone else at Excelsior seemed to gravitate toward?

Jeanine tries not to think about what they did—the fallout. How Audra told them through tears that the headmaster found the answer key in her locker and that he didn't believe Audra when she said she had no idea how it got there. How Esther pretended to comfort Audra at Yasmin's apartment that night, when they all knew she was the one who was responsible.

Jeanine was shocked when Audra was expelled. Horrified. So was Yasmin, who vomited into a little garbage can in her bedroom. Only Esther stayed strong, patting Audra on the back and saying that everything happened for a reason.

That was the first time Jeanine and Yasmin realized what Esther was capable of, how far she would go to maintain her power. Except back then, they didn't see it like that. They only thought it was a prank gone too far. A secret they would have to keep to save themselves.

Now, though, after what had happened tonight, Jeanine was rethinking things. Yasmin, too.

They always knew they had been wrong to go along with Esther's *plan, but now that Audra was dead and her daughter was associated with the Legacy Club, shouldn't they come clean? Shouldn't things change?*

Yasmin blinks up at Jeanine, fear written on her face, but then her gaze moves to the doorway, the one that leads to the back of the Club and the kitchen. Her mouth forms an O in surprise.

Jeanine turns around, ready to chide whichever student found their way into this forbidden room, but when she sees Esther Kaplan standing in the doorway, cool and composed, she feels herself retreating into the girl she was in high school, desperate to please this commanding woman.

Esther smiles and crosses her arms over her chest. "Oh," she says. "Good. I was just looking for you two."

Tori

I DON'T KNOW what comes over me, but sitting here next to this woman who *knew* my mom gives me such a head rush that it's hard to think straight, to remember my speech. Esther looks to the podium as Mrs. Shalcross begins asking students to come up and give their presentations.

There are thirty-six of us in total, and we each have ninety seconds to make our case. At the end of the dinner, Club members will cast their donations, and after dessert service, the winner will be announced, a check handed over.

I pull my notecards out of my purse as waiters perform a precise choreography of passing out plates of filet mignon and branzino, the smell of butter-soaked potatoes permeating the room.

As soon as I start reading over my speech, it all comes back to me, everything I memorized at home with Joss's help. My lips move as I recite the words silently, remembering when to emphasize and when to pull back.

A hand rests on my arm and I jolt up, surprised.

"Tori," Esther says, leaning toward me. "I really do want you to have this." She reaches into her small jewel-encrusted clutch and pulls out the velvet box, the one that contained Bernie's grandmother's diamond necklace. She reaches inside and retrieves the gemstone, holding it up to my neck. "Please," she says. "Let me." I swallow the lump in my throat and let her clasp the necklace around me, feeling the weight of the stone press against my collarbone. "Take it," she says, handing me the drawstring bag.

But we both know I already have.

"Tori Tasso!" Mrs. Shalcross exclaims at the front of the room. I drop my cards and push myself to stand. Esther Kaplan rests her fingers on my arm.

"You'll excel. I know you will."

I stand and make my way to the stage, realizing that Esther is right. I *will* excel, but I'm going to do it playing by my own rules.

Bernie

MY HEART BEATS fast as Tori climbs the steps to reach the podium. I glance at Mom, who's beaming at her nominee, and feel the same sense of confusion I did only moments before. Why is Mom acting like Tori is *her* kid? Like I'm not right beside her, in need of her, too?

But I push that itchy, gnawing feeling aside and try to be happy for Tori. After all, this was what we decided should happen: Tori would take the money and keep it. That would make all of this okay.

As Tori looks out at the crowd, I catch myself inhaling sharply. She's wearing that diamond, and even I have to admit it completes the outfit magnificently, complementing her beautiful navy gown. She closes her eyes and takes a big breath. It's so quiet you can hear the sound of a fork scraping against a plate.

Tori looks around and smiles. "This week, I found out that my mother, Audra Baros, was almost one of you."

Oh no. My heart drops into my stomach, and I feel my mom tense beside me. A titter of surprise breaks out among the room. Jeanine Shalcross's face goes white at her table beside the stage.

"She was an Excelsior student, nominated with five other class-mates. But she did not make it through the end of the week. She was expelled from Excelsior, the school that she pushed me to gain entry to when I was only a freshman." Tori stops, looking around as if putting everyone on high alert. "She wanted me to go to Excelsior because she saw what it could give someone like me, someone who did not grow up in a world where entry to a club like this was a given. She saw the opportunities, the good it could do. But she also knew of its dangers and how, if I wasn't careful, I could lose myself in it."

Tori smiles. "Earlier this week, Mrs. Shalcross reminded everyone that I am the first recipient of one of the Intercollegiate League scholarships to be nominated to the Club, and for that I am grateful. But I am also inspired to continue raising money for these scholarships because I know the kind of good they can do. They can help people like me access a world that was once deemed impossible to penetrate. And yet, I understand what exclusivity can do to a young person and how detrimental it can be to their self-esteem."

Around me, I hear murmurs of agreement, of surprise.

"I'm not so naïve as to think I can change this place, but I like to think that if you were to continue supporting the Arts and Letters scholarship in my name, I, along with all the other students whose places here aren't predetermined, might help you understand how your generosity impacts us in every way. The scholarship made it possible for me to not only attend Excelsior, but thrive there academically—albeit not always socially."

Someone laughs and Tori smiles, like she's playing to the audience. "I'm honored to be among you and grateful to my nominator, Esther Kaplan. But tonight, I also remember my mother, Audra, whose love for her children was boundless. To be nominated by Esther, who knew her, is an honor. Thank you."

Mom rises in her chair and lifts her hands out in front of her, clapping them together with effusive pride. I want to tell her to calm down, but I find myself doing the same thing, reminding myself this is all part of the plan.

Isobel

WHATEVER SKYLER GAVE me is *not* sitting well. I feel like I'm sweating out of every pore of my body, and I can't seem to get comfortable, no matter what seat I find myself in. A wave of nausea hits me so uncontrollably, I keel over at our table and try to breathe.

"Are you all right?" my nominator whispers in my ear.

I nod, feeling woozy. "Just cramps."

She pats me on the hand and turns back to the stage. But all I can think of is getting to the bathroom as quickly as possible.

Mrs. Shalcross announces that we'll be taking a quick break, and I push my chair back and rush down the hall to a large bathroom with a few different stalls, the kind where the doors go all the way from floor to ceiling so it feels like you have complete privacy.

I shove open the stall at the end of the row and land on my knees in front of the toilet. As soon as I get the seat up, a river of vomit streams out of my mouth. I retch once, twice, three times. Almost immediately, I feel better. I flush and rest my head on the cool porcelain of the toilet bowl and breathe deeply, trying to bring my heart rate down.

I feel for my phone in my pocket and pull it out, texting Skyler, What the hell did you do? Poison me?

He doesn't respond, and just as I'm about to leave to wash my hands, I hear the unmistakable clip-clop of high heels entering the room, resting handbags on top of the countertop, running water at the sink.

"Well, *that* was quite a show." It's an older woman, one of the nominators, but I can't quite place her voice.

"She did great, I thought, clearly well enough to win." *Esther.* I'd recognize that trill anywhere. They must be talking about Tori. Even though I was basically comatose through her presentation, it was obvious Club members were smitten by her honesty.

"Oh, she'll definitely win," the other woman says. "But really, Esther, you think this is good enough to make the lawsuit go away?"

Something inside my body goes on high alert. *What are they talking about?*

Bernie's mom sighs. "Once she realizes what I've given her, yes."

"Please don't tell me it's anything illegal."

Esther laughs softly. "Not illegal. Just irreplaceable. Valuable beyond what she could ever ask for. Access to this. The Club." She smirks. "Now her kids won't have to grow up working at a diner. A worthy trade to get her family off our backs. Hawkins Kaplan will be *fine.*"

She must be talking to Lulu Hawkins, Skyler's mom. She clears her throat. "Emphasis on *our* backs. Don't forget you're tied up in this, too."

Esther pauses. "I'm serving Rafe the divorce papers next week."

"So, that's why you went underground. You didn't tell me."

"How could I, Lulu? You're his partner."

"And you're my friend."

There's an unsettling quiet, and I hold my breath to keep from making any noise.

"I'm not even supposed to be talking to you right now," Esther says, curt.

Lulu clucks her tongue. "Come on, Esther. You can't be serious."

"I'm protecting myself," Esther says. "You should, too."

Lulu makes a grumbling sound, and then I hear the sound of a door opening, their voices getting softer as they make their way out and into the hallway.

Finally, I bust open the door and am greeted by my own reflection in the mirror. I wipe the spit from the corners of my lips and reapply lipstick with shaky hands. But all I can wonder is *What the hell is going on with the Hawkins and Kaplan families?*

AFTER THE BALL

ESTHER GUIDES JEANINE *and Yasmin back to the ballroom, where she insists they must keep up appearances and act as leaders.*

Jeanine feels resentment grow inside her belly, but she does as Esther says, like she always has done, and she begins refreshing water glasses, breaking open extra bottles of wine, calming down the remaining Club members.

But after Esther Kaplan disappears into the kitchen, a detective approaches Mrs. Shalcross with a stoic look on his face, wondering if this is the woman he needs to break the news to. She seems like the event planner, the person who knew the ins and outs of the evening even if it was clear to him that she wasn't the mastermind.

He lowers his voice, aware that eyes are on him, necks craned in his direction.

"Do you have cameras that show what's on the roof?" he asks.

Mrs. Shalcross shakes her head. "We respect privacy here."

"Not worried about thefts? Break-ins?"

She looks aghast. "Not on the roof."

"Well, we've been up there and found evidence that more than a few people went up there tonight. By the looks of the footprints, some people in high heels. We need answers."

Mrs. Shalcross doesn't look as concerned as the detective thinks she should be, but little does he know, she's just glad this isn't about what they did to Audra all those years ago, though that would be silly, she reminds herself. It's not like they did anything illegal. Only immoral.

She's about to speak, but suddenly the room goes quiet as all eyes turn to Bernie Kaplan, who has stood up from her perch on the marble staircase. Her hand is still wrapped around that diamond necklace, and her pretty face is stained with tears as she walks toward the cadre of detectives huddled in the lobby.

She clears her throat, announcing her presence, and waits for them to turn around. When they do, she tilts her chin up and says loudly enough so everyone can hear, "I was up there. And I'm ready to talk."

Tori

MY HANDS ARE shaking as I move little bites of tiramisu around on my plate, keeping my eyes glued to the table. All around me, I can feel people looking, staring, gawking, and I wonder if I just jeopardized everything.

My phone buzzes and I see there's a text from Joss.

How'd it go? she asks.

I'm about to respond, but just then, Bernie's mom sits back down in her seat with a big sigh. "Well, that was wonderful," she says, turning to me. "You sure excited everyone here."

"Maybe it was too much?" I ask, though I'm not quite sure why I feel the need to seek her approval.

She smiles. "Too much is always the right amount in this room. Right, Bernie?"

On the other side of Esther, Bernie has been sitting there, still. Like a doll, she responds, "Right."

The rest of the presentations go off with all the excitement of a half-empty matinee. Skyler, Lee, and Kendall speak about the value of philanthropy and nothing much more. Bernie talks about her family history with the Club, and Isobel flubs her presentation quite badly, fumbling over lines she clearly didn't memorize. When she returns to her seat, her nominator whispers something in her ear that makes Isobel laugh.

After every single student has presented, Esther reappears on stage and leads the room in another round of applause.

"Now comes the fun part," she says, grinning widely. "Nominators, it's time to cast your votes in the form of donations. You will all find envelopes with donation slips inside them under your seats. Please fill them out and bring them up to the ballot box in the front of the room. Happy voting!"

The room erupts in a moment of excitement as chatter breaks out among the nominators. I scramble to stand with the rest and wonder if I should be schmoozing or trying to gain any points in any way. But when I look around the room, I see the rest of the students have gathered into a corner, so I follow Bernie to join them.

"What's going on?" I ask.

"We're not supposed to talk to them while they cast their ballots," she says. "Something about tampering or whatever."

When I look back out at all of those adults, the people who signal our future, I spy Esther and Lulu Hawkins flitting around the room, laying soft pats on the elbows of nominators, whispering behind cupped palms.

A flutter disturbs my stomach and I can't help but wonder—hope—that they're convincing them they should vote for *me*.

Bernie

MOM IS FOLLOWING through on the plan. Good.

We came up with it when I was still in her hotel room—how easy it would be to convince all the nominators that Tori was the obvious winner of the evening. After I learned all that about her mom and about how her family *still* hadn't received the settlement money, I wanted to do something, to help. When I told Mom about it, she thought it was a great idea and was eager to go through with it, even agreed that Tori should buck convention and *keep* the money that winners usually donate back to the scholarship funds.

Now, all around the ballroom, I see her using the same expression she makes when she's subtly persuading someone to do something for her. It's how she gets her favorite personal shopper at Bergdorf's to leave another customer mid-purchase to tend to her, how she gets seated at Marea after being told her table isn't quite ready yet. It's a face that manipulates with suggestion, effortless and docile. Mom's always been known as whimsical, a "breath of fresh air on New York society," as one Page Six columnist wrote after she hosted a fundraiser for the Children's Hospital. But only those close to her realize that those assumptions give her strength. Power. They allow her to walk into a crowd and leave with whatever she had deemed hers. I always thought that quality was a secret weapon, one I yearned for but could never quite attain thanks to being more tightly wound, more self-conscious and contained. But tonight . . . maybe tonight is the moment I learn we're more alike than I thought.

Streams of nominators head up to the donation box and drop their envelopes inside before flitting off to the bar. Few of the students around me seem to care what's happening, who will win, but when I look at Tori, I see she's biting her lip, her gaze focused on the ballot box.

"You did great," I say. But she just shrugs and crosses her arms across her shoulders.

"She's right." I turn around and see Skyler approaching. "You killed it, Tori."

"Shut up," she says, not looking at him.

He turns his focus to me. "Guess our moms are working the room, huh?"

My whole body tenses.

Skyler seems to be thinking this over. But then he turns to me and leans in, his mouth almost grazing my ear. "Can we talk?" he whispers.

Something inside me unlatches, and for a second, I think I might be able to pretend that we're the same as we've always been. That whatever happened between him and Opal doesn't matter. That I can get past the fact that he turned Isobel against me, used Tori, too. I agree before I can think better. "Okay."

Skyler takes my hand and leads me away from the group, down a hallway and through a back door. All of a sudden, we're in a dark passageway alone, somewhere deep inside the Club, and I wonder if I need to be scared. If Skyler would *do* something here, to me.

But then we reach a little corridor, and he pauses, holding my hand tight. He turns around so our faces are close together. I can feel the warmth from his breath, the heat from his body. There's very little light, but I can just make out his face, that strong jaw and jutting cheekbones. I shiver, a chill whipping through my skin, and Skyler shrugs off his tuxedo jacket, wrapping it around my shoulders.

"Thanks," I say, my voice a whisper.

He leans his head down toward mine, his eyes full of regret. "I'm so sorry, Bern," he says softly. "I wish I could take it all back."

A pang of regret hits my stomach, and all I want to do in this moment is forgive him.

"What can I do?" he asks, his voice warbling. "I'll do anything. I just want you back." His hands are shaking as they pull me to him, so close I can feel his pelvis against mine.

It would be so easy to say *I'm here. I'm yours.* We were destined to be together . . . until we weren't. Because that's the thing. Destiny is only as real as you make it. Disregarding our own choices, that we have the power to *make* choices . . . well, then you'll end up with a boyfriend who lies and cheats and thinks a few tears will be enough to make you forget everything horrible he did to hurt you.

I step back, out of his grasp, and shake my head, coming to my senses. "Nothing," I say. "I don't want this. I don't want you. Not anymore."

Skyler looks shocked, but then his face turns to fury.

On instinct, I run.

I head back from where we came, hearing Skyler's footsteps behind me. "Bernie," he calls. "Wait!"

But somehow, I make a wrong turn in this maze and push through a door I've never seen before. I stop short, realizing I've been spit out into the wings of the stage where the presentations took place. Skyler must have followed me, because all of a sudden, he crashes into me from behind.

"Bernie," he starts. But then I see on the stage that my mom is at the podium, and the room is hushed. She's about to read the winner.

Skyler realizes it, too, and snaps his mouth shut.

Mom opens an envelope, the sound ricocheting off the microphone out over the crowd, and takes out a thick piece of card stock. She smiles widely and looks up. I let the tension in my neck ease, knowing the name she's about to read out.

"Tori Tasso!"

The room erupts in applause, and I glance out from behind the thick velvet curtains to see Tori stand at our table, a little look of surprise and pride on her face. Mom motions for her to walk toward the stage, and as she approaches, people stand to welcome her, to praise her.

Skyler lets out a puff of air behind me. "Shocker."

I spin around. "How'd you know?"

"Well, yeah, with the lawsuit and everything."

A pit forms in my stomach. "How do you know about the lawsuit?" I pause then, thinking over his words. "Wait, what does Tori have to do with it?"

But before he can answer, Tori takes the stage. "I just want to say thank you to the nominators and everyone who has welcomed me here tonight. I know this is only the beginning of my experience with the Club, but it's a good one."

More applause, more celebrations, and then my mom ushers Tori offstage as they both walk toward us in the wings.

I ask Skyler again, "What do you know about the lawsuit?"

He looks at me, surprised. "Tori's dad is suing Hawkins Kaplan. Didn't you know?"

AFTER THE BALL

BERNIE PERCHES ON *a couch in the lounge, the skirt of her dress falling over her knees. She looks up at the detectives, her eyes gleaming with tears. Her gaze is direct but soft, making the officers comfortable. She exudes glamour and poise, with her hands folded neatly in her lap. Almost as if she rehearsed for this exact moment. Perhaps . . . she did.*

But before any of the detectives can question her demeanor, Bernie leans in with dramatic affect and begins to tell her story.

"We went up on the roof to hash things out," she says. "I take it you've already learned that things were tense this week between us. We wanted some privacy for once."

One detective leans in but tries not to appear too eager. "You said 'we' went up on the roof. Who exactly are you referring to?"

"The four of us," Bernie says with confidence. "Skyler, Isobel, Tori, and me." She shifts slightly in her seat, moving her weight from one side to the other. A more trained detective, someone skilled in reading body language or subtle movements, might take note. They might pinpoint this exact moment as the one where Bernie begins to slip. But the cops in this room . . . they can see only her pretty face stained with tears, hear the mournful lilt in her voice. They see only what she wants them to see.

"The four of you," the detective repeats tenderly, reaching to hand her a tissue. "And only three of you made it down alive?"

But before she can answer, the door swings open and Esther Kaplan stands in the entryway, hands on hips, face aflame. "Bernie Kaplan, what on earth are you doing?"

Bernie doesn't look to her mom. Instead, she glances down at her fingers. "It wasn't supposed to be like this."

But when her eyes move up, she sees that the detectives' gazes have shifted. They look upward, curiosity written on their faces. Concern. They aren't paying attention to her, don't care what she has to say.

"What?" Bernie asks. "What is it?"

The detective sniffs, then looks to her partner. "Smoke," she says. "I smell smoke."

Tori

ESTHER'S HAND IS pressed against my back as she guides me off-stage, but I can't stop looking at what's in my hand: a check for twenty-five thousand dollars. All I can think about is the look on my dad's face when I hand it to him.

"Congratulations!" Esther says once we're in the wings, clapping her hands together. When I look up, I see Skyler and Bernie standing there, slack jawed. Bernie's staring at me, dazed.

"Are you okay?" I ask her.

Bernie cocks her head. "Did you know?"

"Know what?" I ask, an unease settling in my stomach.

"Your dad," she says, stepping toward me. "The lawsuit." Bernie looks at her mom. "This is why you nominated her, isn't it? It wasn't just because you felt sorry for Audra. You wanted to get Tori in your good graces, persuade her dad to drop the suit."

"Bernie, maybe we can talk about this privately?" Esther says, lowering her voice. "I think you're mistaken."

Bernie turns to me and her eyes flit down to my collarbone, where the diamond necklace hangs against my chest. On instinct, my fingers fly up to touch it, feel the cool, sharp edges against my skin.

"You're buying her off and she doesn't even know it," Bernie hisses to her mom.

Nerves fire in my fingertips, and suddenly I feel so hot, so dizzy, like it's a feat to stay upright. "Can someone please tell me what's going on?"

Bernie looks at me hard. "Your dad is suing Hawkins Kaplan. Says they've stolen the settlement money they owe you."

I shake my head. Dad would have told me that. Wouldn't he have?

But maybe . . . if he knew it involved Bernie and Skyler, people in my class, maybe he would have wanted to shield me from the truth, make it less awkward. Especially once my Club nomination came in the mail.

"Mom found out about it and wanted to keep all this quiet, so she devised a plan to bring you into this, to *buy* your loyalty." Bernie nods to the envelope I'm holding. "Who do you think gussied up donations for you?" She slams her palm on her forehead. "I told her to do that."

I look down at the check, the one that gave me so much hope. So much promise. But what if Bernie's right? What if this was all a ruse? A lie at my expense?

Skyler scoffs. "As if twenty-five thousand dollars would make a dent. That suit is for millions."

I snap my head around. "How the hell do you know?"

He starts to open his mouth, but Bernie steps in.

"And now, Mom has given you that necklace. Do you know how much it's worth, Tori?"

I shake my head, feeling the diamond heavy against my skin.

Esther sighs, resigned. "Seventy thousand dollars. You'll see the insurance slip and deed transferred to your name in your email soon."

My jaw drops open as I try to make sense of all this. "I don't understand. How . . . why . . ."

Esther steps so close to me I can smell her perfume—lilac and expensive—and see the faint lines beaming from her eyes. There's a shift, like she's changing course, unveiling a mask. She narrows her brows and speaks quietly, slowly. "Your father's actions could jeopardize the entirety of Hawkins Kaplan," Esther says. "Our families. Our futures. I did all of this"—she gestures around the room—"with the hopes that it might persuade you to put an end to it. It's not everything your father thinks you're owed, but it's a start. You could sell the necklace, or better yet, wear it to all of the events that just opened their doors to you." She sweeps her arm around, gesturing to all . . . this. "See, Tori, I've given you entrée into a society that never would have been yours otherwise. I'll personally make sure you get what you need out of this. Something no amount of money could buy. Status. Class. Belonging."

My heart is in my throat and I can feel my spine tingling, my fingers twitch. Earlier in the day she had sounded so supportive, so ebullient. But now, she's not asking me to consider her request. Even through this guise, I can see she's demanding.

"Plus," Esther continues, "your father probably hasn't even thought of all the legal bills that will follow. He'll be up to his eyeballs in retainer fees for years all because Hawkins Kaplan is a little late on the funds? They'll come. They *always* come. Is this all really that big of a deal?"

I look at this woman, the one who *knew* my mother and then put a price tag on her death, who is no more than a criminal in sparkling Jimmy Choos. She's tempting me. Throwing every single thing she knows that I want right into my grasp. But then it dawns on me why she wants the lawsuit to go away: Because she knows we'd win. She knows Hawkins Kaplan has done something wrong. And suddenly, the answer to her question is obvious.

"No."

Before she can lunge for me, I take off running.

Isobel

WHERE THE FUCK *is everyone?*

The whole party has loosened up, and the lines at the bar are now filled with students who are being served without any sort of oversight. The mood has shifted, ever so slightly, from that of a stiff intergenerational work event to a celebratory holiday party where the rules are more like suggestions. Lee is deep in conversation with some of the Tucker Day kids, sipping on what looks to be Scotch served in crystal tumblers. I turn away, eager for a distraction. A waiter walks by with a tray of champagne flutes, and I grab a full one, downing half of the bubbles in one swig.

Now that my stomach has settled, it goes down easy. I finish the glass and reach for another, from a different tray. It hits me fast, which makes me realize I should find something to eat since I just puked up my entire dinner. I drain the second glass of champagne and ignore the dizzy feeling in my head as I follow the sound of pans banging and utensils scraping food off plates.

I can see the kitchen just down the hall, but all of a sudden, there's a commotion in the stairwell. A flash of blue—Tori—running up the stairs of the mazelike building.

I pause, wondering where she's going, but it doesn't take long for Bernie to run up behind her, the train of her green dress trailing, and Skyler to bring up the rear.

"Bernie!" Skyler calls. "Wait up."

They ascend the stairs behind Tori as Bernie calls after her, a desperate plea in her voice. "Can we talk about this?" she calls. But Tori doesn't answer, just disappears farther into the bowels of the building.

I know I have two options: turn around and head back into the ballroom, or run right after them. But there's really no time to decide, because my body propels me forward, following their footsteps even deeper into the Club.

Bernie

MY HIGH-HEELED FEET burn as I follow Tori, listening for her footsteps as the noise from the party below recedes into the background. Skyler is right behind me, his breath labored as we move quickly up the stairs.

If she'd only stop. If she'd only let us talk to her. Maybe then she might understand that dropping the suit could be *good* for her. She would realize that our parents aren't withholding any money. It takes *time* for cases to be paid out. I've seen it over and over with Dad's clients. They always get the money, even if it takes a little while. So much red tape. Bureaucracy or whatever. That *must* be what's happening here. There's no way Hawkins Kaplan would do anything illegal.

Skyler lets out a frustrated growl behind me. "What?" I ask over my shoulder as we climb another set of stairs.

"I just never thought Tori Fucking Tasso would be the reason our parents go to jail," he says, panting.

I stop short and swivel my head to look at him. "Jail?"

Skyler looks at me, his head cocked. "The lawsuit," he says. "Her dad is right. They don't have the money. They spent it all."

"What are you talking about?"

"You don't know? Hawkins Kaplan has been doing this kind of shit for years. Stealing money from their clients." He shakes his head. "They just always came up with enough funds to cover their asses. Not this time, though. The firm's broke."

My jaw drops open. "How . . . how do you know?"

Skyler begins to laugh, his head tossed back.

"What could possibly be so funny right now?" I cross my arms over my chest, panic building in my stomach.

Skyler leans forward, resting his palm on the handrail to steady himself as he finally stops laughing. "Bernie, how could you not know? There have been signs for years."

I shake my head. "You're lying."

"You're joking, right? All the Hamptons houses, the private jets to vacations, the yacht? You thought that was just through our parents' work? Your mom's inheritance?" All of a sudden, a look of pity comes across Skyler's face, and I want to smack it right off his skin. "Bernie, there's no way in hell we'd have all that stuff if our parents *didn't* steal."

"You're wrong," I say, blinking back tears. "Hawkins Kaplan *helps* people."

Skyler purses his lips. "Remember back when they won that water case in Idaho? The first big one?"

I nod. That was the case that put them on the map, that made them stars.

"That was the only legit one," Skyler says. "After that, they started skimming a little off the top of each settlement, taking a bit more than they should, using the next case fees to pay out their clients. It was wild."

"How do you know this?" My voice is a whisper, hoarse and fearful.

Skyler shrugs. "I asked Mom about it last year. She came clean, said I'd find out eventually and that lots of legal firms do it. I thought you knew, too." I blink back at him and he sighs. "Look, it's only a big deal because they fucked up this time. They took too much, didn't have the funds coming to cover themselves right away, and now we're screwed thanks to Tori and her dad getting a bit too eager to get that cash."

"Are you joking?" I ask. "Listen to yourself. You're a monster. Don't you think they deserve that settlement money?"

Skyler shrugs. "That's not my role to decide."

"Your *role*? Who do you think you are?"

"Look, I'm trying to save our families' asses, and I feel like you should be, too." Skyler reaches for my hand, but I pull away, disgusted to even be this close to him. "That's why your mom gave her the necklace as a gift," he says. "Free and clear, no strings attached."

Blood money.

Our eyes lock, and a realization washes over me: Tori's dad was right. Hawkins Kaplan did steal from the Tassos. Other clients, too. And their whole empire is about to come crumbling down, taking us innocents with them, too.

Looking at the terror and the understanding in Skyler's eyes, I know that we're both well aware what could happen if Hawkins Kaplan goes down in disgrace: Not only would our families lose ungodly amounts of money that have kept us comfortable all these years, but perhaps worse, we'd lose our standing. Our stature. The respectability that comes with being on the right side of wealth, the side that *helps* people fight bad guys, as our parents always said they did.

But in a matter of minutes, it's dawned on me that all along they *were* the bad guys.

And yet, I can't quite reckon what might become of us without them, the power we've been given because of them.

I swallow hard. "She could ruin us."

Skyler nods.

He extends his hand toward me, and as I look at his palm, familiar and warm and full of betrayal, I feel a push and pull deep within me. I can take Skyler's hand. We can confront Tori together. We can persuade her to stop the suit, to take the money and leave our families out of it. Or I can go against everything that's been ingrained in me since I was a child—I can defy my mom, Skyler, the entirety of Hawkins Kaplan, and help Tori, tell her to go after what's hers.

But maybe, just maybe, there's a third option, too, that will somehow leave all of our futures intact.

I take Skyler's hand, and together we push farther into the Club, as I hope with all my heart that my instincts are right.

Tori

I CAN HEAR them close, trailing behind me, and I have no idea where to go, what to do, except follow my body telling me to *run*, to get away from these people—these monsters—as fast as I can. I reach the second floor and see a wide-open living room with leather couches and bookshelves that extend from the floor to the ceiling with nowhere to hide.

My breath starts to give way as I climb the next set of stairs. I throw open a door and am spit out on the top floor, where a felt-lined pool table is surrounded by mahogany armchairs and a wet bar. I look around, searching for a way out, and see, in the corner of the room, a narrow set of stairs. I dart to them and start to ascend, realizing quickly that they lead to the roof.

"Tori!" Bernie calls, out of breath. Footsteps clod up the stairs behind me. Fear pounds in my stomach, and I can't quite figure out why. It's not that Bernie or Skyler would put me in *danger*, but as I push open the door to the roof and feel the heavy summer air warm against my skin, I can't help but wonder if they might. After all, my family is about to rip theirs apart.

But when I think about it, haven't they already done that to mine?

Up on the roof, I look out at the skyline. This city. This fucking city. It's the place that people think will make their dreams come true, where they can come to be whoever they want. But no one will tell them the truth: that there are so many people here who already have what you want, and they'll do anything to make sure you don't get it.

The door opens again with a resounding thud against the brick wall, and I see Bernie and Skyler rush toward me.

"Stop, Tori," Bernie says. "I just want to talk."

I spin around, looking for a way out, an exit, and then finally I see a fire escape ladder that leads down, down, down. As I make a move toward it, I feel the hurtling of limbs and pressure as I'm thrown to the ground, a body smack down on top of me. I smell sweat and mint and hair gel and realize it's Skyler, tackling me to the ground. His arm is pressed against my throat, tightening my airway, and I gasp for breath. *Help*, I try to scream. *Help*.

Nothing comes out.

Fear takes over.

Is this how it ends?

Isobel

I DART THROUGH the dark maze of the Club, bumping into side tables and chairs as I hustle up the steps, where I heard them go before. I burst through a door and see a pool table. This must be the top floor. Nowhere else to go. But where are they?

I fumble on the wall for a light switch, and when my fingers find one, I flip it, illuminating the room.

The walls are a rich hunter green, offsetting the upholstered chairs, the dark wood billiards table, the thick velvet drapes. The whole place reminds me of one of those lounges you see in old movies where only white men were allowed and cigars were at the ready.

I tiptoe around the room, listening for signs of Bernie, Skyler, or Tori, but I don't hear anything. Where could they have gone?

I run my hands over a marble chessboard, a row of bows and arrows mounted on the wall, a lamp made of ostrich skin. Along the far wall are bookshelves, lined with ancient hardcovers. There are sets proclaiming complete works of William Blake and Aristotle, rare first editions of Virginia Woolf titles. I press my fingers to one and try to pull it out, but the book doesn't move. I try another one, a thin Plato manuscript, but that, too, is stuck in place.

My nerves click on and I try another tactic. I push, and suddenly a creaking sound fills the room. I lurch forward as the whole bookshelf moves inward, revealing a dark room inside the wall. I hear myself gasp but step forward, drawn into the space, until suddenly, without warning, the shelf closes behind me and I'm enveloped in darkness.

Bernie

"GET OFF OF her." I lunge for Skyler and pull at the collar of his jacket so he falls back, away from Tori. She's splayed out there on the ground, the silk pleats on her beautiful dress torn, trying to catch her breath. She pushes herself up and rests her hands against the ground, her chest heaving up and down.

I extend a hand to her. "You're okay," I say. "You're okay."

Tori swivels her head to look at me, her hair mussed and her eyes on fire. "Okay?" she asks, her voice rising. "I am *not* okay. He just tried to fucking kill me." She points a shaking finger at Skyler, and I see she's chipped her manicure in the tussle.

She swats my hand away and stands, her fists clenched by her side.

"You two are made for each other with your fucked-up parents." She shakes her head. "You really think you can *buy* me? My mom's dead, and your parents said they could help us." Tears are streaming down her face. Her lip quivers. "It's like you're killing her again."

I suck in a breath of air and realize she's right. I can't force her to keep quiet about this, to take the money and run. What would I do if this were *my* mom? If some hawkish lawyers tried to come in and make a buck off her death? I blink back tears, the reality of what's happened crashing down on me.

Skyler's pacing along the roof and I can tell he doesn't feel the same. He's wringing his hands, not looking in our direction. It's like he's trying to figure out what to do next.

"Look," he says to Tori. "You realize that if your dad files this suit, Hawkins Kaplan will probably never recover from this?"

"Are you fucking serious?" she yells. "We're talking about my *mom*, not some random person. I think the least we can do is try to get justice."

Skyler's face is pleading. "Tori, come on. Just take the money and run. That's *cash*. You really want our families to go down, too?"

Tori laughs. "If you think I give a fuck about what happens to your families, you're more delusional than I thought."

Skyler turns to me, insistent. "Come on, Bernie. Right?" He's looking at me with a sense of certainty that I'll follow him, no matter what. That I'm like him—like our parents. That I'll stop at nothing to get what I want, that I'll kick everyone else in the teeth just to do so. He's not wrong.

"Bernie?" Skyler says again, his voice desperate. "Help me out here."

The summer breeze whips at my earrings, warm against my skin.

Tori's staring at me, her eyes huge like saucers, and suddenly I know exactly what to do.

I clear my head, tune everything out, and all at once, I charge straight at Tori, lunging right for her neck.

Isobel

I SWALLOW THE lump in my throat and try to ignore the pounding in my head, the bubbles from the champagne swirling around at an odd clip. *Breathe. Breathe.*

I take a step forward and suddenly a light flickers on, a motion sensor activated. I let out a puff of air and take in my surroundings, my eyes adjusting to the dim light.

It's a tight room, perhaps the size of a walk-in closet, with enough space to fit a writing desk and dozens of filing cabinets that are stacked in neat, vertical columns. Each cabinet is labeled with a year, and when I pull open the most recent one, I see dozens of manila folders with handwritten names on the tabs. Some are stuffed full and wide, and others are slim with only a few sheets of paper. They're filed alphabetically, and there's one for each nominee. I scan the rest of the cabinets and see that they go back to the early 1900s.

Curiosity pools in my gut and I reach for Bernie's, filed in the middle of the row. Hers is full of glowing referrals from many club members and teachers, photos of her hanging out at Legacy-sponsored family events. Nothing that surprising. I clench my fists and stick it back in its place.

Then I glance toward the back, where my eye catches Tori's. I pull it out and find it's thin with only a few sheets of paper inside. I thumb through and stop when I see a piece of paper that says the words NOMINATION FORM bolded at the top. Esther's scrawl is all over it, in great big loops and sloping letters.

Most of the sections are short, but when I get to one that says, *Why should this senior be let into the Legacy Club above all other seniors?* I stop.

Most members know the story of Tori's mother, Audra, Esther had written. *Tori belongs in this club as much as any other true Legacy, any other student whose parents were members of the club, even though Audra did not make it through nominations week. I believe letting Tori, an excellent student and member of the Intercollegiate League community, into the Legacy Club would right that wrong once and for all.*

Tori's mother was a Legacy? *Almost* a Legacy? And Esther knew about it? I scan the rest of Tori's folder for answers, but there's nothing else there. Did Bernie know about this? Did Tori? This was definitely something one of them would have mentioned, but neither one of them did, not during this whole week. But there's nothing to do now except set Tori's folder back in its place, to let those questions go unanswered.

Looking at the folders, my stomach tingles with curiosity. Right in front of Tori's, mine is larger than the others around it, hefty and thick. I pull it out and flip it open to find my class photo staring back at me, half smiling, my dark bob out of my eyes. It was taken only last fall, but I look so different, so calm. My skin is tan and healthy, and my eyes are focused. Direct. I can't look at her anymore—that girl who had so much and couldn't even see it.

I flip the page and find dozens of copies of my artwork, printed out from my website and my school portfolio. I feel a flicker of pride as I see my work, bold and stark even in the dark room. Behind that are press clippings from my Brooklyn Museum show, a little clip in *New York* magazine calling me a "young talent." A smile tugs at my lips.

Then I see school transcripts, a referral from my art teacher at Excelsior, and dossiers on each of my parents. There's even a short typed-up memo about Marty, spelling out what he's been up to since high school. It all feels a little invasive, obsessive.

When I reach the end, I find one thin sheet of paper, my own form. I scan the page and see it's been filled out by Rachel Breathwaite, my nominator, who made little notes about why I might be a worthy addition to the Club.

One question says, *What would this person add to our Club?* Rachel had written, *Isobel is a once-in-a-generation artist with determination and focus I see in few young people. With a creative mind and a rebellious spirit, she is unlike others who are sure to be nominated, and she will be unique in this group, which can sometimes blend together in its similarities.*

I let out a breath of air, a tinge of embarrassment at reading these sorts of compliments, so rarely shared with their recipients. I keep reading down the page until I see one final question that sends a shock down my spine.

Please describe any challenges your nominee might face.

Below it, Rachel had written a short paragraph, but as I read her words, my heart rises in my throat.

It seems that Isobel has a penchant for illicit substances—mostly legal ones—and though that does not affect her art or productivity, she is known to be somewhat unpredictable and erratic at times. If her nomination is approved, I would make sure that her habits do not influence her standing as a Legacy member who brings honor to the Club.

My hands start shaking and I drop the papers.

A penchant for illicit substances.

Unpredictable and erratic.

For a second, I can't see. I can't breathe. It feels like the whole world has just seen me naked—that there is a massive spotlight on me, and no matter where I go in this building, I cannot hide. I am a raw nerve, exposed. And there's nothing I can do about it.

I sink down onto my heels and press the heels of my hands to my head. I try to blink, to catch my breath, but my gaze is unsteady and blurry, until I focus on something small and papery, wedged in between the filing cabinets. One of those Legacy Club match-books I saw on the bar. I reach for it without thinking and flip it open, ripping one small stick from its place. I swipe it against the striker, watching the flame ignite. The heat is so close to my fingers, and they begin to sting.

I pick up one sheet from the ground, dipping the corner into the flame. I watch as it burns, as the heat takes over and becomes a pile of ash. I lift another sheet and do the same. Again, again, and again until there are only tiny embers on the carpet. I stand on wobbly legs and turn toward the rest of the files. I see my future, the future of this club, and I want to watch it burn.

I drop the match, burned out to a crisp, and pull out another one. Light it. Hold it so close to the manila folders, so close to the entire tinderbox before me, but then I hear a loud and violent noise just above my head, the heavy sound of metal and bone. A scream.

I let out a rush of air and the flame goes out between my fingers. I shove my shoulder against the bookshelf from which I came and land on the other side of the room, where I hear another sound come from above. A sliver of light peeks out from a ladder on the other side of the room.

The roof.

They must be on the roof.

AFTER THE BALL

BY NOW, DAYLIGHT *has begun to break over the Manhattan skyline, but inside the Legacy Club, there are no urns of coffee. No bacon. No French toast. Instead, detectives fly up the stairs, a frantic call to the fire department made with labored breath. They follow the heat, the odor, the wretched fear that something inside this building is burning.*

When they reach the landing, they stop and see smoke billowing out, improbably, from under a bookcase. But there is no time for confusion. No time for haste.

Esther Kaplan is on their heels and shrieks in horror when she realizes what is on fire. What is gone.

Glass smashes. An extinguisher lets loose, and as soon as the secret passageway is revealed, before the flames engulf them all, the room fills with white, with chemicals. In another season, one may think snow.

As the dust settles, all they see is what was once a room full of paper—of information and power and secrets. It's here, now, that Esther begins to weep.

Tori

BERNIE PINS ME to the ground in a hard thud and wraps her hand tightly around the diamond hanging from my neck.

"What the hell are you doing?" I scream.

Her eyes are frantic and it looks like she's trying to tell me something, to relay some message, but what Bernie's forgetting is that I barely know *or* trust her. The idea of us sharing some secret language is laughable, unimaginable.

But then she leans down close to me, her voice clear and determined but soft so Skyler can't hear. "Don't fight it."

We lock eyes, and in an instant, I catch my breath. I decide to give in. I may regret it, but in this moment, I close my eyes and rip the diamond from my neck, resting it in her hand. Bernie looks at it, eyes wide, and steps back.

Skyler looks at us, confounded. "What are you doing?"

Bernie glances over her shoulder at him, and then turns away from me so her body is between mine and Skyler's.

"Who made us the judges here? I don't want to keep living off stolen funds, taken from people who need it more than we do." She spins around again. "Do whatever you want, Tori. Nothing will change what our parents did."

Skyler shakes his head, incredulous. "You're out of your fucking mind, Bernie. You have no idea what you're doing." He takes a step toward us, eyes narrowed, fists forming at his side. His face twists into something raw and menacing, a look I've never seen on his face before. His gray eyes grow stormy, and his hair is slicked back with sweat.

"What are you gonna do?" Bernie taunts. "Come and get this stupid necklace? It's not even worth a fraction of what she's owed." Bernie backs up against the metal railing that hits the back of her thighs. She seems unsure, holding the diamond in her hand, and looks up at Skyler, her eyes pleading, on fire.

Skyler's face tenses and for a second, I see him for who he really is—a boy who isn't used to hearing no. In an instant, he lunges at Bernie, his fists curled around her shoulders. Terror flashes on her face, but then she looks at me, asking if I understand and suddenly, I do.

Bernie holds onto the necklace, her other hand reaching down to grab around the iron railing behind her, and as she wrestles with Skyler, trying to reach for the diamond, Bernie shoves it toward him and with her free hand, grabs ahold of his forearm. She yanks him toward her, so hard he loses his balance, so hard he . . .

"Bernie!" I yell. My voice carries out into the night. But it gets drowned out by another sound. A scream so loud and soaring, it pierces my ears, the city, the whole night sky. A scream from Skyler as he tumbles over the railing, down, down, down.

Bernie

THE YANK COMES suddenly, without thought or foresight or planning of any kind. It comes through me and out my arm, graceful and quiet, until suddenly, I see a look of surprise come over Skyler's face as he realizes he's going over the low railing of the roof, dropping fast and hard to the ground beneath us in the garden with a resounding, terrifying shriek until his voice fades, echoing into the night.

For one moment, I don't hear a thing, and all I feel is relief. I needed to never be under his thumb again—to retreat from the interconnectedness of our families. I needed to put an end to the idea that our two families will be intertwined for good, forever, through us.

But as quickly as it came, the quiet is broken suddenly by another horrifying wail. The door bursts open and I hear a familiar voice—Isobel's—who yells my name and rushes to me and wraps her arms around me, and I realize the horrible sound, the scream, is not coming from the ground. No. The scream is coming from me.

Tori

HE WENT DOWN so fast. Faster than I thought he might. Almost elegantly, like a feather floating to the floor. And then, in an instant, a sick, wet thud. Skin and bone and brain hitting grass and ground and meticulously planted flower beds.

Then . . . nothing.

Isobel

BERNIE IS A puddle on the ground and my instinct is to comfort her, to shield her, and so I do, wrapping my body around hers. Tori stands behind us, her mouth hung open, her arms hanging limply by her side. She turns to both of us slowly, her eyes wide and on fire. In this light, she looks radiant.

"Bernie," she says. "What have you done?"

Bernie

ISOBEL RESTS HER cool hands on my cheeks and whispers something in my ear. "An accident," she says. "It was an accident."

Tori's face is gray and solemn, but she nods and repeats the word. "Accident."

Isobel looks at me, so cool and comforting. The Isobel I've always known, who can defy reality with her imagination, her talent. The one who, before this summer, was like my other half.

She repeats the words; she commands me to say them, too. "It was an accident."

I repeat after her.

"It was an accident."

Isobel

SOMETHING INSIDE OF me lights up, and it's as if every nerve is firing, alive. I usher Tori and Bernie back into the Club, down the stairs that descend to where the party is—was. Because now everyone is standing on the first floor, staring blankly out at the garden through the floor-to-ceiling windows as Lulu Hawkins sobs on the steps, while a man tries and fails to bring her back inside, to comfort her, to eliminate the pain.

That's when the commotion starts.

An ambulance arrives. The crying begins.

Sirens wail. Red lights flash through the sky like fireworks.

Bernie rushes to the garden and falls to her knees, her emerald-hued dress now stained with mud. She digs her fingers into the ground and lets out a choked sob, and for a moment, I can't tell if she's playing a part. Everyone is watching, their breathing shallow, as Bernie reaches for Skyler—the body—her fingers trailing in the pool of blood.

It's too much, too sickening, and without warning, I vomit thin, yellow liquid onto the floor.

"Shit," Tori says beside me. But no one else notices. No one cares.

Because now the Club has erupted, and someone has rushed to Bernie's side, and I'm standing here next to Tori, realizing that everything is different.

THE MORNING
AFTER THE BALL

BERNIE'S TRUTH SPREADS *fast among the elite, appearing in group chats, on voice mails. Skyler Hawkins is dead. Fell off the roof of the Legacy Club. It was an accident. A tragic accident. A horrible end to a beautiful night. He had been drinking. Mixed alcohol with a painkiller. He had stood too close to the edge, to that low, low railing, and was so devastated that everyone had turned on him, had held him accountable for his actions.*

Rumors swirl, of course.

Perhaps he threw himself off. It wasn't out of the question. His lies had come out, after all. How he cheated on Bernie. How he tried to hide it by blackmailing Tori and Isobel.

But murder? No one suspects murder. Not after Bernie revealed what happened, how the girls confronted Skyler about all his misdeeds, how they left him up there, crying and delirious. How when they last saw him, he was still alive.

Everyone believes her.

Isobel and Tori backed up Bernie's statements in their own interviews, conducted separately, later in the evening.

They all kept saying that word: accident. *It was an accident.*

But if it was, then why did forensics find scratches on his arms? DNA under his fingernails? Why did it look like he had been in a fight? And why had a room full of files burned to a crisp?

No one wants to entertain this theory, least of all the members of the

Legacy Club. When the detective broached it with one of the adults in charge, a towering redhead who said she had known the deceased from birth, Esther Kaplan dismissed it entirely.

"Let us grieve in peace," she said firmly, ending the conversation altogether.

As the sun rises and the caution tape comes down, the detectives close their notebooks. They bid farewell. The Club is no longer a crime scene, just a reminder. And so, the members of law enforcement leave the building, hoping never, ever to return again.

TWO WEEKS
AFTER THE BALL

Tori

"SO, SHOULD WE meet at the bookstore or the diner after school?" Joss is bouncing up and down in my kitchen, two foil-wrapped bacon, egg, and cheeses in front of us on the counter. It's been tradition for us to spend the evening together after the first day of school ever since we were kids, but I know Joss is trying to distract me from what we both know is coming—news of the lawsuit breaking.

"The diner," I say, picking at a stray cuticle on my thumb. A bad habit I picked up after the Ball. The accident.

"Good call. I could definitely use some afternoon spinach pie." She glances at my phone, which I'm clutching in my hands. "Up yet?"

I'm refreshing the *New York Times* homepage, and when it loads, I shake my head. "Not yet."

"Bernie okay?" Joss looks at me with concern. Ever since the Ball, she's been protective, worried that Bernie and Isobel are going to turn on me at any second, throw me under the bus and say *I* killed Skyler out of rage. I've tried to tell her that they won't. That there are so few words to explain what happened between the three of us that night. That for whatever reason, maybe the wrong one, I trust those girls. In spite of everything, I do.

I swallow the lump in my throat and tap over to my most recent text with Bernie, received last night at four in the morning. She doesn't sleep anymore. Neither do I.

Mom's gone again, but at least this time I know where. Holed up in the Hamptons. Kept her location sharing on and everything. She says she'll come back once it blows over.

She sent another one after that.

IF! It blows over. Or they lose the penthouse. Whatever happens first.

I get ping, a text from Isobel, and almost drop my phone when I see it's a link to the *Times*.

"It's here," I say. Joss rushes to my side, and we both watch as an image of my mom smiling and holding me, Helen, and George loads, taking over the whole screen. I see Isobel's brother Marty's headline first and remember how grateful he was when we came to him, when we gave him the scoop. He sat quietly as Dad and his lawyer told him our story, taking notes and looking over the legal documents.

Now the headline is stark and simple: *Hawkins Kaplan Accused of Embezzling Funds from Clients.*

I let out a shaky breath and look up at Joss, my eyes blinking back tears.

"We did it," I say, and let her hug me so hard it hurts.

Isobel

MARTY'S COME OVER this morning to send me off to school so we can read his Hawkins Kaplan article in print, together at our kitchen table.

He hands me a mug of coffee, and we spread out the paper, quiet as the reality sets in. The final paragraph of the story mentions the Ball and Skyler. The accident.

"They wanted you to add that, huh?" I ask.

Marty nods. "Editor said it was contextual, since Rafe and Lulu met through the Legacy Club and all."

"But nothing about Audra?"

Marty blushes and shakes his head. "They didn't really understand how it was connected or why it mattered that Esther nominated Tori." He shrugs. "Too insider-y."

I understand, really I do, because I still don't understand everything either, why it felt significant to read about Tori's mom in those files. But maybe some questions are best left unanswered. I learned that at my ten-day detox program in the Catskills, that sometimes it's better to let things stay buried. The hardest part is knowing *which* things.

But I'm starting to understand. After all, only the three of us know what really happened on that roof.

Bernie

WALKING INTO EXCELSIOR today is unlike any other day I've experienced at this school, the one that raised me. It was the only first day of school that Mom didn't insist on accompanying me. She's hardened, since I gave her back the diamond necklace and she realized Tori wasn't going to do anything to stop her father from filing the lawsuit.

But we did have one real conversation, tucked in her bed wearing matching silk pajamas the night after Skyler's funeral. We were lying side by side, our heads propped up on three pillows each, not looking at one another, only forward at the TV playing Bravo on the far wall. I was numb. Exhausted from the summer, from knowing my life as I knew it was over, and in this tender moment, I wondered if Mom was, too.

But then she cleared her throat and told me she was decamping for the Hamptons as soon as she gave my dad divorce papers.

I knew it was coming, but that didn't stop the tears from stinging my eyes.

"It's for the best, Bernie," she said, reaching for my hand.

I pulled away from her knowing that if she were to finish that sentence out loud, what she might really say was *for me. It's for the best for me.* My eyes roamed the room, searching for something to hold on to, and then I saw in the corner on the floor, the photo of her and Audra, the one that used to sit in her office, now lying on the carpet, half hidden by a silk scarf.

"Why did you keep it?" I asked.

"Keep what?"

I nodded to the frame. "After everything . . . why?"

The sheets beside me rustled and Mom sat up. "It was a reminder," she said. "To always look out for myself."

That's when Mom told me the truth about what she and her friends did to Audra all those years ago, how she really did want to make amends with her—even in death—by having Dad's firm get them the best settlement she could. She knew they took extra bonuses, as she called them, every now and then. How could she not? But the clients always got their money. Always. Until this time. Until they juggled the books the wrong way.

I hated her in that moment, but I also understood her better than I ever thought I wanted to and for one moment, I felt calm. So, when she left for the beach house yesterday and Dad received the divorce papers while he was sitting with me at the marble counter eating breakfast, all I could feel was relief that at least this time I knew where she was going. At least this time, I had answers, and maybe when she returned, we could start to rebuild.

I vow to tell Tori about my mom, not today but sometime soon. When I get the strength. But I can't think about that now, not as I head into school on a day that's so different, so strange, so empty because for the first time in my life, Skyler is no longer by my side—and I'm the reason why.

People don't know how to treat me now. I can see that as I ascend the marble steps, past the Wall of Fame and through the corridors. Underclassmen turn to look at me, whispering to their friends, *That's her.* I throw my hair back and set my mouth into a trembling frown. I welcome their gazes. Because what else can I do? Admit what really happened? Explain that I did it on purpose?

"There you are." I turn and see Isobel rushing toward me, her bob neatly in place, her skin a little brighter than it was a few weeks ago. She hands me an iced coffee and wraps me in a fierce hug. "You . . . ?"

She knows better than to ask if I'm okay because she knows I'm not. We've been *us* again since the Ball, the weight of what happened at that Shelter Island party suddenly so insignificant, so paltry compared with the reality we're experiencing now.

I shrug and Isobel accepts this, looping her arm in mine as we walk toward the amphitheater for our welcome-back assembly. I scan the crowd and spot Lee standing off in the corner, talking to some of the guys from his Environmental Science Club. He wanted to get back together with Isobel after what happened, but I was proud of her for saying no, for admitting she liked his family more than she liked him. And soon after, she left for the Catskills instead.

She said the program is working, that she told her parents about her habits and asked them to help hold her accountable. She said she wants to stay clean so I decided to join her sobriety, which I think will be good for us. But we'll see how it goes, how she heals.

Lee looks at both of us, his eyes full of sorrow, and I can't hold his gaze for too long or else I'll start to feel bad, to understand what I ripped away from him, too. So, I blink back tears and set my sights on Kendall, who's got his nose in some novel that seems bigger than his backpack. He looks up and smiles at Isobel, who blushes.

I won't push her on that one just yet.

Isobel and I slide into velvet theater seats, our shoulders touching as everyone else takes their places. Someone approaches our row and clears their throat. "Mind if I join?"

I look up to see Tori, her face flushed and a small smile dancing on her lips. She's wearing the same Doc Martens she wore all last year, her white button-down cuffed up to the elbows. She plops down, and I reach over Isobel to grab her hand. I don't say anything—there's nothing that could convey what I'm feeling, the kind of enormity and guilt and heartache that comes over me when I look at her and when I think about what my family did to hers, what she's been through. But when she squeezes back, I know things will be okay. She will be okay.

The lights go down, and the velvet curtains that were shielding the stage come up, revealing a ten-foot-high image of Skyler projected on the screen. My stomach tenses and I feel like I might throw up.

His piercing gray eyes stare back at me, taunting, furious. I want to look away, to rush out of the room and flee, but the spectacle is impossible to ignore. *He* is impossible to ignore. The boy I knew. His beauty and his flaws, his terrible, ugly insides. It's a tragedy what happened. But after all he did to Tori, to Isobel, to Opal, to me . . . well, I have to imagine they would have done the exact same thing I did.

THE NEXT MORNING

MOST OF THE *residents in Astoria are still sleeping when the mail carrier arrives at the Tassos' home. She gathers a stack of envelopes from her cart and leaves them in a hanging metal box as she does most mornings before going on her way, stopping at every building on the block to deliver bills, coupons, and the occasional handwritten letter composed with care and affection.*

But although this is a regular morning just like any other, she has no idea that the bulge of mail left for the Tasso family will change the teenage girl who lives in that home forever.

Inside one of those envelopes is a note, written on the personalized stationery of Yasmin Gellar, her words scrawled in a felt-tip pen across page after page.

When Tori awakes, excited for her second day of school, she is surprised to find Mrs. Gellar's letter left in a pile of mail on the counter. It's addressed to her in neat cursive handwriting, an ode to the past, to the formality Mrs. Gellar employs in every aspect of her life. Tori sits down at the kitchen table with a bowl of cereal, expecting a letter about the Legacy Club—about her winnings. But as she reads the words, the stories about her mother and her friendships, the devastation her mother endured at the hands of women she trusted, Tori's breakfast grows limp and soggy, forgotten.

When Tori reaches the end of the letter, her fingerprints visible on the edges, she lets out a shaky breath. What she holds in her hands is the truth. Answers to so many questions. And so, she reads it all again, just to make sure she has it right, that she finally knows her mother's story.

Dear Tori, *Mrs. Gellar has written.* I've wanted to tell you this from the moment I knew you existed, and I finally have the courage. It's time to explain the truth about your mother and what we did to her all those years ago . . .

ACKNOWLEDGMENTS

I am so very grateful, once again and always, to Alyssa Reuben for guarding and steering my literary career with care, precision, humor, and honesty. I dare not think about where I might be without you in my corner.

Thank you to Rūta Rimas, who pushed me to make this story work because you knew I could (that we could). I am in awe of your editorial prowess, your thoughtfulness, and your magical ability to make everything—truly, everything!—better. Thank you to Simone Roberts-Payne, a fierce editor in her own right, whose insights elevated *The Legacies* in ways big and small.

Elyse Marshall, my trusted publicist, thank you for moving mountains on my behalf and for so many comforting phone calls and emails.

To Jen Klonsky, Jen Loja, and Casey McIntyre: Thank you for giving me, time and time again, a home within Razorbill, and for continuing to champion my work.

Working with the wonderful team at Penguin Young Readers has been one of the best parts of this job, and I would be remiss not to mention those whose tireless work has contributed to my own success. Thank you for your support in helping authors shine in every aspect of this industry: James Akinaka, Kristin Boyle, Christina Colangelo, Rob Farren, Olivia Funderburg, Alex Garber, Deborah Kaplan, Misha Kydd, Bri Lockhart, Summer Ogata, Emily Romero, Laurel Robinson, Shannon Spann, Felicity

Vallence, and Jayne Ziemba. Thank you to Lisa Sheehan for your work on this fantastic cover.

I am indebted to Liv Guion at WME, who answers every message without hesitation and, always, with the help I need.

Thank you to Olivia Burgher and Sanjana Seelam for helping me dream big and for believing in these stories. How lucky am I to work with you?

I am humbled by the remarkable places I leaned on while revising this book, even when it felt like the end was just out of reach. Gratitude goes out to INNESS for the beautiful setting and the desk in the corner, Mill & Main for all the midday treats, and the Root Strength community for showing me I can do (and lift) heavy things.

Thank you to my family for understanding how much I love and need this work, and how much I love and need you: Halley, Ben, Luke, Charlotte, Mom, and Dad.

Thank you to Ziti, whose cuddles comforted me when the words wouldn't come, and to Maxwell, whose love keeps me afloat.